WHITE RAVEN

THE RAVEN SERIES, BOOK 1

J. L. WEIL

Published by J. L. Weil
Copyright 2015 by J. L. Weil
www.jlweil.com/
All rights reserved.
Third Edition 2017
ISBN-13: 978-1508970866
ISBN-10: 1508970866

Edited by Kelly Hashway & Allisyn Ma
Cover Design by J. L. Weil
Photo credit: http://lisajen-stock.deviantart.com/

ISBN: 978-1-5089-7086-6

❀ Created with Vellum

ALSO BY J. L. WEIL

THE DIVISA SERIES

(Full series completed – Teen Paranormal Romance)

Losing Emma: A Divisa novella

Saving Angel

Hunting Angel

Breaking Emma: A Divisa novella

Chasing Angel

Loving Angel

Redeeming Angel

LUMINESCENCE TRILOGY

(Full series completed – Teen Paranormal Romance)

Luminescence

Amethyst Tears

Moondust

Darkmist – A Luminescence novella

RAVEN SERIES

(Full series completed – Teen Paranormal Romance)

White Raven

Black Crow

Soul Symmetry

SINGLE NOVELS

Starbound

(Teen Paranormal Romance)

<u>Dark Souls</u>

<u>(Runes Universe KindleWorld novella)</u>

BEAUTY NEVER DIES CHRONICLES

(Teen Dystopian Romance)

Slumber

For my hubby.

PROLOGUE

I t only took one heartbeat to change my whole life. One chilling phone call in the middle of the night.

The screams. I'll never forget that bloodcurdling sound. It echoed in my head, like a train horn in an underground tunnel, bouncing from one wall to the other. It wasn't until TJ wrapped me in a hug that I realized those screams of pain and sorrow were mine.

On more nights than not, my own screams haunted my dreams. I'd lost count of the number of times I'd woken up in a dead panic, icy cold and clammy. All because my mom had been murdered.

It was gut-wrenching.

Mom had been my best friend, my world, and when she had been shot at point blank, in what the cops had said was a robbery on West Twenty-Fourth Street, my world crumbled. Hearing the words "Sorry, honey, your mom is dead" from a complete stranger made the air stall in my lungs.

Chinatown had been one of my mom's favorite places in Chicago, mostly for the food. Carrying an order of sweet and sour chicken and beef lo mein, she had been on her way home that Friday night, walking down the same street we'd walked countless times, only five blocks from our little condo. Five measly blocks—that was all that had stood between my mom and her life.

There were perks to living in the city: public transportation, museums, shopping. Virtually everything you needed was at your fingertips. But then again, there were huge sacrifices.

I learned that the hard way.

Grief came in waves, choppy and fierce, breaking the heart. It was time I swam before I simply sunk—the waves devouring my soul.

CHAPTER 1

The ferry rocked over the crystal blue waves, splashing and spraying the salty water up the sides of the big white boat. My stomach rolled with the waves, and I could feel my face turn an unflattering shade of green, like split pea soup. Gross. The sea and I, we didn't mesh. But who did I have to impress? The captain? Hardly.

Impressing anyone was the furthest thing from my mind. My current problems were monumental. Before my father had announced that TJ and I would be "taking a trip," I had gotten my nose pierced at a less than reputable establishment. That got me tons of brownie points with the Pops ... not. He had looked me over with sad brown eyes and a scruffy face, shook his head, and then went back into his painting cave, shutting out the world—including me. No sweat off my back, because that was how I preferred it lately.

The less we saw of each other, the better.

I guess he felt the same.

And here I was, miles and miles away from Chicago, with the wind in my face on my way to what I considered my summer of doom. I was sure plenty of seventeen-year-old girls would probably kill for

3

the chance to spend their summer vacation on an island off the New England coast. Maybe even have a summer fling.

I wasn't like most girls—not by a long shot. I wasn't exactly sure what it was that made me different. I just knew, like I knew my favorite color was purple or my favorite food was Chinese.

Sighing, I stared into the clear blue, watching the fish jump in the wake left behind by the boat, and immediately I missed my cramped, dusty apartment in Chicago. I missed my best friend, Parker. And most of all, I missed my mom's vibrant presence, the smell of her perfume, and her laugh. A sound I would never hear again, no matter how much I willed it. The hurt was still an open wound, so much so that tears stung my eyes.

"You got a bug in your eye, Piper?" my younger brother TJ sneered, seeing my eyes well up.

There were only two years separating us, but most days it felt like twenty. He made my life a living hell. What else were little brothers good for? I screwed up my face as I stared up at him. It still burned my butt that he had surpassed me in height this year. I hated having to crane my neck to look at him. "It's the wind, snotnose."

He snorted, his messy, sandy hair blowing in the wind. "If you say so."

Using the back of my free hand, I wiped my eyes. We both knew it wasn't the salty air that was bothering me. It was everything.

The loss of our mom.

Being shipped off to a grandma we'd never met.

Constantly feeling pissed off at the world.

The list went on and on.

This was going to be our first summer without *her*, and I didn't think any of us had a clue how to move on, least of all Dad.

Hence, here I was, on my way to the remote island of Raven Hollow, courtesy of my grandma, a woman I barely remembered. Grandma Rose was Mom's mother, and let it be noted that she was filthy rich. Money meant nothing to me, especially since I spent most of my life without it, and I had been happy … before. My whole life, Rose had been nothing but a check in the mail during holidays and birthdays. Big whoopee. Not precisely a doting grandma. If it hadn't been for that photo Mom had framed on the wall, I wouldn't know what the woman looked like.

She looked like Mom.

And that depressed me.

After the … um … accident, as I liked to refer to it, Rose had finally been able to break my father down and convince him that we should stay with her, at least for the summer.

Ugh. What a horrible idea: strip us away from everything we'd ever known, our friends, our home, and our lives. I didn't think it took much convincing, honestly. I was a constant reminder that Dad had lost the love of his life.

Grandma Moneybags thought that it would be best for TJ and me to get away, to start fresh from the painful memories of losing our mom.

That was utter BS in my book.

But what did I know? I was just a kid. Yet, it was me these last months that had taken care of everything. Hell, without me, we would have starved. We would have had no clean clothes. The bills wouldn't have been paid. And someone had to make sure TJ *actually* went to school. But I didn't get a say in *this*—on where *I* wanted to spend my summer?

Ridonkulous.

Dad was an utter mess, and who could blame him? The man had lost his wife. My parents had been very much in love, but since her *accident*, he had become unreasonable. So I gave up. Newsflash: He wasn't the only one suffering here. It was possible that TJ and I might have pushed him over the edge. We hadn't exactly been model children the last few months—TJ with his dicey choices in friends, me with my pierced nose and late weekends at the clubs. But I couldn't help feeling like he was checking out of life, too. So what if he didn't make much money or any money for that matter? Struggling artists weren't exactly making it rain dollar bills, no matter how talented, unless they were selling.

And he hadn't sold a single piece since that night.

5

But what right did he have giving up on us? Sending us to a complete stranger, how was that going to fix anything? I would probably come back from this summer more damaged than ever, because that was what I was: damaged.

It was the summer before my senior year. Not that long ago, I'd had dreams of going away to college. Now I only dreamt about Mom.

How was I going to survive on an island that didn't even have a mall for God's sake? TJ tried to put on the tough guy act, but his room was next to mine, and the walls in our old apartment were thin. Hearing his cries at night broke my heart, though I would take that secret with me to the grave. The less ammunition I gave TJ to use against me, the better we got along.

This was the first time in forever that TJ and I had both agreed on something. Neither of us wanted to be here—uprooted.

The ferry skipped over the choppy waters, hitting a killer wave that caused me to lose my balance. I stumbled against the side of the boat, my hair falling into my face. *Cursed boat.* I was dying to get off this hunk-a-junk, afraid I might embarrass myself and hurl over the side.

TJ would never let me live that down.

That was when I saw it. Through the misty fog rising from the waters, a shadow emerged: Raven Hollow. The sight was bittersweet. My combat boots were ready to touch solid ground, but the knot in my stomach wanted me to hop on the next plane back to the Windy City.

"Thank God. We're almost there," I whispered, ignoring my belly's internal turmoil.

"That's where we are going?" TJ said in outrage, his brown eyes narrowing. "What a craphole."

Off to the right, you could see the beginning outlines of homes, a lighthouse, and civilization. My hand gripped the edge of the railing. "Yup." And truthfully, there was nothing crappy about it. The outline of the island was breathtaking.

TJ shoved his hands into his pockets. "This sucks."

Did it ever.

He pulled out his phone. "We better get cell service, or I am taking the next boat back to the mainland."

I might just be right behind him. "Tell me about it."

"I don't understand why Dad didn't come with us," He rehashed the same question we had bounced off each other for days.

I shrugged. "He said he needed to figure stuff out."

A fire started in his irises. "That's such a cop-out, and you know it."

I did. It was code for: I need to find a way to keep us from being homeless. "I know." I sighed, leaning my face on my hands. "Let's get to the jeep. I think we are about to dock."

"Aye-aye, Captain Bossy Pants," he said mockingly.

I socked him in the arm. "Knock it off. You might be taller than me, but I will still kick your ass."

A small smile tugged at his lips. "Dream on."

We found my jeep Cherokee right where we had left it, lined with the other cars crossing the ocean. Josie had seen better days. The red paint was chipping, and there were rust spots growing on the lower frame. Climbing behind the wheel, I was glad for a little shade. Another five minutes under this scorching sun and I would be well-done.

TJ slammed his door as he got in the passenger seat beside me. The hinge didn't latch. It was notorious for being a stickler. The door squeaked, swinging back open. He swore under his breath and gave it a harder jerk. My whole car rocked back and forth.

"Hey. Not so rough. Josie needs a sensitive touch," I reminded him for like the umpteenth time and petted the dash. "Don't you, girl?"

TJ shook his head. "You need serious help, Pipe. Talking to cars is not normal."

"Neither is your face, but I still tolerate you."

He made a stupid expression at me. "Funny."

This was how our conversations usually went.

We waited for the ferry to be anchored at the dock. Water sloshed from all sides, and the large boat swayed from side to side. When the captain finally gave the signal—a blow horn—I started up the engine. It turned over a few times before purring like a kitten. Well, a really sad, deranged kitten.

"This car is such a piece of crap. I hope no one sees me." He slunk lower in the seat.

I rolled my eyes. "You don't know anyone, and at least I can drive."

Grabbing a baseball cap from the backseat, he pulled it down lower over his eyes. "Doesn't mean you're good at it."

And here we go.

I dropped my sunglasses over my eyes and shifted Josie into drive. The moment my two front tires touched ground, an electric shock rippled through my body. I shuddered. *What was that?* It felt like I'd been struck by lightning, charged with a bolt of energy. The sensation lessened as I kept my foot on the gas.

Strange.

We rode in silence, each caught up in our own mixed-up feelings. Piled in the back seat of the truck, and every available nook and cranny, was my whole life. I took in the new sights as we drove along the road. It was really beautiful, more so than I wanted to admit. TJ was pretending to be uninterested, but I caught him a few times glancing up from under the brim of his Cubs cap.

As we rounded the last bend, the only thing I felt was dread.

I stopped Josie in front of a driveway with two white columns on either side. One of the pillars had the numbers 1-1-8-5. There had to be a mistake. This couldn't possibly be her house. Digging through the cup holder, I pulled out a wrinkled sheet of paper, skimming for the address. There it was: 1185.

Holy. Shit.

The engine idled as I sat there gaping. I might have swallowed a fly or two.

This was the house (correction: mansion) I was going to spend the next three months in? Someone pinch me—hard. I didn't know whether to ask which room needed to be cleaned first, or do an embarrassing happy dance in the middle of the road.

I opted to sit there like a nincompoop with my mouth hanging open catching flies.

"Fuck me," TJ said, doing some eyeballing of his own.

"Language," I scolded.

"This place is seriously sick," he added as any fifteen-year-old boy would.

I'd never seen a house like this before—only on *MTV Cribs*. It was a pristine white that shone against the sparkling ocean. Three brick chimneys jutted from different levels of the charcoal roof. There were so many porches and balconies I lost count. The yard was immaculately manicured, and a glitzy, lipstick-red sports car was parked out front. It was nauseatingly expensive. I was afraid to breathe in fear of setting off the security alarm.

"Pipe," TJ said, grinning, "this is the first time I've seen you at a loss for words."

"Whatever," I replied sarcastically, clamping my mouth shut.

Together we climbed out of Josie, standing side by side and ogling the oversized palace. I'd never felt so unsure and out of place. This wasn't me. We looked like a pair of misfits washed ashore. Fretful, I shifted my feet and glanced down at my tattered black jeggings and white tank top. Oh boy. Granny was in for the shock of her life.

I hope she didn't croak at the sight of us.

Wouldn't that be our luck?

"Nervous?" TJ asked.

I bit my lip. Of course I was. Inside, I was a bundle of knots. "Let's go greet Her Grace," I joked and made a mental note to ask if she was in fact royalty or something. I mean, I knew that my mom came from money, but there was a difference between being rich and being billionaires. Swinging one of my black duffle bags over my shoulder, I strolled up to the massive double doors. TJ was right behind, his sneakers scuffing on the concrete.

A woman with long white and silver hair greeted us in a great hall. Circular tiles covered the floor, and the woman's heels clicked as she walked toward us. There was something powerful about the way she carried herself, and the tilt of her chin. A billow of emerald fabric flowed behind her, soft and fluid. She oozed importance and something else. Something I couldn't form into words. I hated that I felt insignificant. This was my grandma—my blood—but a stranger all the same.

"Welcome to Raven Manor." She held out her arms, the jingle of bracelets echoing with her movements. "Now come give your grandmother a hug."

There was an awkward silence where no one did anything. Then finally, I stepped forward and found myself engulfed in arms that were surprisingly strong for her age. She smelled of expensive floral perfume. There was something quirky about her underneath all the dollar signs.

Self-consciously, I ran a hand over my wind-blasted hair. "It's nice to, um, see you, Grandma," I said, my ingrained manners coming to the surface. I guess I hadn't buried them deep enough.

She smiled, her Irish eyes sparkling. "Please, call me Rose. I've never been much for titles."

I snorted, maybe a little too loud. It was just that I found that hard to believe. She lived in a home that could house half my neighborhood comfortably. It was probably fully staffed with a butler and chauffeur. Please. I've seen *The Real Housewives of Beverly Hills*.

TJ nudged me in the shoulder. He probably didn't want us to get evicted before we had a chance to be shown our rooms. Rose gave him a hug, and afterward he cleared his throat. "Nice digs you got here."

Digs? I wanted to thump myself on the head.

Luckily, Rose didn't bat an eye. "Why thank you, TJ, I think. I can't tell you how grateful I am for the chance to get to know the two of you. It has been a long time coming."

You could say that again.

It was on the tip of my tongue to ask why it had been so long, but TJ seared me with a glare, so I checked myself.

"Now, I am sure you have had an exhausting trip and would like to get your things settled in." She walked to a panel on the wall and hit a button. "Thomas, please help Piper and TJ with their bags."

Turning back to us, she lifted her hand, the bling on her fingers blinding me.

Holy ten carats.

My grandfather had died when my mom was a teenager, and Rose had never remarried. If that whopping ring on her finger was any indicator, she probably never would. It was kind of sentimental, if you were into that kind of thing.

"It's cool," TJ said, going to the door. "We don't have a lot. I can grab our stuff."

I couldn't keep the shocked expression from my face. *TJ ... offer to help? What has the world come to?*

"Nonsense. Let's get you to your rooms." Her thin fingers framed my face. "You, my dear, look just like your mother."

My throat constricted, and I fumbled with my necklace.

There was nothing slow about this woman's movements. She was the liveliest old woman I'd ever seen. "I had each of your bedrooms specifically designed for you. I want you to be comfortable here. This is your home."

I wasn't sure I could ever consider this mausoleum *my home.* And how the hell had she had time to organize rooms? The decision for us to come here had only been made a week ago. What? Did she have magical faeries working for her?

"Piper."

I whipped my head around at the sound of my name.

Her eyes met mine, and I couldn't help thinking they were so familiar to me, minus the crinkles at the corners. "I have put you in the west wing, dear. I think you will find it to your liking."

I swallowed.

What the heck was I going to do with a whole wing to myself?

Already the prospect was lonely. On the upside, TJ and I would have an entire wing between us. That was great because TJ snored like a freight train.

"Follow me. I will show you to your rooms," she said with a gagging cheerfulness. The mass of bangle bracelets at her wrists chimed like a gypsy as she began to lead the way.

I glanced over my shoulder one last time to look out the open front doors. It suddenly felt like I would never see my old life again. If I kept going, deeper into this house, my world would never be the same—everything would change.

I sighed and followed behind TJ.

CHAPTER 2

Two right turns, one left, and I knew I was going to need a map or a GPS. Getting lost in this place was imminent. The corridors just kept going and going. There should have been street signs assigned to each hall.

It was impossible to imagine my mother living here in this maze, everything so cold, immaculate, and ... breakable. Mom had been vibrant, colorful, and a klutz. Our home had been crammed with things she had made or picked up at a flea market. As I tried to picture her living here, I saw her drowning in so much space. She adored our cramped apartment in the city. No wonder she had said adios to Raven Hollow and never looked back.

Marble and wrought iron decorated the winding staircase. I ran a finger along the banister as I climbed. No dust. None whatsoever.

It was unnatural.

Awestruck, I hiked my duffle bag higher on my shoulder as we came to the top of the stairs. I was a little out of breath. How Grams was able to make that hike without breaking a sweat was sort of impressive and made me think I needed to hit the gym. I couldn't let Granny have better stamina than me.

That was just pathetic.

Rose and TJ were prattling as we walked, but I stayed silent, observing. There wasn't a shy bone in my brother's sinewy body. He was inquisitive by nature and had more questions than an investigator. He got that from Dad. I was used to tuning him out.

My interest piqued when Rose came to a doublewide door with silver scroll handles. A hand on each knob, she threw open the doors and said, "This is your suite, TJ."

A suite?

She was joking, right?

One glimpse of TJ's room and I knew I wouldn't see him all summer. Who could blame him? It had everything a boy his age could ever dream of: monstrous TV, Xbox console complete with a video game library, a fish tank bubbling in the corner with neon lights and one of those little scuba guys.

"I can't believe I am going to be living here," TJ beamed. It had been a long time since I'd seen such a ridiculous grin on my brother's face. He might be a pest most of the time, but I was glad to see one of us was going to enjoy the summer. At least while it lasted, because I was positive when we went back to Chicago, we wouldn't be able to afford the clock on the wall.

And we were going back.

Crossing my arms, I leaned on the doorframe, watching TJ touch everything.

"Are you looking forward to your freedom this summer?" Rose asked, standing beside me.

I lifted my brows, uncertain what she meant, because *free* was most definitely not what I was feeling. Stuck was a more appropriate description.

For someone in her sixties, she looked amazing. The hue of her gypsy-style dress made her eyes intense, yet, on her, the dress was elegant not shabby. "I know you have had a huge amount of responsibility on your shoulders. It's time you let someone look after you for a change."

Hmm. I wasn't sure how I felt about that. I liked my independence

—a lot—and I wasn't used to people waiting on me. "Is there a curfew in this … joint?"

I wasn't certain, but I thought I caught a hint of a smile on her rosy lips. "No. I just ask that you call and leave a message with the staff. Do you have a cell phone?"

Duh. Did she think we came from Bedrock? "Yeah, we both have phones," I replied flatly.

I got the feeling she was amused by me, which had not been my intention. My grand scheme since Dad dropped the bomb had been to be rude, intolerable, and a pain in her ass so she would send us back home. But now … seeing how genuinely happy she was to have us in her gargantuan home, my need for sabotage started to dissipate.

"Good. Your room is this way." She gave a nod to the left.

Onward, oh mighty one.

We continued on down a wide hallway, my boots clomping on the marble floors. Her long silvery blonde hair trailed down her back, swaying with her graceful movements. She was a woman of importance, and I found that intimidating. As we progressed through the house, I admired the art that hung on the walls. Dad could have spent weeks exploring this place, gazing at each piece for hours. He often lost himself not only in his own work, but in the masterpieces of others as well.

I had been so caught up in my surroundings that I didn't notice she had stopped. Well, not until I bumped into her. Thank God I didn't knock her flat on her ass.

"Sorry," I mumbled. "There's just so much to take in."

She brushed a strand of my blonde hair behind my ear. "Give it time, and before long, it won't seem so overwhelming. Your mom and her sister used to—" She stopped, taking a long breath. There was a flicker of emotion in her piercing eyes before she quickly masked it.

I wanted to ask her to finish what she was going to say. Mom had rarely talked about her family, and the mention of a sister caught me off guard. Suddenly, I needed to grab onto any memory of my mother, even if it was someone else's. I longed to feel a connection again with my mom, even if it was with the woman who raised her—a stranger.

Rose tipped her chin and ran a hand down the side of her hip, smoothing invisible wrinkles and composing herself. "This is the west wing," she stated, a soft smile highlighting the curve of her cheekbones.

For the second time today, my jaw hit the ground, along with my bag. Any thoughts of pressing her about my mom and her mysterious sister flew out the window.

Peering into the doorway, I was extremely relieved to see there wasn't a drop of pink in sight. But that didn't mean it was precisely *my style*. Three of the walls were a milky white with a lavender stripe cutting across in the middle. The wall housing a queen size bed was the same color as the painted border. A crystal chandelier hung over the center, sparkling against the lights. White sheets covered the mattress, and a purple knitted blanket was folded at an angle near the end of the bed. Under a bay window was a deep velvet bench seat with a stunning view of the ocean. On the other side was a white desk housing a laptop. There was an adjoining bathroom just as posh as the bedroom with a stand-up shower as big as my whole bathroom at home and a soaking tub with more jets than Carter had pills. (I wasn't positive what that phrase meant, but it sounded cool.)

Sure, my room was to die for, but I felt like a bloody princess, and there was nothing royal or angelic about me. I could be the princess of darkness, if there was such a thing. I liked loud rock music, black nail polish, body piercings, and dark eyeliner, not tiaras and lace.

Yet each of my silver-ringed fingers itched to put my stamp all over the room, and that was unexpected. The only thing I thought I would feel for the bedroom I was assigned was contempt. I moseyed back into the main room and spun in a circle, trying to take it all in.

"Will this be acceptable?"

I jumped, forgetting I wasn't alone. Rose was standing in the doorway, watching the range of emotions cross my face. "It will do," I replied.

Her hand reached down, gripping the handle. The cluster of bangle bracelets chimed at her wrists, echoing through the room. "I'm glad. Tonight, I'll let you get comfortable and unpack. Tomorrow, I'll give you the tour and show you around town."

Let me. I wasn't sure she meant that as an order, but it rubbed me the wrong way. I had a problem with being told what to do. In my eyes, I was already an adult—not by choice. The last year had thrown me into adulthood.

"Great," I mumbled dryly. I was tired and cranky, the long trip catching up with me, so I rationalized. Life-altering moves did that to me.

She didn't show any reaction to my less-than-pleasant tone. "If you need anything, this panel is hooked up to every room in the house, including TJ's."

Fan-freaking-tastic. Now he could annoy me at the push of a button.

"Thanks," I said, the weirdness coming back. I stood in the middle of the room, wide-eyed and tongue-tied, not knowing what to say next.

She faced me, her eyes studying me. "I've waited seventeen years for this moment, Piper. I can't tell you how happy I am to see you here with me in Raven Manor."

And with that completely unexpected speech, she shut the door behind her, leaving me by myself with my wandering thoughts. I flopped onto the bed, the blankets immediately wrinkling under my weight. I started to smooth out the creases before I stopped myself. If I wanted a messy bed, then by God, I was going to have a freaking messy bed. I didn't have to change who I was. Rose wanted to get to know *me*, then have at it. She was going to get every one of my fabulously bad habits, and there were plenty.

Alone, I lay there staring at the porcelain ceiling, wondering just what my dad had gotten us into. There were so many thoughts coursing through my mind I thought my head might pop. I lost track of time, until there was a soft rap on the door.

Startled, I swung into a sitting position, shaking out my hair. "Come in," I called.

Behind the door was a short man with olive skin, dark hair, and dark eyes. He was carrying the rest of my measly belongings. Ugh. I did not look forward to the task set out in front of me: unpacking. No siree, Bob.

I let out a gorilla-sized groan. Who in their right mind actually enjoyed unpacking? So my organization and tidying skills might suck a teensy bit. Oookay, fine. They sucked a lot.

Hauling my duffle bag on top of the bed, I unzipped it, digging out my clothes and tossing them mindlessly onto the bed. Through the mess, a round black circle caught my eye. I grabbed the old Minnie Mouse T-shirt I had gotten for my birthday two years ago. Burying my face against the soft cotton material, I inhaled deeply. It smelled of home, cinnamon apples, warmth during cold winters, laughter. A deep longing filled my chest, and I wanted to hold onto those precious memories forever. I wanted to live in the past because the present was unbearable without Mom.

Quickly burying the pain before it could surface, I went to one of the drawers and stuffed the shirt at the very back. "Three months," I whispered.

For the next hour I hung, folded, and re-folded the rest of my stuff. There was only one small box left, so I tackled it with about as much gusto as I had the rest, grumbling and bitching the whole time. What could I say? I was being a poor sport about this whole thing.

At the bottom of the box were my colored pencils. There was a time when I had dabbled in drawing, anime mostly. I had no idea why I'd brought them with me. It had been months since I'd drawn anything, but maybe this place would be as dull and boring as I imagined. Nothing like boredom to strike inspiration.

There was another knock on the door just as I finished putting the last piece in its place: a picture of Mom. I was miffed by the interruption and swung the door open with more force than necessary. This place felt like Grand flipping Station.

"What now—?" I stopped my rant when I saw a young woman slightly older than me holding a tray of food. "Oh shit, I'm sorry ..." I paused, realizing I didn't know her name and I'd sworn. My eyes scanned the top of her polo shirt, looking for a nametag.

"Estelle," she supplied, smiling. Her hazel eyes twinkled. "Ms. Rose thought you might be hungry."

My stomach rumbled, and I softened the scowl on my face, realizing my lips were still turned down. "Thank God, I'm famished." Then because I'd never had anyone bring me food before, I shifted on my feet. "Um."

Luckily, this wasn't Estelle's first rodeo. She waltzed into the room, hips swaying, and set the food on the desk. The savory smells wafted in the air, hitting my belly, and I thought about my brother. "Has TJ—?"

"He has already eaten," she said before I could finish.

TJ was a bottomless pit. It didn't matter what you put in front of him; he would eat it. Even though he was my irritating little brother, I still felt a sense of responsibility for him.

I exhaled, my shoulders relaxing. I hadn't even realized how tense I'd been. "And there was enough for me?" I joked.

She laughed, but quickly stopped as if she had done something wrong.

Was laughter forbidden?

There was something about this girl that made me feel at ease. These walls didn't seem so lonely knowing there was someone my age. I wanted very much to ask Estelle to stay, to keep me company. Eating by myself sounded miserable, but I was afraid I would be overstepping the house rules.

I didn't want to shake the foundation just yet.

Figured I would give it a week before I set the whole house in an uproar.

Estelle tiptoed out of my room while I had an internal debate, taking the decision out of my hands. I stared at the closed door, my stomach again rumbling, reminding me it had been hours since I'd last eaten. I managed to finish half of what I had been given.

With a full belly, I meandered into the bathroom to shower, hoping it would help me sleep. The multi-head spray hit me from all angles, and my entire body went limp from the heat. I let the pressure massage my tired muscles, thinking that if I could live in this shower for the summer, I'd be blissfully happy.

Geez, I was lame.

By the time I was finished, the bathroom was foggy with steam. I took my towel and smeared the mist from the mirror. There I was, my reflection staring back at me. Green eyes, usually round and large, were heavily lidded. The tiny beauty mark above my lip winked back at me. Pretty much like every other teenage girl, I had insecurities. I was too thin and lacked curves, and my hair never did what I wanted it to. I wished for killer legs, not pencil sticks. And my mouth and my brain never communicated.

Drying my long blonde hair, I tossed it into a messy bun and slipped into my "Coffee is my BFF" PJs. As I walked back into the adjoining room, my eyes locked onto the window seat. It looked too inviting to not take advantage of. My butt sunk into the velvety cushion, and I pulled my legs up against my chest, getting comfortable. My forehead rested against the cool windowpane while I stared out into the vast blue waters. The waves were much darker now that the sun had set. Even with the sparkling stars dotting the night's sky, the water appeared almost black.

An emotion I refused to acknowledge came over me: sadness. Before I could swallow back the wretched feeling, tears were blurring my vision and streaming down my cheeks.

Angrily, I swiped at them with the palm of my hand. I'd promised never to shed another useless tear. Not ever. Not for some idiotic boy who breaks my heart. Not when I feel such excruciating pain that it makes me call out. Not when I am alone and feeling lost.

I'd bawled enough tears to last two lifetimes, and for it, I was stronger. I refused to let myself travel down that dark path ever again.

Through my muddled eyes, I saw a beautiful spark of icy blue. At least I thought I did in the shadows. I was mesmerized. Squinting, I swore there was something out there, moving with the darkness. Inching closer on the seat, I thumped my head on the glass.

"Dammit," I cursed.

My eyes shot back up as I rubbed the tender spot on my forehead, searching.

Confused, I blinked.

Nothing.

It was gone.

That was when I knew I was on the brink of losing my mind. Moving to Raven Hollow had tipped the scale. There was something about this place, about this house, that my mom had run from, never to return. I wanted to know why. She must have had a very good explanation to cut herself off from her childhood home and her mom … but what?

A chill ran over my arms.

Secrets. This place was brimming with them.

CHAPTER 3

I jerked straight up in bed, confused and disoriented, my hair curtaining my face. It had been near 3:00 a.m. when I'd finally been able to fall asleep, and I had no idea what woke me. Flopping onto my back, I glared at the ceiling tiles, knowing that once I was awake, there was no hope of ever falling back to sleep.

Buzz. Buzz. Buzz.

I frowned. What the hell was that annoying sound? Was the freaking house on fire? Should I look for an emergency exit? Throwing off the covers in a mad panic, I swung my feet to the floor. My damn toe got caught up in the sheets, and I nearly cracked my two front teeth on the wood floor.

"Holy shit," I cursed. "That was close."

"Piper." My name echoed through a small speaker by the door.

I lifted my head, staring in the direction of the voice.

It was Rose.

"I require your presence in the blue room," she informed me.

I groaned and thumped my forehead on the floor.

Good grief. I hadn't had my first cup of coffee or the chance to wipe the sleepy gunk from the inner corners of my eyes, and she wanted to talk to me. I wasn't fit to talk to humans until after at least one dose of caffeine. Everyone in my family knew that if you woke me up before noon, it turned me into a bitch-a-saurus—except Rose. There was more excitement and fun at night. The whole city came alive and I with it. I missed my late nights with Parker sneaking into clubs. I missed our midnight lattes at the café across from my apartment, gossiping about his newest manga.

Did I mention that Parker was a geek? A sort of cute geek. His shaggy brown hair always hung in his eyes, and he always had his nose in a comic book.

Crawling back into bed, I snuggled deeper into the covers, making an inaudible response. Day two and already Rose was making demands. I lay there another few minutes, debating whether to get up or stay in bed all day. Finally, my curiosity about this house and the town itself got the best of me, remembering that Rose had mentioned something yesterday about a tour.

Twisting over, I glanced at the blue neon lights on the alarm clock situated on the nightstand. Was she kidding me? Nine o'clock? It was indecent. I'd had a long night. Being in a new place with a bad case of homesickness, sleep did not come easy, and now my body was paying the price.

Dragging a hand through my tangled hair, I pushed myself up, dangling my feet over the side. I blinked. Still groggy, it took a few flutters of my lashes before it sunk in. I wasn't in my own room. The walls weren't the color of red wine; I wasn't sleeping in my snuggly daybed with a view of the skyline, and the chakra crystals weren't dangling above my head. This wasn't a dream.

Hell's bells.

A gentle breeze from the ocean blew through the balcony doors, flapping the lace curtains. Strolling across the room, I quickly rummaged through the closet, almost afraid I would fall in and never return or end up in Narnia. Fortunately, I didn't have much stuff, so it just looked pitiful. I had never been on time to anything in my life. Why start today?

Still in a zombie-state, I tugged a shirt from the hanger, whipped it over my head, and wiggled into my favorite pair of jean shorts.

Combing my fingers through my hair to loosen a few of the snarls, I tied my hair up into a ponytail on top of my head. Considering that it was before noon, this was the best it was going to get.

My bare feet padded over the wood floors as I opened the door to the hall, looking left then right. *Downstairs where?*

I was going to need more specific instructions, like latitudes and longitudes, if I was going to get around in this place. It took me twenty minutes to locate the *blue room*. I didn't know why they just didn't call it a sitting room, because that was basically what it was. If it hadn't been for the voices, I might have still been aimlessly wandering about.

True to its name, the walls were royal blue, and the focal point of the room was a floor-to-ceiling brick fireplace in a pristine white. When I more or less stumbled my way in, TJ and Rose were sitting on a cobalt paisley couch. It was the ugliest thing I'd ever seen. If being rich meant having horrible taste, then by God, I was glad we had grown up just scraping by. I would take our worn leather sofa from Goodwill over that stiff looking thing any day of the week.

Above their heads hung a tiered crystal chandelier. At my less-than-stellar entrance, both heads turned my way. It made me squirm. I fumbled with the chain around my neck. "Sorry, I'm late."

"She's always late," TJ snorted.

I thumped him on the back of the head as I took a seat beside him, curling my legs underneath me.

He scowled.

With her hands primly folded in her lap, Rose began to lay out the agenda for the day. "We are having lunch at the club, and I thought afterward I would show you around the island."

Lunch at the country club? What the hell did one wear to a country club? My head started to fill with images of tennis skirts, polo shirts, and khakis. I owned none of the above, nor would I actually ever wear any of the above.

I couldn't keep the sourpuss expression from my face. "Um. I hate to be the rain cloud, but I left all my party dresses in Chicago," I replied.

TJ's frown deepened. He was pissed at anything that might jeopardize his suddenly posh summer.

But Rose had thought of everything. "Not to worry. I had Estelle pick you up a few things. You'll find them already in your room."

It was on the tip of my tongue to ask just how she had known what size I was. Had she snooped around in my drawers while I slept, gone through my panties?

Ew. Gross.

Now I was scowling.

TJ bounced off the couch, ready for just about anything. "I'm starved. When do we leave?"

"In an hour ... on the dot," she added for my benefit.

I did a mental eye roll.

As far as I was concerned, TJ was adjusting too fast and was too accepting. In a way, I sort of felt betrayed. Why was he so eager to get to know a woman who never once bothered to visit us?

Irritation flaring, I looked down at my outfit. Why did I have to change? I liked how I dressed, how I talked, and how I lounged on the couch. Couldn't I just be me? It burned my butt. And for the second time today, I was faced with a decision all before I'd had a caffeine buzz. This could go two ways. I could be difficult and refuse to change —my gut reaction. Or for TJ's sake, I could haul my ass back upstairs and put on one of Rose's silly dresses. Heaving a sigh, I chose the high road, which didn't happen often.

"It will be fun." Rose attempted and failed to make lunch sound enticing.

Fun was subjective.

Unfurling my legs, I more or less stomped up the stairs, but not before giving TJ the stink eye and walking into a wrong room or three. When I finally found *my* room, I swung open the door and snorted. There it was. Laid out on my bed was a pink sundress, sticking out on the white bed like a pink spotted giraffe at the zoo.

Pink!

I vomited in my mouth.

Of all the colors in the rainbow, why did it have to be cotton pink?

Standing in the center of the room, eyeballing the very girly material, I reconsidered my choices.

Option 1: I show up to lunch in jean shorts and a tank.

Option 2: I don't go to the country club at all.

Option 3: I suck it up and wear the damn dress.

Really, in any other color it would be acceptable … but pink? I didn't care about impressing her uppity friends. I didn't care about what others thought about me. But what I did care about was TJ. The last thing I wanted was to make this any harder for him. Not that he was having a hard time, but he'd already had a traumatizing year. I owed it to him to try to make living here as smooth as possible. He might be a royal pain in my tush, but if he could survive the summer, so could I.

Ugh. I was going to grit my teeth and bear it. After all, it was only one day—one meal. How hard could it be? It was not as if I would melt like the Wicked Witch of the West if I wore pink.

Sixty-five minutes later I was sitting in the back of a black town car on my way to the country club in an itchy *pink* dress. Yep. I was late.

Served her right for making me wear a dress.

Rose's hair was tied up in a sophisticated bun, not a flyaway in sight. TJ's sandy hair was combed, looking clean and polished, something that never happened at home. We were lucky if he showered once a week. And then there was me. The best I had done with my long blonde hair was run a comb through it. There hadn't been time to work miracles.

Sinking into the plush seat, the same thought looped on repeat. *What the heck am I going to do at a stuffy country club?*

Mingle? Doubtful.

Dine on exotic cuisine? Don't hold your breath.

Tennis? No stinking way.

My kind of club was an underground one with flashing colored lights, floor-shaking mixes, and half-naked peeps. This *club* was called The Black Crow. To me, it sounded like a strip joint, but what did I know about hoity-toity places?

On the short ride from the manor to the country club, Rose rattled off all the amenities the club offered from tennis to boating lessons, and it was all at her expense, since she had added us to the approved guest list.

Dollar signs beamed in TJ's eyes. I gave him a stern look. "Does that include a booze tab?" I asked smartly.

TJ kicked me with his shoe. "She's joking," he said, seeing Rose's displeasure.

Actually, I wasn't, but no harm in letting them think I was.

I didn't know what it was, but everything in Raven Hollow rubbed me the wrong way. Even Rose. Sure, she had been nice; however, I hadn't forgotten that never once had I seen this woman. Unlike Dad and TJ, my trust had to be earned. I didn't just give it away because of the size of her wallet. I hated feeling like a charity case. There was a very good reason my mom hadn't ever wanted to return to Raven Hollow, and I was determined to unearth it.

The Black Crow was not as seedy as the name suggested. Tall white pillars flanked a set of stairs that led to a huge wraparound porch in a plantation style, perfect for lazy afternoons or quiet evenings. From behind the black wooden building, I heard the crashing of waves against the rocky shore and a boat horn in the distance. The club was on the harbor, its smooth windows sparkling in the sunlight.

We were seated on the back deck with an impressive view of the waterfront. The golden glow of the sun flashed off the rippling waters as sails from boats whistled in the winds, coming and going from the dock. I loved the water. It reminded me of the lakefront.

A warm breeze blew over my bare shoulders, the sun basking on my skin. It felt nice, a change from my usual crazy Chicago summers where you wore shorts one day and a sweatshirt the next. My complexion could use a righteous tan. Maybe that would be my goal for the summer: sunbathe on the beach and drink all the Shirley Temples my stomach could handle. I sipped my pinkish drink and twirled the umbrella thinking that was exactly what I was going to do. The less time I spent at the manor, the better.

TJ and Rose kept the conversation rolling as I gave the appropriate one-word responses or a head nod. I didn't have much of an appetite, mostly picking at my chicken Caesar salad and gazing out at the ocean, until …

His hair was black as a wintry night, eyes icy blue as a gypsy's heart. He had a lazy saunter about him and a glint of humor twinkling in those heart-melting eyes. There was nothing loose about his body, muscles bunching as he tethered a boat to the dock. I twiddled the straw, staring brazenly.

Good God. I wanted to have his babies. Not now, but most definitely someday.

And just like that, my summer got a billion times hotter … and interesting—way more interesting. I bit my lip, mulling over how I was going to accidentally fall into his pants. Um, I mean, path or even his lap would do, anything to get that one's attention.

Drool hit the table in a mad case of fangirl, and I didn't even know his name.

As if he sensed he was being slobbered over, his eyes scraped over me, and I held my breath. Holy hot tamales. An electric bolt of—lust maybe?—I really didn't know what it was but it coiled through my body, making me shudder. A flicker of an unidentified emotion crossed his face right before a secret smile appeared on his lips. Oh man, don't get me started on his lips.

Elbows propped on the table, I rested my head on the edge of my palms, continually gazing and getting lost in the depths of his eyes. He hypnotized me. I followed his movements, my eyes glued to him. Then one of my elbows slipped off the table in classic Piper form and down I went. I caught myself just before my chin whacked a corner of the patio table.

Only me.

Mortified, I closed my eyes.

TJ laughed. "Smooth, Pipe. I think you made a lasting impression."

My cheeks stained my face an unflattering shade of pink, and I narrowed my eyes at TJ from across the table, wishing we were closer so I could pinch him. Unable to resist, I glanced back up, praying my future husband hadn't witnessed my finest moment. My belly sunk. A burst of humor lit his eyes, and a flush raced over my body—part humiliation but more anger. I hated looking like a fool.

Rose delicately dabbed a napkin on her mouth. "It's not polite to stare, Piper."

"I lack more than just manners," I grumbled.

If she had heard me, she ignored the comment. "Did you not find the salad to your liking?"

"Who is that?" I asked, unable to help myself. My curiosity was beyond piqued. It was bordering stalker.

She didn't look pleased, but on Rose, frown lines didn't make her look any older. "That would be Roarke Hunter's second oldest, Zane. He works down at the docks," she informed me in a way that said Zane was beneath her class. "And he is trouble."

Good thing I liked trouble. A lot.

TJ saw the glint that sprang into my eyes, the one that made me want to do something just because someone told me not to. I'd had plenty of those looks lately. "I think you dropped something, Pipe," he said.

"Uh, what?"

"Your standards," he sneered.

"Funny, douche—" I stopped myself before I called my brother a douchebag in front of Rose in a sophisticated club nonetheless. This fine establishment probably had rules about having a potty mouth. Now that I knew what the club *really* had to offer, I didn't want to risk getting kicked out. One day I would learn to control my tongue.

TJ laughed at my blunder.

Once Rose had noticed my distraction with the boat staff, she hurried lunch along. We left the club shortly after. She had her driver take us around the island, showing us the hot spots. It was only about seventeen miles long, not a lot to see, especially when there was only one thing on my mind: Zane.

How was I going to finagle a meet and greet without looking like a total dork? Asking Rose for an intro was about as lame as you could get. Not an option. Especially since Rose had made it perfectly clear she didn't approve. I was not to associate with club employees. I was on a members-only social restriction.

Yeah right.

What did I have in common with rich girls and trust funds? I'll tell you: nada. Zilch. But a guy who worked for his money, *that* I understood. Whether Rose liked it or not, she couldn't dictate who my friends were, and I was going to be spending a lot more time at the club than I had planned. Like every day. Tennis lessons might just be added to my summer to-do list.

By the time Rolo parked the town car in front of Raven Manor, I realized I hadn't *really* seen a single sight in Raven Hollow. My mind was so awestruck by the bluest eyes I'd ever seen that I hadn't been able to focus on anything else. His perfectly sculpted cheekbones. That I-just-woke-up messy hair. Those kissable lips that hinted of mystery. He had rough edges that only drew me in more. It wasn't likely to be a face I would ever forget. Zane defied the laws of nature.

Holy smokes.

I was acting like I'd never seen the opposite sex before. Okay, so I'd never actually had a boyfriend. Parker didn't count. We'd never hooked up or even kissed, but I guess he was sort of more than just a friend. At least, there had been a time when I considered things moving into more of a boyfriend/girlfriend status, but that had been before *the accident*, before my life took a sharp turn in the wrong direction.

Alone in my room, I stared into thin air, thinking of Parker. His light brown hair, coffee-colored eyes, and boy-next-door smile, which was funny, because Parker had been the boy next door. He lived in one of the condos on the floor below mine. I was determined to return to my former life, to my best friend, but a little summer distraction couldn't hurt.

Parker had always been there for me. From before kindergarten, he had been in my life. Just as I couldn't imagine a world without my mom, I couldn't imagine my world without Parker. He was steady, dependable, caring, considerate, and funny. We had completely opposite tastes in just about everything, but our friendship worked. He listened to country. I loved Paramore (girl bands are the shiznit). He liked Italian food. I craved Chinese. He was the yin to my yang.

I missed the crap out of him, and it hadn't been a full day since I'd been gone.

Rolling over, I plopped on my stomach, immediately falling in love all over again with the softness of the mattress. Before I completely forgot because my mind decided to start planning my wedding to Zane, I picked up my cell phone and hit Parker's name.

CHAPTER 4

I t rang twice before he picked up. His familiar voice washed over me, causing me to miss home more than I thought possible. "Pipes."

My heart thumped. I savored the sound of my name a moment before I responded. "Hey."

"Summer is going to suck without you."

The corners of my mouth turned up. It was the same phrase we had rehashed over and over since I had found out I was leaving. "How's everything?"

"The same. And don't worry. I won't forget to feed your Venus flytrap." I could picture him in his bedroom, staring at his ever-growing superhero collection. While I dragged Parker to underground dance clubs, he lugged me to every single Marvel movie made, sometimes more than once.

"Parrrker." I elongated his name. "You have got to give me something, anything. Even the most mundane dirt." I wanted just the smallest connection to home.

"Well," he drew out, thinking, "Mrs. Youleg locked herself out of her apartment again."

I laughed, my feet dangling in the air. "I bet the super had a

32

conniption. That's like the third time in the last month."

Sounds of the TV came through the other end of the phone. He was probably watching reruns of *Supernatural*, our favorite show. He liked the gory creatures, and I liked the eye candy. It was a win-win. "So what's *she* like?" he asked.

I sighed. "Rose is"—I started, not because she didn't want to be called Grandma, but because I refused to acknowledge that she was family—"classy, elegant, and eccentric. Everything I'm not." Or would ever be.

"You don't give yourself enough credit, Pipes." His voice was disapproving.

"Everything is different here."

"Good or bad?"

"I can't decide," I admitted, drawing lazy circles on the bedding. "Sure, it looks like paradise, and I'm living in a palace bigger than the White House, but it's too much. None of it feels real. I keep thinking that any minute I am going to wake up in *my* room."

"You might get used to all that luxury and not come back," he said.

"Never," I vowed, but my mind immediately went to Zane.

"Thank God." He exhaled in relief. "Because I'd come get your ass and drag you home."

I smiled into the phone. "It's so good to hear your voice, Park. I really miss you."

"Maybe I could visit," he fished, hoping for an invitation.

For some reason the idea of Parker in Raven Hollow didn't thrill me as much as it should have. I hesitated. "Maybe."

"Or not," he added, sensing my lack of enthusiasm.

It had not been my intention to hurt his feelings, because I did really want to see him. The crappy part was I couldn't rationalize why I didn't think it was a good idea. Something about this place, this island ... "Whatever. Don't be like that. You'd hate it here," I said, trying to lighten the suddenly serious mood.

There was a bit of a pause. "Not if it's where you are."

I swallowed. There it was, the inkling that Parker liked me more than just as a friend. He had been patient with me, not pushing, but lately he had been dropping not-so-subtle hints. I was still not ready to take that huge step. Parker was important to me; he was family. If we crossed that line and it went sour, I wouldn't be able to forgive myself if I lost him. Selfish, but I needed Parker in my life, and I was taking the safe path for now—friends.

"It's just three months," I reasoned. "Ninety days. I should be able to survive without ending up in juvie or on Google's homepage."

"Not funny," he moped.

"Tough crowd tonight," I mumbled. "I should go. It's getting late. Text me later?"

"Ditto." His voice was laced with concern.

Click. There went home.

I had expected the ache in my chest to lessen after talking to Parker. Sadly, that was not the case.

I'LL ADMIT, life was better in flip-flops. And with a maid. And a chef.

But that's where better ended.

Rose spent every second she could criticizing my wardrobe, clucking her tongue at my hairstyle, and picking apart my mannerisms—or more appropriately, lack of. She wanted to mold me into a miniature, younger version of herself. Christ. No wonder my mom had skedaddled the first chance she had gotten. Rose was smothering. It could be she was trying to make up for the last seventeen years, but if I had to hear her say one more time, "Piper Brennan, that's not how a lady acts," I was going to clobber her. Old woman or not, I could only bite my tongue for so long. And this was most definitely the longest I'd gone without lashing back.

I was having sarcasm withdrawals.

The use of my full name brought painful memories of my mom. They shared the same eerie tone and disapproving glare. The only consolation … she adored TJ, and he seemed genuinely happier here than he had in months. At least a change in scenery had done one of us some good. I, on the other hand, suffered, missing her more that we were so far away from the only place I'd ever lived. There was not a single piece of Mom inside this museum.

The longer I stayed locked behind the walls of my room, the more I seemed to gasp for air. Too much space. Unfamiliar surroundings. Too much time alone with my thoughts. I needed to get out of here —pronto.

Throwing on a pair of shredded jean shorts and a black tank, I headed out onto the balcony. How freaking convenient was it that my bedroom had its own entrance? As I raced down the stairs, I sent TJ a text, letting him know I had gone out, not to worry, blah, blah, blah.

Warm sunlight kissed my skin as I tucked my phone into my back pocket and flipped a pair of sunglasses over my eyes. The heat felt good after being inside the air conditioning all day. I lifted my face, letting the balmy breeze whisk over me. Ducking under the security gate, I set forth on foot toward the boardwalk, remembering a glimpse of shops.

They lined both sides of the wooden walkway: ice cream, souvenirs, seafood grills, and a giant Ferris wheel that overlooked the entire island. You name it, they had it. People strolled up and down, meandering in and out of the local vendors. With nothing but my cell phone and a debit card with less than a hundred bucks in my back pocket, I began my mission.

There were so many things I didn't know. Living here for just a few days, I realized there was a part of my mom's life I knew nothing about. Raven Hollow was her hometown—where she had grown up. I wanted to experience the island as she had, on my own terms, and if I could unearth any information about Rose or my mom, that would just be a bonus.

The island wares were tempting (New England at its finest) and so different than the shops in my neighborhood, but I could see little elements I never realized my mom had brought into our home. I was drawn to the glitz of a jewelry vendor, the gold and silver sparkling in the setting sun. Beside me, a guy dribbled mustard down the front of his white polo shirt. Oh man, that sucked. I bit back a smile, eyeing the felt displays of handmade jewelry. With a gentle touch, I ran my hand along the delicate silver chain of a necklace, trailing to a teardrop pendant. It looked much like the one I wore. Where mine had a white stone in the center, this one was light green.

A spark of electricity shot through my fingers, traveling up my arm. I jerked my hand away, taken by surprise. *What the hell?*

The bohemian lady behind the counter watched me intently, her long dishwater hair flowing past her waist in silky strands. Hair like hers took serious dedication. I never would have had the patience.

"You have her eyes," the woman said. She had a husky quality to her voice, and as she looked at me, it felt as if her gaze pierced my soul.

She suddenly had my full attention. I placed the tips of my fingers on the edge of her booth, leaning forward. "You knew my mom?"

A flicker of sympathy crossed her gray eyes. "Aye, I did, but that was not who I meant. It's the White Raven I speak of."

"Uh." Okay. It was official. The woman was off her rocker. *Just move on*, I told myself.

White Raven?

No clue.

But it was the first time all day anyone had said more than two words to me. I got the feeling everyone knew who I was and avoided me. "White Raven?" I echoed.

"The winds whisper about you, a warning you would be wise not to ignore." The skin around her eyes seemed to darken.

I squinted, leaning forward and thinking the light must be playing tricks on my eyes. A hundred questions tumbled through my head, and as I tried to sort out which to ask first, a lyrical voice came from behind me.

"You're Rose's granddaughter." There was a hint of old Irish or something close, like Welsh. Honestly, I couldn't tell the difference. It was very light, but beautiful all the same.

I spun around, startled that someone recognized me, and was momentarily robbed of speech. Wow. She was gorgeous in an intimidating way: striking black hair, ocean blue-green eyes, and dark tan legs that went on forever, not much younger than me. It was her friendly smile that set me at ease. "Yep. The one and only," I replied with a touch of sarcasm.

She giggled. "Why do you sound like you're not thrilled about being related to Her Highness?"

My eyes popped out. "You call her Your Highness?"

She scrunched her button nose. "Not to her face."

I could see an instant friendship forming. Anyone who wasn't kissing Rose's feet was a friend of mine. "How did she earn such a prestigious nickname?" I assumed it was because she had money pouring from her tatas.

Eyes glittering, she said, "It's pretty obvious. If I owned an island, I'd consider myself royalty."

My jaw dropped. I was dumbfounded. "The whole island?"

"Yep." A shopping bag dangled from her fingers. "That makes you royalty, Princess. I'm Zoe, by the way."

"Piper." Now it was my turn to screw up my face, but I did so less cutely. "And there is nothing royal about me."

She smiled. "I sensed that about you."

"Do you live on the island?"

A flicker of wistfulness and sadness crossed her eyes. "Born and bred. My family owns The Black Crow."

Ah. The country club. "I was there yesterday."

Like we'd been old acquaintances, she looped her arm through mine. "I heard."

I groaned. "What did you hear?"

"Your arrival has the whole island in an uproar—Rose's heir."

My face paled. I'd never thought about that. And Zoe never did tell me exactly what was being said about me. So what if I was someday to inherit Rose's wealth? It's not like she was on her deathbed. The woman was as fit as a fiddle, for Christ's sake.

"Do you want to go to a bonfire?" Zoe sprung on me. My expression must have showed my hesitation, because she added, "Come on. It will be fun. I'll introduce you to everyone. I know they would love to meet you. You're all anyone around here has talked about for weeks —the arrival of Rose's only granddaughter."

I scoffed, thinking this small town needed more interesting things to gossip about than me, but then again, my mom's death had probably been headline news. "Will there be hot guys there?" *Particularly one with dark hair and icicle eyes*, I added in my head.

She made a funny face. "*You* might think so, but I've known them my whole life, so the idea just grosses me out. However, you never know, there might be a few newbies vacationing."

Hell, why not? What else did I have to do? "I guess I could."

"I have a feeling about you, Piper," she said, grinning. "We're going to be fast friends."

Fingers flying over the buttons on my phone, I sent TJ a text, letting him know I was going to be gone a few more hours. Not that I expected him to care. It was habit. I was sure he and Rose wouldn't even miss me.

Zoe and I walked down the beach less than a quarter mile when I started to see the smoke billowing from the fire. Around a bluff, the orangey flames came into focus, popping against the blue and yellow horizon where day and night meet. It was awe-inspiring. Waves lapped, rising and falling in a lulling melody, mixing with the snapping of firewood and Brantley Gilbert's smooth, crooning voice singing about kicking it in the sticks. Sand squished over my flip-flops, wedging between my toes as we approached a group. Bottles of beer and wine coolers were being passed around. The chatter and laughter of carefree youth filled the air. It was hard to deny that this place was close to paradise.

And I was about to trip into utopia, figuratively. A tingle skipped down my spine. My gaze scanned the many faces, flames from the fire shadowing their inquisitiveness. Who could blame them? I was the shiny new toy.

A hasty chill blew in from the ocean, and I rubbed my hands down my arms. Lifting my head, my eyes clashed in a sea of blue, and suddenly, I was drowning. I swore a symphony of violins played in perfect harmony in my head. Even my soul sighed.

O.M.G.

I bit my tongue to keep from moaning. It was Zane, the hose-me-down hot guy from the club yesterday. He was here. Activate internal girly scream. *Holy crap, Piper. Get ahold of yourself. He is just a guy. No need to freak out.*

Zoe lightly bumped her shoulder against mine. "Let me give you a word of advice. That one leaves scars. Stare too long at that one, and you'll get burned."

If I was being honest, a chance to see him was the entire reason I'd come. And wowzer, he was mind-bendingly gorgeous. "Do you speak from personal experience?" My head felt like it was floating in the clouds.

Zoe giggled. "Zane? Not exactly."

"Does he have a girlfriend?" I wanted to hit my head on the wall as soon as those words left my mouth. God, I was acting a little too desperate. What was wrong with me? It was like I'd never seen a guy before. *What a way to make a first impression, Pipe.*

If Zoe thought I was odd, she didn't show it. "Not that I know of. But he doesn't always tell me. Brothers tend to suck that way."

Didn't I know it?

Wait. What?

I choked.

My face flamed ten different shades of red. *Her brother?* Oh God. I had more or less admitted I had the hots for her brother. "I'm so embarrassed."

She laughed lightly. "You shouldn't be. I'm used to it. He has that effect on the female population, but then he opens his mouth and poof, the drool-factor is shattered. I'm warning you, Zane is a prickly bastard."

I didn't know if I should thank her or hide my head in the nearest sand hole. "Duly noted." It wasn't like I had come here looking for a spring fling, but it didn't mean I couldn't have a little fun. Warnings kind of rolled off me like water off a duck's back.

Zoe waved at a girl with perfect auburn ringlets. "Come on. Let me introduce you to everyone."

Why not? I mean, how much more could I humiliate myself in one day?

CHAPTER 5

Moving closer to the roaring fire, I was hyper aware of Zane. I could feel his eyes on me, but I kept mine averted, knowing I would probably stumble and face-plant in the sand. Lord knows what he already thought of me. It was my mission to erase any preconceived notions that might be swirling in that head of his, because there seemed to be a lot of assumptions about Rose's granddaughter.

No doubt, they had me all wrong.

Zoe rattled off names while we weaved in and out, but it was the small group around Zane that I would remember, and not because they were all incredibly good looking, which they were, but because they were all family.

"Did you bring in another stray, Zoe?" The light-hearted timbre belonged to a dark-haired cutie. He was as breathtaking as Zane, but there was a playfulness in his aqua eyes that Zane lacked.

"This bonehead is Zach. My twin," Zoe informed me.

"Twin?" I looked between the two of them measuring their features. It was obvious by their coloring they were related—same midnight hair and aquamarine eyes, a stunning contrast.

"Trust me. It's not as cool as it sounds," Zach said teasingly. "Just wait. Zoe drives everyone around her crazy."

She pinched Zach, rolling her eyes. "Don't listen to him." A mischievous glint lit her eyes.

I froze.

Her smile brightened. "This brooding eye-candy is Zane, my slightly older brother."

I coughed, trying not to let my cheeks turn a cherry red. I was going to kill her later, if I didn't die from mortification by the end of the night.

Our eyes engaged. Before this moment, I had wondered if seeing him would bring forth those tingles of interest and lust. It was strange. I'd never had such a sharp reaction to anyone. My heart caught in my throat, a mess of emotions slamming into me, turning like the tides.

Well, I guess that answered my question. Hell yes, seeing him brought a mess of emotions, and I thought for sure my knees were going to buckle.

The color of his eyes was mesmerizing, reminding me of a frozen cavern. Hues of crystal blue refracted from the firelight. I wouldn't have been surprised if there was drool dripping from the side of my mouth. He looked edible, even in just jeans and a T-shirt.

"We sort of met." He was frowning, but the sound of his voice did funny things to my belly.

"You failed to mention that you two met," Zoe added, giving me an inquisitive glance, the kind that said, "We are so going to talk about that later."

Keep cool. I angled my head, meeting Zane's cool gaze head on. "Right. The country club. I was warned about you." I couldn't believe I sounded so calm and flirtatious, especially since I was quivering inside.

"For good reason." A chill settled over his words, hardening those eyes to chips of ice.

Zoe thumped him on the chest in warning. "Ignore him. He's always an ass."

"But I'm not," said an amused voice to the right of Zane.

Zoe's smile widened. "How could I forget about my big brother? Oh wait, I can't. He always makes his presence known. This, Piper, is Zander."

What the heck was with all the Zs, and how many were there?

And good grief, did they all have to look like dark Celtic gods? The accents … Irish? Welsh? I was no scholar. It was faint, but enough to make most girl's hearts wobble. Zoe had a trio of troublesome brothers. I didn't know whether to envy or pity her. So, of course, instantly, I liked them, well, except for Zane. My feelings for him were undetermined. "Please tell me there aren't more of you."

Zoe handed me a drink. "That is a loaded question."

I gave her a puzzled glance.

Zach chuckled. "Zoe is just sore that I'm older by four minutes. She hates being the baby but uses it to her advantage at every single chance."

"Hey," she protested, "that is not entirely true." But her tone wasn't very convincing.

"So what do think of Raven Hollow?" asked Zach.

I swirled the yellowish liquid in my cup, which I figured was lemonade and probably vodka. Parties were my thing, but drinking, not so much. I hated the fuzziness and tripping over my feet. Add in the puking my guts out and the killer hangovers, and one time was enough for me. Poor Parker. I didn't know what I would have done without him watching out for me and taking care of me.

The memory made me miss him that much more. "It's not home."

Zach pulled a swig from his cup. "I'm going out on a hunch here, but you don't seem like the typical summer girl."

"Summer girl?" I echoed.

He waved his drink in the air with his movements. "Yeah, you know. The rich girls who come here for the summer, looking for a righteous tan and a hookup with a local." The smile on Zach's lips said he had been one of those local hookups more than once.

"I am definitely not one of those," I assured him.

"Gross." Zoe wrinkled her nose. "Are you hitting on my new friend?"

Zach wiggled his brows.

I laughed, pegging him for a harmless flirt. Anyway, I was more interested in another Hunter. There was a strange pull inside me, confusing and unnerving. I didn't understand why my body was on high alert when it came to Zane. We'd barely met, and yet I was ready to go under the dock with him for some intense, reckless lip-locking. What I wouldn't give to get my hands on his totally touchable abs. Perfection.

I'd never even had a boyfriend before, and then, overnight I became a hussy. Not likely. I had standards, and it was time I took control of my raging hormones. Taking a sip from my cup, I hoped it would clear my head.

"Ignore him," said a husky voice. It belonged to Zander, the eldest Hunter. "He hits on everything with a skirt." It took me a moment to realize he was talking about Zach, not Zane.

"Good thing I left all my skirts in Chicago." Needing to steady my legs, I took a seat in one of the empty lawn chairs beside Zoe.

She laughed. "I knew I was going to like you."

Me too. Zoe was very easy to talk to, and normally girls and I didn't mix—too much jealousy and drama. I didn't need either in my life. Thank goodness for Parker, but having a guy for a best friend had complications in itself.

Zander took the seat on the other side of me. A piece of me was hoping Zane would have occupied the empty seat, but he couldn't be farther from me.

The party was pretty tame compared to the ones I normally attended. No blinding rainbow lights. No Parker. No skimpy-dressed, boyfriend-stealing, bimbos. And someone had a serious love-fest with Brantley Gilbert, as another one of his hits pumped over the beach. Most of the people were nice, but standoffish. The ones who did talk to me did so for only a minute for polite chitchat or a nod before speaking with Zander. If it weren't for Zoe, Zach, and Zander (the triple Zs) making me laugh, it would have been the pits. Zane didn't say two words to me, but I caught his eyes on me constantly, and each time his scowl deepened.

WTF?

What was with this guy?

I was starting to think all he had going for him was his extraordinary face. He had the look of a guy who left a string of broken hearts in his wake, and I didn't want to be one of his victims. Or did I?

The next time I caught him glaring at me, I held his with one of my own, raising a challenging brow, not that I thought he was the kind of guy who backed down from a challenge. And he wasn't.

Glowering, he didn't look away, and I hated to admit that his arctic glare was making me uneasy. I blinked. It must have been a hell of a blink, cause the next thing I knew, he was standing in front of me, blocking the heat from the crackling fire.

"Zoe, she shouldn't be here," he snapped.

I was taken aback by his harsh tone. It made the kitty cat inside me throw out her claws. "Are you always this welcoming, or are you just a classic douche?"

"Oooh," his other two brothers chorused, bumping fists.

He shot me with icy daggers that were probably very intimidating to most, but I didn't back down easily. Parker could attest to that and all the sticky situations he'd gotten me out of, except this time I was on my own.

"Douche," he repeated. "How charming."

I lifted my chin. No one pushed me around or told me where I could or couldn't be. I wasn't one of those placid girls. The sooner Zane Hunter realized that, the better, or we were going to be having many more confrontations. "I call it like I see it."

Zane's eyes flashed—similar to the blue center of a flame.

"Take a chill pill." Zander stood, putting himself between the son of Satan and me. They were almost the same height, topping at over six feet. "Nothing is going to happen with me around."

Huh? Happen?

What did he think I was going to do?

It was clear from Zane's straight expression that he wasn't convinced. "Oh, how could I forget? Zander is above the laws. It's your funeral." And with that lingering unpleasant thought, Zane sauntered his jean-clad butt into the shadows, giving me his back.

I didn't know why I was even thinking about his butt. Asshole. I mentally flipped him off. "What the hell was that about? What is he talking about?"

Zoe offered the lamest excuse I'd ever heard. "I told you my brother was moody."

I wanted to shake her. Moody? That was downright rude, hurtful, and senseless. "Maybe I should go. I don't what to cause problems." I shifted in my seat to get up before I made a bigger scene.

Zach stopped me. "Don't let him get to you." His eyes narrowed at Zane's back. "He's the black sheep of the family."

"He's heinous," Zoe added with a cute pout that would have looked ridiculous on me.

I don't know what it was about her, but I felt like I might have just made a legit, girl friend. Look at me. Two days on this island and I'd made a friend and an enemy without even trying. I decided to stay.

"So what's it like living in that enormous house?" Zach asked, smiling at me. The light from the fire caught strands of his raven hair. The Hunters all had that in common: dark, dark hair. And the accent.

Toying with my necklace, I replied, "I wouldn't call it a house. It's atrocious."

For the next hour, the triple Zs kept me busy with the thousand question game. The sun had completely disappeared over the oceanic horizon, and the burning wood snapped. *He* pretty much stayed out of my way and I his. As the crowd began to thin and the fire dwindled, Zane emerged from the shadows, appearing beside me.

And just like that, my body was on pins and needles again. Damn him. I wrapped my arms around myself, trying to chase the sudden chill that prickled my skin.

Zach nudged him in the shoulder. "Zane, stop sulking for two seconds and give the lady your hoodie. She's cold."

I started to protest, but he had already scooped it off a wooden log and handed it to me. "Here," he said, dark and sinfully beautiful.

I hated it. Hated him.

Liar. Liar. Pants on fire, my subconscious chanted.

It was on the tip of my tongue to tell him I didn't need his stupid hoodie, but before I could utter the words, a shiver tore through me. It would be pointless to pretend, but what he didn't know was the shudder was more because of his presence than the cold breeze blowing in from the oceanfront. "Thanks," I grumbled, slipping my arms into the sleeves and tugging the soft material over my head. The fabric hung past my fingertips. Then, as if someone else claimed my body, I lifted the ends to my face, inhaling.

My heart missed a beat. It smelled of summer rain, smoky firewood, and a scandalous Zane. The three blended in an exotic fragrance that teased all the senses, making me completely forget myself. I lifted my eyes, and I wanted to climb into the nearest sinkhole.

Zane had been watching. He arched his brow.

I couldn't believe I'd gotten caught sniffing his hoodie, especially after he'd made it very clear he didn't want me here. Classic. Only me. My cheeks flamed. The darkness hid most of my face, but still, it was awwwk-ward.

"You're in over your head, rich girl," he murmured.

The claws came back out. "Good thing I'm not a rich girl."

He snorted. "The big-ass house you're staying in says otherwise." He leaned forward, his face inches from mine. "You even smell like money."

I exhaled the breath I'd been holding, his nearness causing a fleet of somersaults. That was funny, because I knew for a fact that I smelled like a five dollar bottle of Pantene. "Shows how much you don't know about me."

"Why are you here?"

What's his deal? "Did I do something to piss you off?"

His eyes roamed curiously over my face. "You should leave before you get hurt."

"Hurt?" Was he …? "Is that a threat?"

He shook his head. "No. A warning. One you should take seriously."

Did I detect a hint of sadness? Of regret? I hadn't been sure anything could break his frigid exterior, so to hear actual emotion did something funny to my belly. "And that's my cue." I stood up. "I would like to say it's been a pleasure, but it hasn't." Then I turned to leave, but not before I thought I caught a glimpse of a smirk.

Argh. Boys.

I gave a slight wave to Zoe, letting her know I was heading home. The night's air washed over my face as my feet squished in the cold sand. If it weren't for the huge moon tonight glowing gently, I would be walking around blindly. Its reflection cast an orb onto the vast waters. There was a peacefulness in the night here that the city lacked.

I had gone a whole ten steps when I heard footsteps behind me. Lifting my head, Zane's looming form materialized. "Oh, here." I started to shrug out of his hoodie, thinking that was why he had come after me.

"Keep it." A slow grin tugged at his lips. "It looks better on you."

Did he just compliment me?

Secretly, I was glad he didn't want it back. Not only was it chilly, but there was something cozy about wearing a guy's hoodie. Even if that guy was a drool-enticing ass.

He matched his strides with mine. "You shouldn't walk home alone."

My steps faltered. He wasn't going to start this again. Biting back a groan, I tried to reason with him. "It's only a few beach houses down." Being alone with Zane had to be hazardous for my health—if not, then definitely my heart.

"Still, it's not safe at night, Princess."

I scrunched my nose at the pretentious nickname. "You really know how to shake a girl up, don't you? Guys like you need to come with a warning. And if you call me *Princess* again, I'll probably unman you with my knee."

He ran a hand through his already messy hair, but on him it looked dashing. "You are not at all like I expected."

"I could say the same about you," I mumbled.

He gave a soft chuckle.

We had just reached the street, and I could see the front gate of Raven Manor. It was hard to miss. A smart girl would have been cautious about walking alone with a guy she barely knew. I couldn't explain it. There was nothing about the way he looked that should make me feel safe, but that was precisely how Zane made me feel. And that pissed me off. I wasn't a damsel-in-distress kind of gal. I *was* the kind of girl that took care of herself. No one was going to intimidate me or make me feel inferior.

The universe must have wanted to test my so-called, self-proclaimed bad-assness, because just as I was feeling pretty damn good about myself, a noise clattered through the street. To me, the sound was like a cannonball, explosive and life-threatening, danger becoming a tangible thing in the air. My stomach ended up in my throat.

I jumped, bumping into Zane, and my pulse went wild.

"Hey, you okay?" He placed a hand on my wrist, steadying me.

A bolt of static vibrated up my arm, but I hardly noticed as my eyes darted over the empty road. Nothing stirred. "Yeah. I'm fine," I said in a trance, convincing myself as much as him.

His lips twitched. "Good. I would hate to have to carry you home."

I rubbed my eyes. "Sorry. I didn't mean to freak out on you. It's just sometimes, since my mom—" My voice choked. I couldn't finish the sentence. I never talked about her, especially to a guy I barely knew. What was wrong with me?

Great. He was going to think I was a basket case.

Aren't you? whispered a dark voice inside my head.

"You don't have to explain. I get it." His fingers casually stroked along the inside of my wrist. It was like the Fourth of July. Fireworks exploded inside me.

He did? I forced myself to meet his hypnotizing gaze. "Right. I guess you heard." I had forgotten how small this island was and how fast news of this magnitude must have traveled. Obviously he knew about my mom.

"Maybe. And even if I hadn't, it's not my business."

Now we'd come to the awkward good-bye. This was far from a date, so why was I stressing? Between Zane and my overactive paranoia, my palms were sweating. "I think I can take it from here." I placed a hand on the gate.

Zane leaned a shoulder against the brick post. "Let me give you a piece of advice. Stay on your side of the block. Night, Princess."

I gaped. It was amazing that he could so easily wreck an almost palpable ending to the evening. To think I had almost forgiven him for being a dickhead.

Shaking my head, I pivoted, showing him *my* back, and walked away, but not before I got the last word, or in my case, gesture. I stuck out my hand, giving him the one-figure salute. *Eat this.*

I heard him laugh. Dark. Dangerous. Desirable.

It was obvious Zane Hunter was going to be a thorn in my side. To think I thought I was going to have a boring summer. He didn't know it, but Zane had declared combat. His dark, brooding, and fierce eyes might work on everyone else, but not me.

I glanced over my shoulder, slitting my eyes, prepared to give him a dirty look. He was gone. What the—?

There was no way he could have disappeared so fast. It was just not humanly possible. Then again, the jerkwad probably wasn't human.

I thought about checking in on TJ, but after the strange night, I just wanted to stew alone. So instead of going through the house, I went toward the terrace that led to my bedroom stairs. I had to admit, it felt like I was sneaking in—a concept that wasn't foreign to me—but this time, I knew my mom wouldn't be waiting on my bed to scold me.

I wished she were.

Flipping the switch, a soft light chased away the lurking shadows. I was exhausted, more mentally than physically. My so-called detective skills sucked. I had learned nothing about my mom, nothing about

Rose I didn't already know, and the guy I'd been crushing on made my head spin. He had a dizzying presence. One minute he was showing me the door, and the next, he was securing my safety.

Guys like Zane were hazardous to my emotions. I collapsed on the bed, fully clothed, my eyes fluttering shut, and the scent of Zane following me into sleep. He was such a d-bag. A hallelujah-have-mercy, smokin' hot d-bag.

CHAPTER 6

Within seconds, the dark whisper loomed over me. The nightmare was always the same. Mom and I were walking home, smiling and laughing, the wind from the lakefront teasing our identical shade of blonde hair. It wasn't called the Windy City for nothing, but it was one of the great things about living here. Brick condos lined either side of the narrow street. In the distance, an impatient driver honked his horn. Ahh. The sweet, bustling sounds of Chicago.

In the dream, we were happy, just the way I remembered her. She laughed as we strolled down the road—a sound I will forever cherish —each carrying a plastic shopping bag filled with the delicious smells of Chinese food. She looped her arm through mine, maintaining our Friday night family tradition. Since before I was born, Mom and Dad had spent their Friday nights exploring the city's culinary wares, and Chinese was a family fav.

It was the sudden change on her face that sent the first signals of alarm: genuine fear. She had stopped walking and was tugging on my arm, pleading with the men who came out of the shadows to let me live.

A gun.

One of them shoved it in her face. She stood rigid, shoving me behind her, our food splattering over the sidewalk. Sweet and sour sauce dribbled down the city drains, fried noodles spilling out of the container, and egg rolls rolling down the street. Needles of dread stabbed my gut. No matter how hard I tried, I could never get a glimpse of their faces.

The gun went off, vibrating on the brick walls of the alley, followed by my hair-raising scream. Mom crumbled to the ground, and I fell to my knees beside her. It was at that point everything went fuzzy. But there was one moment that was crystal clear.

Blood covered my hands. Her blood. Hot. Thick. Sticky.

I bolted awake, prickles of terror beading along my skin.

THE RECURRING NIGHTMARE brought forth a memory from my childhood that I rarely allowed myself to dwell on: ghosts. When I was little, I was convinced that I saw dead people. Bizarre didn't come close to how seeing them made me feel: like a freak, curious, scared, uncertain, sad, disturbed. The list of emotions went on. I made the mistake of telling my mom. It was the one and only time she ever raised her voice at me and the last time I ever brought it up. As I grew, those glimpses became less and less frequent until they stopped all together.

It was easier to pretend it had never happened than face the reality that I saw things other people didn't. Parker was the only one who believed me. But then again, Parker believed in aliens and Superman. He wasn't exactly what I would call levelheaded.

I awoke restless with the smell of sizzling bacon tickling my senses. Everything was always better with bacon. And chocolate. Better yet, chocolate-covered bacon. Yum, now I was starving.

Given the size of this house, I knew food had to be close. I narrowed down the smell to the mahogany tray on the dresser, a covered white plate on top. Sitting up, I pulled a hand through my hair, staring at the tray, willing it to magically float into my hands. When I finally gave up on my nonexistent superpowers, I padded across the room, the hardwood cool on the bottoms of my bare feet. There was a handwritten note cushioned between two prongs of what looked like a placeholder.

THOUGHT you might like breakfast in bed, since you missed actual breakfast.
    Rose.

A SMALL SMILE worked its way across my lips. I uncovered the plate and sighed at the same time my stomach growled. Blueberry pancakes, scrambled eggs, two strips of crispy bacon, and a side of ketchup. Eggs without ketchup were a crime in my house.

I could so get accustomed to all this five-star food that wasn't cooked by moi. Rose was going to ruin me—spoil me so much that my life before this would be dull in comparison, and I refused to let that happen.

Staring down at the plate of my favorite foods in a battle of wills, my belly and I both agreed that my act of rebellion could start tomorrow. I carried the tray to my bed, snuggled back under the covers, and dug in.

A quiet knock sounded just as I licked the last crumb off the fork. "It's open," I called.

Estelle peeked around the door, hazel eyes warm and sparkling. "You're up." Her envious auburn hair was swept up into a stylish, messy bun. When I attempted the style, it just looked like a bird's nest.

I set the empty tray on the nightstand. "It's late, huh?" Not everyone was on owl-time as I was. Mornings were difficult for me—understatement. I was downright inoperable. Parker swore I was part firefly. I only came out at night, and that was when I shined.

Estelle grinned. "Depends on who you ask. If I didn't have to work, I'd be sleeping too."

I stifled a yawn. "Do you like working for Rose?" I asked, curious if Rose treated her employees well.

Her shoulder lifted in a one-sided shrug. "It pays. Actually, I'm really lucky to have this job. There aren't a lot of opportunities available on an island this small. My father is acquainted with your grandma and helped me get the job."

I was glad she was feeling more relaxed around me.

Soft freckles dusted either side of her nose. "It's my second summer here. I've been saving to get off this blasted island. Go to college somewhere exciting, like Paris."

I could see the stars in her eyes. Estelle had big dreams. "Who doesn't want to see Paris?"

"Your dad is an artist, right? You seem so worldly."

"Me? This is the first time I've ever been outside Chicago." But unlike Estelle, I hadn't wanted to escape.

She sat on the edge of the bed, one leg tucked underneath her. "Well, you would never guess it. You seem so sure of yourself. There's this cool edge to you."

"Trust me. I'm anything but cool. I choke around hot guys. I have more bad hair days than good. And I have a slew of insecurities." Did I ever. Apparently, I could put on a good front. I had body image issues like every teenage girl. Mostly, I lived in fear of being alone. Forever.

Her smile brightened. "Thank God. I was beginning to think you weren't human. Did you have a nice day yesterday at the boardwalk?"

I kind of liked the way her mind bounced from one topic to the next. It was refreshing. "Interesting." I shifted on the oversized bed, sitting cross-legged. "What do you know about Zane Hunter?"

Estelle stiffened, her eyes averting to her lap. "More than I care to. We grew up together."

"You did?" I didn't know why I was surprised. Of course all the locals knew each other, and maybe Estelle could dish on the goods. "Was he always a prick?"

If she was offended by my unfiltered mouth, she didn't show it. "I'm guessing you had your first run-in with Death Scythe?"

"Death Scythe?" I repeated.

"He's lethal."

"That he is," I mumbled.

Estelle grinned. "A lively bunch, the Hunters. A word of warning, Zane is not boyfriend material. Don't get swept away by that face of his. You would be better off flirting with Zander—less chance of getting burned, unless you're just looking for a wham, bam, thank you ma'am."

I was never good at taking advice, but maybe this time I'd make an exception. I was no one's booty call. Then again, maybe I could learn a thing or two from the famous Zane. "What is it that makes bad boys so appealing?"

"When it pertains to Zane, it would be a shorter list to name his redeeming qualities, if any."

"Yeah, I kind of got that feeling. Did you and he ever …?"

She made a face. "Ew. God no. He's not my type."

That got me thinking. Did I have a type? Zane couldn't possibly be *my* type, because then that would mean my type was douchebag. "And who *is* your type?" I asked.

A dreamy smile lifted the corner of her lips. "Jensen. He's a re—" She stopped midsentence before starting over. "He's the complete opposite of Zane. Do you have a boyfriend back home?"

I got the feeling she was hiding something, and I vowed to get it out of her sooner or later. "Uh. No, not really."

She pursed her lips. "You don't sound so sure about that."

Pulling my knees to my chest, I hugged my legs. "There is this guy, but we've been friends since diapers. It would be weird, you know? I'm not sure I want to cross that line."

"Maybe distance is just what you need. It might put things into perspective." Standing, she reached for the empty tray on the night-stand. "I should get back to work. And you should take advantage of the sun. Go down to the beach and work on that tan, pasty."

I laughed.

That sounded like a good idea. "I just might."

I GAZED at the rugged jag of cliffs jutting over the ocean, watching the waves swallow them. Tiny flowers fought their way through the cracks, blooming along the rough terrain alongside small patches of wild grass. Twirling a dark gray colored pencil, I tipped back my head, deep in thought. Waves hurled themselves against the sandy shore, slapping my feet, the deep, deep blue water going on forever.

I nibbled my lower lip, staring down at the sketchpad in my lap, a pretty girl clutching a wicked-looking scythe. My favorite kind of anime: a girl who could kick major ass and wasn't afraid to get bloody. It was always the same sleek, deadly weapon, just a different heroine. Her face never really mattered because the weapon always stole the show.

Death's weapon.

A psychologist would probably tell me it was ironic—my mind projecting my mother's death, a symbol of her horrible murder. I would probably tell that shrink to stick to his bullshit analysis, and then I would be promptly asked to never come back.

But today, the weapon made me think of Zane. It was wacky weird. What were the chances he had a nickname about my favorite anime accessory? I'll tell you: a gazillion billion to one.

I angled my head, using the natural light to shade in the shadows on her face. As the creative juices flowed, I envisioned her with bright purple hair, something punky—the colors not yet on paper working in my imagination.

As my strokes flew over the paper, a shadow fell over my pad. I silently cursed the soul stupid enough to invade my peace and block my soon-to-be fading light. Lifting my pencil from the page, I glanced up. The silent curse became a mutter under my breath, and a body planted itself down in the sand beside me. Zane's body.

"Did you come to run me out of town, or just irritate me?" I huffed.

One corner of his lips tipped as if he were secretly laughing. "Both." He snatched the sketchpad from my lap before I realized his intent.

"Hey," I protested, attempting to steal it back from his grubby fingers.

He put up one of his python-sized arms as a roadblock. Ten seconds passed while his eyes scanned my drawing, exposing a piece of myself I wasn't comfortable opening up to a jerk. Ten whole seconds. It felt like ten minutes. "This is really good." He traced the outline of the scythe.

Huh? A Compliment?

"Hang on a minute. I think I might spontaneously combust," I said dryly.

Zane stretched out his legs, and the dark material of his shirt pulled taut against his chest. "Are you always this much fun?"

I thought about jabbing him with my pencil. "Do you always treat people like they have no feelings?"

"Not usually."

I snorted. "You have a funny way of showing it."

He handed over my sketchbook, his bright blues on mine. "That's because you're different."

"Different how?"

Unruly dark hair fell over his forehead. "You being here causes a whole lot of problems for me, and I don't like it."

His words went right through my flesh like a cold wind. What I heard was, I don't like *you*, and it was a blow to my womanhood. "Screw you." I grabbed my stuff and started to push to my feet.

"Piper, wait." He reached out, placing a hand on my arm, neither of us prepared for the static tremor of his touch. Quickly, he snatched his hand back. "That came out harsher than I intended."

I paused, my back to him.

"Don't leave."

Holy cow. I had never imagined that two words, said in just the way he had, could have such a powerful effect on me. They reached deep inside me. Maybe it was the accent. Yep. It had to be the accent. A few heartbeats passed as I collected myself before I turned to face him.

Surprise and bewilderment burrowed in his brows. "You really don't know," he said.

I squinted, wondering if I had set myself up for another trap. "Know what?" I asked.

Curious eyes roamed my face. "Who you are."

Hugging the sketchpad to my chest, I asked, "And just who do you think I am?" If this was his idea of a twisted game … but his dark expression appeared so sincere.

He shook his head. "You confuse me." Lifting his hand, he froze in midair, stopping just short of stroking my face, second-guessing whether he should touch me again. He looked at me without a trace of irritation or loathing.

"Me?" I stated, feeling a rise in my blood pressure. "You're the one who is speaking in circles. You're the one who has been nothing but rude. And now you are telling me I confuse you. You're joking, right?"

He leaned in, the scent of him a sensory overload. I wanted to press my nose to his neck and inhale a deep, drugging breath. "I wish things were different," he murmured.

My heart pranced. What was he doing to me? Just a few minutes ago, I had been ready to punch him in the nose. He had done nothing but insult me since we met, but here I was drifting toward him, captured by his crystal eyes and the warmth of his nearness. It didn't matter that nothing he said made sense. I couldn't comprehend it, anyway.

The pad of paper slipped from my grasp, and I bit my lip.

Sweet baby Jesus.

Was he going to kiss me? Was I going to let *him* kiss me? Did I want Zane to kiss me? The kiss I would never forget. The mere thought of his lips on mine, of him kissing me brainless—because boys like him definitely kissed with fervor. His hands wrapped around my waist …

My gut twisted in a wild need I'd never felt before. He hadn't even touched me, but his eyes caressed every part of my skin. I held my breath, waiting, poised on the edge of reckless stupidity. I barely knew Zane, yet here I was. He stirred a dark passion I had never known lay inside me, opened my body to a world I had never explored but desperately wanted to. Right here. Right now.

I wanted to close the small distance between us. I wanted to feel the craziness his lips promised. I wanted …

A dog barked.

At first, I thought I'd imagined the sound. It was so faint, hardly heard above the pounding of my heart and the waves lapping and foaming on the shore. Then it came again. And again. Louder. Clearer.

I couldn't believe what I was seeing. A fluffy, white pup nuzzled its way between us, yapping in excitement.

I blinked.

The spell was broken.

Shit.

I shook my hair, letting the breeze pick the loose strands off my face. The pooch, oblivious to what she'd interrupted, licked Zane's face, and I about lost it until I saw the scowl. I was getting quite acquainted with that particular look. He shot to his feet as if he couldn't wait to get away from me. Standing, I brushed the sand off my shorts and mumbled, "Thanks for the hand, dillweed."

Zane's lips curled menacingly. It was infuriating that he constantly seemed to be laughing at me. "I think we can both agree that bad things happen when we touch, Princess."

What did that even mean? How harmful could the simple gesture of a hand be? It wasn't like I was asking him to bang me on the beach, well not in words at least. What my body had been begging for moments before was another story. What the hell was wrong with me?

"Oh, I'll show you bad," I snapped.

"You should be careful what you say. I wouldn't want to misconstrue your words."

"Blow me."

A single brow arched. "If you knew what was good for you, you would turn around, walk off the beach, and never look back. You would get off this island before …"

Before what?

At this point I was too furious to care. Emotions were high, and mine swiftly turned to rage. *Oh, I'll show him my back all right.* "Kiss ass, Zane. And stay the hell off my beach."

I thought that was a heck of an exit. Score one for Piper. I gave myself a mental high five as I stomped in the sand. Zane Hunter didn't have the first clue as to who he was messing with.

CHAPTER 7

Not even the walk from the beach to the manor did the slightest to cool my temper. Zane Hunter was the most infuriating guy I'd ever met. Just like a million other moments in my life, I wished my mom were here to listen to me vent, offer me advice, or at the very least, make me laugh. I may not be able to make a lick of sense out of guys like Zane, but a bowl of mint chocolate chip ice cream loaded with all the fixings might help ease my wrath.

It was what Mom would have done: stuffed our faces and made horrible jokes until whatever was bothering me no longer seemed important.

I sighed and made my way down one of the hallways I hoped led to the kitchen. My hunt had barely begun when Rose found me. I cursed under my breath.

To say I wasn't in the mood was an understatement.

"Piper," she said. "Just who I was looking for."

"Oh, goodie," I mumbled tartly. My rumbling belly was pissed, seeing my calorie indulgence fading from existence.

"I've been meaning to talk to you. I know things have been hard …" she started until I slumped against the wall.

Ugh. I didn't want to have this conversation, not while my emotions were high and close to the surface. It wouldn't take much to push me over the edge. As silly as it was, I did not want to cry in front of her.

Rose sensed my hesitation and overall indifference to sharing my feelings. I *was* making it overly obvious. You would have had to be dumb as a rock to not get the message my body was conveying, and Rose struck me as anything but dumb. The old bag was as sharp as a razor. What did she expect? That I would just pour my soul out to someone who suddenly decided to pop into my life? If that was the case, she should be talking with TJ. He had inherited my dad's blabbermouth and sensitive genes; they kind of went hand-in-hand.

I was cautious, guarded, and cynical. "We really don't have to do this now. Or ever," I added, pushing off the wall, hoping she would let me go.

Rats. No such luck.

"Since you've been here, we haven't spent any time together," she said. "I wanted to give you a few days to get settled and explore the island. Now that you have ... why don't we have ourselves a woman-to-woman chat?"

Joy.

My favorite kind.

Spinning back around to face her, I dragged my butt, following her into the yellow room. I liked to color-code each room. It was the only way to keep them straight. The room itself had soft sunny walls and was more of an enclosed porch than a room. Windows lined the walls from floor to ceiling. Transparent white curtains fluttered in the breeze, and the room smelled like sand dollars and seashells.

"Were you just coming in from the beach?" she asked, taking a seat on one of the distressed wicker rockers.

I slunk into its twin, a little square glass table between us. "Yeah. I was hungry."

She folded her delicate hands in her lap. "Great. I'll have Annette whip us up something. I'm a little hungry myself."

Fan-freaking-tastic. Tea and crustless cucumber sandwiches. Just what I wanted. I kissed my ice cream good-bye.

As if her employees had a sixth sense about them, Annette walked in carrying a tray of lemonade. She carefully set it down on the table, and Rose asked her to bring in something for us to nibble on. Annette nodded.

Did she just do a small curtsy?

I felt like I was living in the 1940s.

Rose crossed her legs. "How was your trip into town the other day? Did you enjoy the boardwalk?"

I left my lemonade untouched and stared at my sandy feet. "Are you spying on me?"

She reached for one of the clear glasses, her blush-colored nails tapping on the glass. "Now why would you think that?"

I had expected her to flinch at my snotty tone. She didn't. Eventually I was going to get a rise out of this woman. She was not as easily provoked as Zane and not nearly as fun.

"Your safety is my main concern," she added.

"Why wouldn't I be safe?"

She took a breath and held it. Released it. "Until the men responsible for hurting my family are brought to justice, I will make sure nothing happens to you or TJ."

Finally. Emotion. Anger. That was one I was very, very familiar with. Yet I had to wonder if she knew something I didn't. Were TJ and I in danger? "Have you heard from my dad?" I tried to keep the hopefulness out of my tone, but failed. Maybe he had called with information about Mom's case. It had gone cold, but ...

Her emerald eyes softened. "No. I am sure he is carried away with his art."

My heart sunk. No matter how many times I told myself that I'd hardened my heart against disappointment, against hope, it struck back like a venomous viper. "Why did she leave here?" I blurted. Let's get to the heavy stuff. Why stop when we were on a roll?

There was a soft rap on the door. Annette strolled in with a tray of fruit kabobs, pretzels, and beer dip. My taste buds danced. This was my kind of "tea time." It was more tailgate than tea party.

Rose smiled. "What were you expecting? Cucumber sandwiches?"

Bull's-eye. "Sort of," I admitted, popping a pretzel into my mouth.

"You remind me so much of her. Your spunkiness. Your fearlessness. Your recklessness. And your appetite. I bet she was so proud of you." Her chest rose in a deep sigh, and there was a glint of regret in her eyes—unexpected. "Your mom did not want the responsibility and the stress that came with her name. Being a Morain comes with a price. Letting her leave was the second hardest thing I've ever had to experience."

I assumed her death was the first. It was for me. The single worst day of my life, and I still lived through the pain every day. "You never answered my question. Why did you let her go then?"

Rose might be old, but her skin still had this beautiful glow about it, almost unearthly. Her eyes held a sad smile. "For love. What else?"

The stick of strawberries and bananas was suspended halfway to my mouth. "My dad."

She gave a slight nod of her head, her white hair falling over one shoulder. "I always thought she would be back one day. How wrong I was. Never did I imagine that the last time we said good-bye it would be forever."

There was pain inside her, hidden behind a tough wall, but it was there nonetheless. I didn't know how I felt sharing the loss of my mother with her. We had more in common than I thought. We had both thought we would see her again, only to have that chance stripped from us by a couple of ass-faces. "Life's a bitch."

Rose gave a sophisticated chuckle. "That it is." She plucked a piece of fruit off the kabob. "Well, this turned into a much heavier discussion than I had planned, but I guess we both needed it."

I still ached, and no amount of beer dip was going to help, but it didn't stop me from popping pretzels like crack. "I guess," I agreed, still uncertain what had happened. On one hand, misery loved company. On the other, it felt sort of fake. I didn't trust Rose, and my gut instinct told me there were things she was hiding from me.

And I wanted the truth.

"You'll be the matriarch of this family someday, Piper."

"Matriarch? What is this, a feminist protest?"

"The females in our family have run things for generations. It isn't to be taken lightly. Like I said, there is a great amount of responsibility that will be yours," she informed me.

My ears perked up. I wasn't a fan of responsibility. "Like what?" Let it be known that no one even asked me. She just assumed I would take her place. Boy, was she in for a rude awakening. I had plans for my future that did not include slumming it in this mansion.

She set aside her half-drunk lemonade, her sharp eyes on mine. "You will learn soon enough when you've had time to get adjusted."

Hmm. I pursed my lips unhappily. Patience was not one of my virtues. Neither was doing as I was told.

Uncrossing her legs, she stood up. "I'll see you tonight. The chef is making a special dinner. TJ's request."

"Great," I grumbled, slouching into the back of the wicker chair. "Meatloaf and mashed potatoes. Can't wait."

Her lips lifted. "You know your brother well."

AFTER A RIVETING DINNER, complete with a meal I barely managed to swallow in a dining room that couldn't have felt emptier, I retreated to my suite. The air was easier to breathe as soon as I walked in, surrounded by things that were mine.

I ignored the unmade bed. Why make it when you were just going to mess it up again? Clutter never bothered me. It meant I was christening the room as my own, which was the exact opposite of what I wanted—to be comfortable here—which only furthered my bitchy mood. Without a second thought, I closed myself into the mammoth bathroom.

As I walked past the mirror, I caught a glimpse of myself, the soft light from the chandelier catching the glittery pink of my tiny nose ring. Look at me. Unbelievable. A few days away from my life and already I could see the changes. It wasn't my outer appearance but what was inside that was changing. I twirled the little stone on the right side of my nose. *I am still me.*

What I needed was a hot, steaming shower to loosen my tense muscles. I stepped directly under the waterfall spray, letting the beads of water rain down on my upturned face. Time ceased. Even after the water began to run cold, I didn't want to leave. Pink-skinned and polished to a shine with some French soaps, I turned the water off and slid the glass door open. The entire bathroom was filled with the mist of steam. There was a white terry cloth robe hanging on a hook just to the right of the shower. I hadn't noticed it before. My fingers touched the material—not just terry cloth, but something silkier. Three violet letters were stitched at the breast. P.L.B. Those were my initials: Piper Lynn Brennan.

I didn't know whether to be touched or creeped out.

A robe seemed personal, almost like buying me panties, but it didn't stop me from slipping the cloud of fluff onto my skin. The indulgent material quickly absorbed droplets of water. After I braided my damp hair, brushed my teeth, and put some moisturizing gunk on my face, I curled up on the bed. Tugging the covers to my chin, I lay there trying to get snuggly, but the sheer size of the room made it nearly impossible to have that cozy feeling. There was too much space with me in the bed. My back wasn't butted up against the wall. It felt more like sleeping in a hotel. I stuffed the extra pillows alongside me, cocooning me. Then I wiggled to get comfortable and closed my eyes.

It didn't help.

My mind wandered, as it often did when I was alone with nothing but my thoughts. Why couldn't I be one of those people who dropped off to sleep the moment their head hit the pillow? I was restless, and this time I knew whom to blame. *Thank you, Zane.*

Never had I been so boy-crazed. There was something about this particular guy that drew me in. I was attracted to him, but I didn't want to be. He was pigheaded. Deplorable. Arrogant. Disreputable.

While counting all of Zane's flaws—and there were many—I drifted off to sleep.

IT WAS PITCH BLACK, and for a moment I didn't know if I had opened my eyes or not. A dark whisper called my name. *Piper.*

"Zane." His name tumbled from my lips.

The balcony door was open, white lace curtains dancing with the whistling winds. My eyes darted over the room, searching the shadows for movement, a burglar, or the boogieman. That door had been firmly shut when I had gone to bed. I was sure of it.

I don't know how long I lay there with my heart in my throat, just waiting to switch into ninja mode. When nothing jumped out at me, I slowly swung my feet over the side of the bed. As I padded over the cool tiles toward the open door, a familiar scent tickled my nose—fresh rain and a hint of mint, a refreshing combo. My feet moved soundlessly, only murmurs of the balmy wind and the swishing of the tide.

But I swore I had heard my name.

Under the twinkling stars, I looked out over the grounds, nightfall blanketing it as far as I could see. Through the darkness, a speck of winter blue stood out.

I stumbled, and that was all it took for the little light to vanish. My eyes scrambled to find a trace of it, as I refused to believe I was imagining things. I gripped the doorway for support, the thundering of my heart throttling my chest. The second I felt a tingle crawl down my back, I closed the door, bolted the lock, and drew the curtains shut.

Sleep was out of the question.

CHAPTER 8

I managed an entire week without one run-in with Zane. That took skill. This small island was impossible to roam about without bumping into a Hunter at every corner. Lucky for me, none of them were the six-foot, moody, perfect male specimen.

Then why was a part of me bummed each time it wasn't him?

I blamed it on lack of sleep.

Since that night, I'd been not only avoiding Zane, but also sleep. It was a lot harder to do than it sounded. My eyes and my body refused to cooperate, but that night had triggered a new nightmare where a masked man loomed over my bed. And it was the moon glinting off the gun pointed at my head that caused pandemonium to be set off inside me. The paranoia might all be in my head, yet it was very difficult to wake up in a dead sweat, your heart hammering in your throat. I wouldn't recommend it night after night. It wasn't a look I rocked well. Baggy eyes. Dark circles. Bloodshot eyes.

There was one other explanation my brain mulled over, but it was just as frightening as the masked man. It kept me up as well, but in a different way.

Zane had snuck into my room.

Crazy, right?

It made very little sense. What reason did he have for creeping into my room in the middle of the night? I couldn't wrap my brain around it, but that scent ... it was one I knew well, and I was doubtful I'd ever forget it. I might have inhaled the material of his sweatshirt until I was high on Zane. That exact smell had been lingering in my room. Explain that.

On the seventh day, I gave in. There was an unexplainable urge to see his face, even if all we did was bicker. My heart and my head needed a reminder as to why Zane was bad news. Time had lessened the volume of his douchery. As I headed to Josie, keys spinning on my finger, I contemplated going the straightforward method, but asking him if he was sneaking into my room sounded nutso, even in my head.

Of course, I still had to find him.

Whenever you were looking for someone, they were nowhere to be found, but when you wanted to avoid someone, they were everywhere.

He wasn't at work. I checked. The boardwalk—nada. This casually bumping into him idea was turning out to be a bust. Maybe I should have just texted Zoe. It was sounding a whole lot easier, but I didn't want to appear desperate, because it was most definitely not like I had to see him or I would die. Or I could stalk him at home, but that posed a problem in itself: I would actually have to know where he lived, and I didn't.

I figured that was a sign.

Today was not the day I would run into the dark and mysterious Zane Hunter. There was always tomorrow. It's not like I had any idea what I was going to say if, by coincidence, I found him.

I cut around a corner, taking a shortcut down a one-way street I was pretty sure led back to my jeep. The very last thing I needed was to lose my car. That would just make my day. The sun was slowly receding behind the horizon, and I didn't want to be roaming around in the dark, for obvious reasons.

At a walk just short of a run, I came to the parking lot where I was darn sure I'd parked. Searching the lot, I found Josie easily enough, except my jeep had a new ornament that hadn't been there earlier. A body was lounging against the rear bumper, and for a heartbeat I thought it might be Zane, but as I got a clearer look, he had shaggy blond hair, not raven black. He wore torn jeans with a muscle tee. Thick leather strands hung around his neck. His face looked slightly familiar, and I wondered if he had been at the bonfire. A curious gaze aimed my way in a not-so-friendly way. He sucked on a long drag from the cigarette dangling from his lips. The tattoo of a red hawk on the inside of his wrist captured my eye.

"Smoke?" he asked in a husky voice that led me to believe he had been puffing away since birth.

What a way to end what was turning out to be a shitty day. Let's be real. I was having a shitty year, and today of all days I was letting it get to me.

I shrugged. "Why the hell not?" I was going to give rebellion a run for its money while I was still young. Truthfully, I didn't want the cancer stick. I hated smoking, but I thought if this guy had been at the bonfire, then maybe he knew Zane. Okay, he definitely knew Zane, as everyone here knew everyone, but he might be able to give me an idea where I might find him. It didn't make sense, but suddenly it became important that I find Zane.

And something told me this guy hadn't casually ended up using my car as a resting spot. This guy knew who I was. The question was: what did he want with me? I fumbled with the strap of my cross-body bag, taking little comfort in the fact that I never left home without my mace.

With a coolness as fake as my smile, I took a cigarette from the pack he held out.

"Piper, right?" he asked.

I was getting tired of walking around with a giant nametag stamped on my forehead. "And you are?" I prompted since he wasn't offering.

A ring of smoke escaped his lips, traveling up and still keeping its shape. Cool trick. "Names really aren't important."

I positioned the cigarette between my fingers like I'd done it a million times before. "It just seems a little unfair. You already know mine."

"Life's a bitch."

He wasn't going to get an argument from me. "And so am I."

Bad-habit guy leaned forward, interest lighting his smoky eyes. "I hope so."

If he wasn't going to volunteer information, then I was going to cut to the chase, put him on the spot. "You're a friend of Zane's, aren't you?"

"I wouldn't go as far as to say we are friends."

The hair on the nape of my neck stood on end, and a chill had moved through my blood. I had a horrible feeling that I was treading on a slippery slope with bad-habit guy.

He flicked his lighter, the orange-yellow flame jumping to life. I put the slim paper between my lips, leaning forward, never taking my eyes off him. Just before the torch reached the tip, I heard a voice that had my skin sparking.

"I would think twice before taking a puff. It's probably laced." Zane stepped out of the shadows.

I blinked a few times as his form came into focus. Words couldn't express what was happening inside me. Seeing Zane caused a chain reaction of fireworks, booming and sizzling. The cigarette I'd been holding between my fingers slipped, tumbling to the ground, forgotten. I had not taken one drag from the nicotine stick, yet I was short of breath.

Then his words registered in my brain, and my eyes bulged. *Laced?* I tore my eyes from yummy Zane to glare at bad-habit guy. "Did you —?" Dumbfounded, I couldn't even complete a sentence. I'd hung around some questionable people before, but this was a first. Drugged?

What would he possibly gain from drugging me, other than violating me? My mind went off on a tangent, envisioning all sorts of slasher quality scenarios.

He pushed off the frame of my jeep with his foot, closing the distance between us. "Don't get your panties in a wad, little Raven. It's not personal."

I flinched.

Personal?

I'd say trying to slip me a drug was kind of personal. "What the hell is wrong with you?" I demanded, mortified that I had been naive enough to trust this ass-tard.

He leered. "How much time do you have?"

Smartass.

Zane growled at my side. "I'd back up, Crash. Unless you want me to break your nose."

"Interesting." He threw the half-smoked cigarette to the ground, smashing the cherry out with the heel of his boot. "Took you long enough," he said to Zane.

The two of them sized each other up, clearly not BFFs. Zane stiffened and tension crackled between them, thick and volatile. No long lost love, that was for sure. Sandwiched in the middle quickly seemed like a bad place to be.

"Since when did the hawks give a rat's ass about our summer girls?" Zane barked.

My mind couldn't process the situation, Zane's close proximity screwing with my already confused brain cells. And don't get me started on what the texture of his voice did to my innards, until he called me a summer girl.

That really ruffled my feathers, so I pinched him. "I am not some summer girl," I snapped.

Zane groaned. "Will you just keep your mouth shut? I'm trying to help you."

Crash laughed. "No, little Raven, you are most definitely not one of those flighty summer girls. Is she Zane?"

I gave them both my best bitch face.

"Why don't you get the hell out of here before I make you eat that pack of cigarettes in your hand?" Zane suggested very persuasively ... or more like threateningly.

My hands flew to my hips, irritation spiking. "How about one of you tell me what the fuck is going on?"

They ignored me, only fueling my temper. I was Irish. It didn't take much to stoke that fire.

Whatever was going on between them, I couldn't help but feel like I was involved, which made absolutely no freaking sense.

"How cute. She doesn't have a clue, does she, Hunter? Afraid I might spill the beans?" Crash pushed.

Zane flashed in front of Crash, grabbing him by the front of his shirt and hauling him off his feet. Zane's eyes darkened.

And Crash's ...

Crap on a graham cracker.

Just when I didn't think things could get any more f'd up, I noticed something on Crash that my mind couldn't explain. His eyes ... I blinked and blinked again, but his eyes looked the same.

The veins around them darkened a deep crimson like blood, spidering down his cheeks. "Should I tell her or ...?"

Zane's back was to me, but I saw his fists tighten. He didn't strike me as a guy who reined in his anger. Kick ass now, and who cared about taking names?

After a count of silence, Crash said, "That's what I thought. Take your bloody hands off me, mate." He jerked, breaking out of Zane's hold.

Now that they weren't in each other's faces, I got a glimpse of Zane's profile. Nothing prepared me for what I saw, causing me to suck in a sharp breath. There was a brief moment that I was positive I was sleeping and in the throes of a nightmare, because everything I was seeing was inconceivable.

Zane, too, was sporting some creepy, veiny eyes. Different, but nonetheless disturbing. I should have been scared, running-for-the-hills, screaming-for-help scared. The sight unnerved me; however, I was also curious.

Averting his face, I swore Zane had heard my gasp of surprise. I tried to get a better view, but he cleverly kept himself angled away from me. It was enough confirmation for me. He had secrets. And they weren't the I'm-cheating-on-my-girlfriend kind of secrets. This place was off the grid freaky.

Regardless of what I had seen, Zane's presence gave me courage. Explain that. I could have blamed it on adrenaline, but really, it was just me. I asked the first thing that popped into my head. "What is wrong with your face?"

As Crash's smirk grew, the lines began to diminish. "Better ask your guard dog. I'm not dumb enough to risk Zane's wrath twice in one night." He rubbed the side of his jaw. "I'll be seeing you around, little Raven."

Zane blocked his path, towering at least four inches over Crash. "You come near her again, and I promise, you won't walk away a second time. Hit the road before I change my mind and smear the sidewalk with your face."

Crash leisurely lit another smoke before sauntering down the road. As I watched him go, I was riddled with a gazillion questions. So I turned to the only person left to answer them. "What the hell is going on?"

"A thanks would suffice," he mumbled, facing me as he ran a hand through his midnight hair.

My eyes ate him up like a bag of flaming Cheetos, searching for a shred of evidence, proving I hadn't been seeing things. Naturally there were no traces of the unusual ink-like marks. "Thanks for ruining my night," I replied, giving him a dose of attitude. He didn't need to know I had been looking for him. I would admit to nothing of the sort, not now that he was right in front of me and after what I'd seen.

"You are something else, *Princess*," he said cynically.

To set the record straight, I wasn't ungrateful that he might have saved me from a very unpleasant experience; it was that he made my palms sweat. He made my nerve endings tingle. He made my brain cells mushy. All of the above put my back up. I rubbed the inside of my slick hands on the pockets of my shorts. "What was up with your eyes?" I knew I was being forward, but he deserved it for calling me Princess.

"I don't know what you're talking about," he said, brushing me off.

I snorted. "Don't play coy with me. I know what I saw. You and ashtray both had some kind of freaky eye action going on. Different, but similar."

"I think we better get you home." He grabbed me under the elbow. "You are suffering from some kind of shock. Let's go."

I despised being manhandled. "Shock? My ass! Do you make a point of walking all the girls home?" I asked, attempting to wiggle out of his grasp, and failing.

"No."

His clipped response drove me bonkers. "Why did he call me little Raven?" I asked, sincerely curious.

He opened my passenger door. "How would I know?" Then he more or less lifted me off my feet to get me inside. "Don't think about getting out of the car. I don't have the patience to chase you right now."

Biting my lip, I thought about it before leaning back. "Does everyone on this dreadful island have a bird fetish?" Ravens. Crows. Hawks. What was the deal?

A lethal smile rose on his lips as he hopped into the driver's seat. "Do you have a fetish?"

I rolled my eyes. "What is wrong with this place?"

He adjusted his seat belt and held out his hand. "You don't want to know."

I knew what he wanted, but I didn't remember agreeing to let him drive Josie. "So you're admitting things are weird here?"

"I plead the fifth. Keys?"

"Fine," I huffed, dropping my keychain into his palm.

He eyed the anime charm on the ring, a girl with aqua hair and big, black, twinkling eyes. "Cute." Then he turned over the engine, and my jeep groaned before kicking over.

"She's finicky," I stated, feeling my cheeks turn pink.

Reversing the car effortlessly, he raised a brow. "She? Let me guess. *She* has a name as well."

"Of course, but that is not the point." I was seconds away from ripping the keys out of the ignition. "God, getting answers from you is worse than an elephant trying to squeeze through a mouse hole. I'm going to find out one way or the other."

He stopped fast, and I wasn't prepared for the sudden jerk. "You listen to me, Piper. Don't go sticking your nose where it doesn't belong. I won't always be there to keep you out of trouble."

I blew the hair out of my face. "What trouble?" I demanded.

Silence.

Glaring, I craned my neck, positive I was going to suffer from whiplash. "Wow. You think of yourself as some kind of hero."

The car started rolling again. "Damn right," he replied smugly. "Crash is not someone you toy with—fact."

"I kind of figured that out, genius." I angled myself toward him in the seat. "To set the record straight, I am not a damsel in distress. Got it?"

"Whatever you say, Princess."

My jaw tightened. "Call me that again, and you won't be able to have kids."

The wind teased the hair at his neck. "I don't think I've ever had a girl threaten me as many times as you have."

I smiled. "You haven't been hanging out with the right girls."

His blue eyes snapped with a pristine coldness, darkening. "And you think *you're* the right kind of girl?"

I squinted, not in the least put off by his frigid change. "Uh, your eyes are doing that thing you say they don't do. Should I take a picture?" My hand went to my pocket, pulling out my phone.

Knuckles tightened on the steering wheel and his chest heaved in one long exhale, and I watched in awe as the charcoal lines around his eyes faded. "Have you ever seen a shrink?" he asked, envious lashes blinking.

"Of course not," I lied. "What kind of question is that?"

"I'm just trying to rationalize your foolish behavior." Strained lines wrinkled his forehead.

"*My* behavior?" I shrieked. He was joking, right?

Afraid not. "Done anything illegal?" he rattled off.

I thought about it, hanging my hand out the window to surf the wind. "Define illegal."

His lips twitched as we stopped outside the gate to Raven Manor. Zane put the car in park, and I hopped out, walking around the front of the car. He was still smirking as he stepped out of the jeep.

Finally, an amused emotion. He was capable of having them. I leaned against the side of the car. What I didn't expect was for him to box me in with his body, his arms placed on either side of me. "Do you have any tattoos?" He continued the most random game of twenty questions.

"Do you?" I countered—way calmer than the sparks going off inside me. If he kept looking at me like that, I couldn't be held accountable for what my body or lips might do.

"No."

"Liar." My gaze wavered from the exquisite planes of his face, down his arm, stopping just short of his hand.

He lifted a brow. "So you can see it?" Turning his arm over, he exposed the tattoo on the inside of his wrist. It was in the exact same spot as Crash's, but Zane's was a black crow.

My fingers reached out, hypnotized by the shimmering ink. "Why wouldn't I?" I wanted to trace the lines of the widespread wings. The tattoo seemed to almost move under my gaze, like a shadow.

He swiftly dropped his hand, eyes meeting mine. "Do you sleep naked?"

I swallowed back my disappointment and choked. "I fail to see how that is relevant."

"It isn't." He shot a dark grin. "I just wanted to know."

Why did he have to mention being naked, because now I couldn't get rid of the image my mind conjured of him naked. It only got worse and steamier when I joined that image. I tried to pretend my cheeks weren't beginning to flush and used my best defense: sarcasm. "I guess that is one of life's mysteries you will never know."

One of his full lips tipped. "Is that doubt I hear in your voice?"

My chin jutted out, refusing to let him rattle me. "I warned you." Then I put my fist into his gut.

His shoulders moved in a silent laugh, not in the least bit shaken by my little outburst. "I shouldn't be surprised by your spunk."

Peeved, I pretended my hand wasn't throbbing from the impact of his abs of steel. "Are you going to tell me what is going on yet?"

Sighing, he brushed a strand of hair from my face, tucking it behind my ear. "It's not my place."

My heart skittered through several beats at his touch. Holy hellfire. "That sounds like such a cop-out."

He flicked the end of my nose, just brushing my stud, and I felt the zing all the way to my toes. "Hand me your phone."

I didn't just hand my phone over to anyone. It was my life.

His fingers tapped on the screen before returning it. "In case you get into any more trouble, I put my number in your favorites."

"Wonderful," I said tartly.

He closed the space between us and whispered, "So do you?"

"Do I what?"

"Sleep naked?"

I stood nailed to the spot, digesting what had just happened. Was he flirting with me? "You're a dicknose."

He shot me a smile that would melt the heart of the Ice Queen as he started walking backward down the driveway. "Do you make up insults in your sleep?"

There was only one answer worthy of such a comment. I let my middle finger do the talking. He laughed. As I watched him saunter away, I was left thirsty for more, my mind burning with questions. So frustrating, like Zane himself.

Did he think one flashy grin would redeem him?

Not a chance.

CHAPTER 9

In my room, I strolled over to the desk, half in a daze. The last hour's events didn't seem real. How could they? None of it made sense. Confused didn't come close to what I was feeling. I'd managed to keep calm and collected in front of Zane, but alone, my hands were shaking. Steadying them on the back of the chair, my fingers brushed something soft.

There it was, a piece of Zane. Laying on the back of the chair was his hoodie, the one he had so graciously lent me the night of the bonfire. It hadn't been washed. Gross, but washing it would have been a sin. I picked it up. Unable to resist, I pressed the cotton material to my face and inhaled. Instant nirvana.

Oh boy.

I was in trouble.

Boy trouble. I was falling for a jerk.

A jerk with an unexplainable … I didn't even know what to call it. An ability? A curse? A mutation? But he wasn't the only one. Crash. There must be a reasonable explanation for what I'd seen. I was a reasonable person—well, most days—so I did what anyone in this day and age did when they needed answers. I Googled Zane Hunter.

Wiggling my butt into the plush chair, I booted up the computer, biting my nails as I waited. The Internet speed was surprisingly quick for being so far off the mainland. Typing in his name, I frowned at the search results. Zilch. No Facebook. No Twitter. No Instagram. No criminal records. In cyber world, he didn't exist, which meant he wasn't human.

"Who the heck are you, Zane—or *what?*" I muttered. Determined to uncover his story, I couldn't help thinking he knew things, and not just about what I'd seen, but my family as well. Nothing about Raven Hollow added up.

Zane and Crash were *something*. Their eyes ... I'd only seen something similar on TV. Vampires. What I'd learned from Dean and Sam Winchester was about the extent of my supernatural knowledge, except neither Zane nor Crash had pointy fangs or an extra set of razor sharp teeth, which ruled out vampires. Not ready to give up so quickly, I started a new search on paranormal abilities and then narrowed it down by freakish eyes. Maybe I would find an article, a legend, or a myth that would shed light on what I'd seen. It was a stretch, but what else did I have to go on?

A half hour later, I'd read several websites to no avail. My eyes were glazing over, and the words blurred on the screen as I scrolled through an online newspaper. Most of what I'd found was completely useless crap.

On a whim, I typed *Raven Hollow*. A few seconds passed before a name popped out at me: Rose Morain. I scooted my chair closer, tucking my legs underneath me, lured by the possibility of uncovering dirt on Grams. The mouse clicked on the link, and a moment later I was scanning the headline.

RAVEN MANOR UNDER FIRE

"Rose Morain of Raven Hollow's founding family was interrogated by police about the recent deaths of three teenagers who were found on her beachfront property. The names of the eighteen-year-olds are being held at their family's request. No charges have been filed against the highly respected pillar of Raven Hollow's community."

Rose was questioned as part of a murder investigation? It seemed preposterous. She might have been an absent grandmother, but it only took one look to see she didn't have a murderous bone in her body.

"Are you looking at porn sites again?"

I jumped and whirled around in my seat at the sound of TJ's voice. He was leaning against the doorjamb. "Hilarious," I barked. "You're the horny teenage boy, not me. Sex isn't on everyone's mind twenty-four seven, ya know." I tried to cover the monitor with my body.

TJ pushed off the door, walking into the room. "And that, sis, is your problem. *You* need to get laid."

I coughed, fumbling blindly behind me with the mouse. If I could just switch the webpages .... "Excuse me. Just what do you know about getting laid?"

"More than you apparently if you're searching ..."

My fingers rapidly tapped over the mouse button. *Click. Click. Click.*

He laid a hand on the back of the chair, looking over my shoulder. "Mythical creature responsible for killing spree?" TJ read. "Pipe, you need help."

In a kneejerk reaction, I elbowed him in the gut.

He gave a *whoosh*. "How did I get stuck with such a lame sister?"

"Funny. I was thinking the same thing. Why are you here again?"

He rocked back on his heels, averting his eyes. "No reason. I was exploring and ended up here."

Guilt settled in the pit of my belly. Since we had arrived at this plush establishment, I'd been so caught up in my own worries, determined to dislike Rose and recently dissecting Zane, that I'd forgotten TJ was only fifteen. He was still my little brother who missed our mom as much as I did. We had essentially lost both our parents in less than a year. I manufactured a smile. "Have you made any friends yet?"

TJ belly flopped onto my disheveled bed. "I haven't really left the castle."

The corners of my lips curved as I swiveled the chair to face him. "This place is crazy, isn't it? I find it hard to believe that you're already bored of all those video games."

He gave a one-shoulder shrug. "Nah. Not really. Marco had to go eat dinner with his family. We're getting back online in an hour for a one v. one of CoD."

"Huh? You know I hate it when you speak gamer-geek."

A small snicker came from his lips. "Never mind. I don't have time to educate you."

Marco was TJ's best friend back in Chicago. "You should try to get out and meet people. Who knows? You might find another dork like you."

"What about you?" he pointed out, turning the tables. "You've been moping around in your room all week."

"I have not been moping," I denied.

His brows lifted.

"Fine. But it's been a weird week, okay?"

"Weirder than usual? I find that hard to believe."

Twerp was asking for it. I grabbed the nearest pillow from the floor, where I had kicked it many nights ago, and heaved it at his head.

He ducked, laughing as the fluffy missile zoomed right past him, and I realized it was the first time I'd heard TJ's laugh since we got here. "Your aim still sucks."

I couldn't stop the smile. TJ might be a pain in my tush, but we were family—the only family we had really. "You want to raid the kitchen and watch a movie?" I asked, another family tradition that had vanished with Mom.

Lines of consideration creased his brow. "Sure. Why not?" That was his way of saying he missed me. "Just as long as it is not porn."

"Hardy har har."

MY CELL PHONE buzzed on my dresser, scaring me half to death, not that I was doing anything important, just lying on my bed, counting ceiling tiles. I lost count after seventy-six and had to start over. Thank God for technology.

Eyes narrowing, I read the number that flashed across the screen. It was a local area code, but one I didn't recognize. For a painstaking, heart-stopping moment, I thought it might have been Zane. Then I remembered that he had programmed his number under Dicknose. It made me smile.

I debated whether or not to let it go to voicemail. It was after nine, and like the last few nights, I had just brushed my teeth with the very lame idea of going to bed early. Yep. That was the kind of Saturday night I was having.

Pathetic.

I didn't recognize myself.

"Hello," I answered.

"Hey, girl. Get dressed. I'm coming to break you out."

My mind was slow to place the voice. "Zoe?"

"Duh. Who else do you know on this dreadful island?" Zoe replied.

She had me there. Zoe had a spark for life that was contagious. Enough so, that I was actually contemplating getting out of bed. The more I thought about it, the more appealing it became. Maybe I could get her to give me some dirt. I was getting squat from her brother, and I had so many questions: Zane, Crash, Rose. "Where are we going?"

"You'll see," she sung in that pretty lilt of hers. "Be ready in fifteen."

"Better make it twenty," I answered, staring at my reflection in the mirror. It was going to take an act of God to make myself look presentable. Lazy day equaled no shower. I needed an entire team of professionals to pull me together. Hmm, I wondered if Rose staffed her own stylist. It wouldn't surprise me.

Rolling off the bed, I snuck a quick sniff under my arms. "Ew." I rushed into the bathroom, cranking on the shower to hot. Ten minutes later I was in a towel, staring at a closet three times the size of mine at home.

I pushed aside all the clothes Rose had stuffed the closet with. Lace, pink, and floral were not my style. If there wasn't black on it somewhere, it wouldn't touch my body. Tugging on a pair of self-ripped jeans I'd found shoved in the back, I paired it with a peek-a-boo tank. The outfit definitely accentuated the important parts: butt and boobs.

Highlighting my eyes with a quick coat of mascara and a thick line of black eyeliner, I ran a brush through my blonde hair, adding a little bit of hairspray to tame the flyaways. After an application of my favorite lip gloss, I was ready to paint the town red. I smacked my lips, shoved my ID and cell phone into my back pocket, and checked the clock.

Two minutes to spare.

I took a breath, surveying myself in the full-length mirror. Not bad under short notice. It would have to do, because my phone buzzed. It was a text from Zoe.

I'm outside the gate. Hurry ;)

On my way, I quickly sent back as I opened the terrace doors.

For a brief moment, I felt guilty about sneaking out, but as soon as I saw Zane leaning on the side of a sleek car, I was feeling nothing but the hum of excitement and annoyance.

He wore a dark scowl.

I scuffed the sole of my shoe on the gravel. "Zoe failed to mention you would be with her."

"Zoe is full of surprises," he mumbled.

I rolled my eyes. "And you are full of piss and vinegar."

A lock of wavy hair fell into his eyes as he shot me a crooked smile. "At least you are starting to get me."

I leaned my weight to one side. "I take it she didn't tell you I was tagging along."

"Nope. She knew I never would have agreed."

"And why is that?"

"As long as you stay out of my way, we won't have a problem," he warned through a gritted smile.

"Ditto." I reached for the door handle, but he beat me to it, and I slipped into the seat, trying to disregard my racing heart. "Are you going to tell me where we're going?" I asked Zoe, meeting her smiling aqua eyes as she twisted in the driver's seat.

"I like you," Zach said. "Direct and to the point." He was sitting shotgun, which meant that …

Zane climbed into the backseat with me, frowning. I scooted over to the other side, securing my seat belt. Oh goodie, confined in a small space with Zaney. Why was Zoe subjecting me to such torturous treatment?

She shifted the car into drive and hit the gas. Let's just say Zoe was the definition of a "girl driver." If my seat belt hadn't been strapped on, I would have ended up in Zane's lap. Her long midnight hair was swept up into a ponytail at the crown of her head. "We're going to Raven Hollow's best kept secret. Only locals know about it. You are going to love it."

It was unlikely that I would be having any kind of fun if grouchy didn't get an attitude adjustment. "I'm not going to be shunned by being the outsider, am I?"

"Hardly," Zach snorted. "You are Morain's granddaughter. That makes you freaking royalty and one of us."

That's what I was afraid of. "Good to know." They might not have considered me a summer girl, but that didn't mean everyone else didn't. And honestly, I was a summer girl. This wasn't my home—never would be. At the end of summer, Raven Hollow would be dust in the wind.

I slid my gaze to the guy across from me, who clearly had his boxers in a wad. I wondered if he wore boxers. He struck me as a boxer brief sort of guy. Why was I thinking about his underwear type? At least it kept my mind off other parts of his body.

Eyes of steel pinned his sister in the rearview mirror. "Zoe, this is a bad idea and you know it."

"Do you ever quit?" I snapped, cutting him a death look.

Zane tipped forward, the leather groaning under his weight as he closed the space between us. "Not when I know I'm right, Princess."

I sent him a look of pure hatred.

"Don't make me stop this car," Zoe threatened like a soccer mom. "The two of you need to learn to play nice."

Zach snickered.

Zoe glanced over her shoulder at Zane when she should have kept her eyes on the road. "What harm could it do to show her? I think it's brilliant."

"You would," he grumbled. "Do I need to remind you that all your ideas backfire?"

This was going to be a long ride. Zoe and Zach struck me as double trouble. Must be a twin thing.

Zach hung an arm out the window. "That's because you're way too serious."

Stretching out all of his six-foot-plus frame, Zane settled back into the seat. "You should really reconsider who you hang out with."

My hands itched to smack those icy eyeballs out of his head. "Buzz off."

"If the two of you stopped bickering and just admitted there's something between you, we would all have more fun tonight," Zach said.

Zane's lips thinned.

I clamped my mouth shut, staring straight ahead. Not happening. Tonight, I wasn't going to give him the time of day. I was going to …

Dammit. I still had no idea what we were doing or where we were going for that matter.

The car stopped. Just in time, too. I couldn't be in the car with Zane another second, not without doing something idiotic. It was a toss-up: slap him or kiss him.

The minute I was free and breathing easily again, Zoe looped her arm through mine, leading me down the sidewalk. A sparkle of excitement and anticipation glimmered in her eyes. "You're in for a night you won't forget. I promise."

Zane expelled a menacing sigh.

A small, evil part of me reveled in his exasperation, but there was something about the way Zoe spoke that gave me goose bumps. I smiled. "Great. Just what I'm looking for."

We turned the corner, Zane and Zach trailing behind us, and approached a flight of concrete stairs going down. My hand trailed on the railing until we came to a set of metal doors. Etched on the entrance of each was what looked like two birds, a raven and a crow, but it wasn't the symbols that captured my eyes; it was the glistening prism of color that appeared 3D.

I blinked, positive my eyes were playing tricks on me.

And they were. The raven and the crow were nothing but two stunning marks on shitty metal doors. They weren't moving, flapping their wings, or flying toward me as they had a moment ago.

Wow. It was definitely not a good sign that I was already seeing shit. I hadn't even had a drink yet, and it was hardly late enough to be loopy.

"You okay?" Zoe asked, tugging on my arm.

"Yeah," I said, forcing a smile. I stepped through the revolving metal doors—Zoe on one side and Zach on the other, a twin sandwich.

CHAPTER 10

"Welcome to the Atmosfear," Zach grinned, holding open his arms.

What a lovely name for a club. Cheery.

However, this was not a club, at least not like the ones I'd been to in Chicago.

It was … spellbinding. My eyes didn't know where to look first. There was so much activity and none of it normal.

It was a black light party, the lights dazzling and cascading over the mob of thumping and bumping bodies in rhythmic intervals. At first the flashing was dizzying. Good thing I wasn't prone to seizures and my eyes were used to the erratic beams. The dance floor was packed with bodies, mostly half-naked girls. Their skin shimmered as if they had been dusted with golden glitter, but it was their veins that set them apart. They glowed. Blue. Red. Black. Pink. It was a network of rainbow bodies.

I was mesmerized, unable to take my eyes off the action.

The Twilight Zone didn't have shit on my life. "A club, huh?" I murmured. "Just what I need." A pick-me-up. My step became a little bit lighter.

Zach grinned. "I knew you were cool."

Glad someone thought so. One thing was certain as I scanned the crowd: everyone in this joint had a mark similar to what I'd seen on the entrance—like I'd seen on Zane. Except this time, I knew there was nothing wrong with my eyes. The marks, they were moving. I kept my expression blank, because the last thing I wanted was to be shown the door. The detective in me was dying to uncover answers, and this club was a perfect place to start. Zoe and I were going to have ourselves a girl chat.

Zane shook his head, glancing from me to Zoe. "You're responsible for her. Don't make me say I told you so." Then he took off in ground-eating strides, leaving me with the twins.

"What a prick," Zoe mumbled under her breath, taking the words straight from my mouth. I instantly loved Zoe. She didn't take shit, and that said a lot having three overbearing brothers.

The bitter scent of alcohol was pungent in the air, along with the stench of sweaty bodies and strong perfumes. A mist of colored water vapors was pumped into the center of the dance floor.

"Come on. Let's get a drink," Zoe leaned in and yelled in my ear.

Weaving us in and around the crowd, I trailed behind Zoe, doing my best not to knock into anyone. She grabbed two drinks from the bar, handing me one. I had the glass to my lips when I noticed the cloudy green liquid that filled the cup. Now I'd seen some pretty strange mixed drinks, but not like this. Lifting the glass to my nose, I sniffed. It had a sweet scent like apples with a hint of cinnamon, reminding me of fall. For a brief moment, I missed my home, but then Zoe was clicking our glasses together.

"Bottoms up."

Zach lifted his glass in a toast, and the three of us downed our drinks in one big guzzle. I was going to pay for that later. I had just broken my cardinal rule: no liquor. I was going to blame that on Zaney as well. If he didn't come across as such an asshole, I wouldn't need something to take the edge off. One thing was certain: Parker wasn't going to be here to save me, so I needed to keep it together. I was switching to water.

"Let's dance," Zoe said, grabbing my hand.

I barely had time to set down the tumbler, sloshing water over my hand, as she tugged me onto the dance floor. My body did what it did naturally to the sound of a really good beat: swayed with the music. I threw my head back, spinning and laughing, a sense of freedom I hadn't felt in forever cascading through me. As we danced, Zoe lifted her arms above her head. That was when I noticed the mark. It was identical to the one I'd seen on Zane, my shock causing me to stumble. I knew it was going to be impossible to communicate over the roaring music, but it didn't stop me from asking, "You have a tattoo?" I watched her mouth move in confusion, so I yelled out again.

"What?" she screamed a second time.

I gave up, waving a hand like it wasn't important, but I couldn't help thinking she was dodging the question like her brother. Too bad they didn't know me well enough to know that I never gave up.

After that I just let loose, tucking the little tidbit about the tattoos away in my brain. My hair flared around me as Zoe and I shook our tail feathers. She was quite the mover and the shaker, although, not to toot my own horn, I was a tad better … until the alcohol kicked in. With my blood pumping, the small amount of liquor I'd consumed started to cloud my vision, and the dancing gave me a buzz. I had not a care in the world. It was glorious.

But not part of the plan.

Forgetting my problems and having a good time with new friends was uplifting, but that hadn't been the reason I'd risked sneaking out. I was supposed to be uncovering dirt on Zane and on my family.

My Sherlock Holmes skills sucked.

Zoe leaned into my ear. "I'm going to get another drink. Do you want one?"

I shook my head, running the back of my hand over my brow as Zoe sashayed to the bar. My feet moved from side to side while I people watched, curious. Zach was whispering into a pretty little redhead's ear. I had caught a glimpse of Zander earlier in the evening, but he was nowhere in sight. Zoe was fighting off the advances of some young guy. And then I was suddenly aware of someone's eyes on me, prickles skirting down my spine. I knew who it was. Only one person in the entire universe made me feel like this.

Zane.

My eyes were drawn to him of their own accord. *Bam.* I was hit by the intensity in his eyes, sucking the air straight from my lungs. He was with a group, but it didn't really matter. They were background noise compared to Zane. At first sight, he always stunned me, knocking me off my feet.

I was ogling, but so was he.

We were caught in some parallel spell, my body still moving on autopilot, until a pair of pretty fabulous boobs brushed up against Zane. I saw red. The skank placed a hand on his arm, angling her body toward him.

Oh hell no.

I scowled, ready to kick some ho ass.

There was a giggle behind me, halting my irrational butt kicking, and before I could strut my shit across the floor, a brunette swayed forward, mimicking my moves. Her face was radiant with a sheen of perspiration that only emphasized her attractiveness. She brushed damp pieces of hair off her neck, smiling. "Your mind better catch up with your body, girl, because your body totally wants to have sex with him."

It was impossible to not be envious. She had everything going for her. A slender, killer body. Long, lush hair that whirled as she danced. Graceful, fluid movements. "That obvious, huh?" I replied.

"It's inevitable. The definition of a Hunter: tall, dangerous, strong, and sexy. The female population is unable to resist."

I laughed. "You nailed it."

The crop sweater and low-rise skirt exposed her midsection. "Did I see you come in with him?"

I nodded. "But we can't really stand each other."

She smiled beautifully. "Yeah, sure. I'd almost buy that, maybe if he wasn't constantly scoping you out in the crowd."

"He is not," I argued. Risking a glance back at Zane, our eyes collided. I whipped my head away. *Note to self: do not make eye contact.*

Drop-Dead Gorgeous tossed her hair, laughing. "Right. And you aren't daydreaming about what you are going to name your kids."

"Do you know Zane?"

"I know his type. And that clinging ginger, Venus, is not it." Her slender nose scrunched. "I can't stand that whore."

My eyes twinkled. "And you are my new best friend."

She held out her hand. "I'm Aspyn, bestie."

"Piper." She opened her mouth to say something, but I cut her off. "Don't tell me, you already knew that."

She just smiled. "Guess you've been getting that a lot, huh?"

I winced. "You have no idea."

"It's not every day that a Raven returns to the Hollow."

"So I've heard," I said, pretending I knew what she was talking about when, in fact, I was clueless. What I needed to do was figure out what a Raven was and why everyone thought I was one. Could be another nickname, but I didn't think so.

"Let me give you a little piece of advice," Aspyn said, the beat of the electronic music vibrating the floor. "You want to get his attention? Dance with his brother."

I chewed on my lip. It was a wicked, troublesome plan ... I loved it. "I just might try it."

Aspyn grabbed both of my hands, lifting them over our heads. "I like a girl who isn't afraid to go after what she wants." She sent me into a whirl and yelled, "Good luck!"

My eyes focused on Zander who appeared out of nowhere, looking at me with irises tinged with purple. I liked purple. But I wasn't sure how I felt about the eldest Hunter, let alone using him to make his younger brother jealous. I highly doubted he would be okay with that scheme as well, and something told me that Zander was a good guy. My body tensed for a moment before relaxing as he smiled warmly and placed a hand firmly on my back.

It was too late to change my mind now. We were moving over the dance floor.

"This saves me from having to ask you to dance." He had a pleasant timbre to his voice that lacked Zane's edge and cockiness.

Was I doomed to compare every male to him?

I even detected the same touch of Celtic accent, yet it didn't make my pulse jump. My laugh wasn't entirely forced. "You were going to ask me to dance?"

He shifted just a fraction of an inch. "I've been working on an excuse to come talk to you all night."

"You have?" I asked, startled.

He cracked a smile. "Don't sound so surprised."

My stomach did a topsy-turvy thing. I wanted Zander to like me, but not *like* me. This was shaping into an awkward situation. "Well, I am."

"You're a great dancer. Are you having fun?"

Compliments made me nervous. I tucked my hair behind my ear. "Actually, I am."

"Atmosfear hasn't frightened you off?"

Zander made me nervous. Like a klutz, I stepped on his shoe. *Bet he no longer thinks I'm a good dancer,* I thought, blushing. "I'll admit it is different, but sometimes different can be good." I was thinking of Zane. Zander was nothing like Zane, which was exactly what I needed. Zander wasn't the kind of guy that would crush my heart into a million little pieces and then scatter the fragments into the street.

"We should go out sometime," he suggested. "Grab something to eat and watch the sunset." He made it sound casual, but I knew what he was asking.

Warmth rose like summer's heat. Zander was asking me out on a date. Too bad he wasn't the Hunter I wanted. Yet, I found that my mouth was not saying what my brain told it to say—just the opposite. "Sure. I'd like that."

Holy guacamole. Did I just agree to go on a date? With Zander? Too late now. This wasn't elementary school—no take backs allowed. I barely knew him, and I wasn't really interested in him that way. But seriously, going out with Zander didn't mean I had to marry him. Or be his girlfriend. And it would be nice to get out of the house.

He smiled sweetly. "Great. How about tomorrow? I could pick you up at six."

Tomorrow? I shrugged, my gaze flicking up to meet his. The purple flecks in his eyes were nowhere near as vibrant as Zane's. I shouldn't be thinking about him. "Why not?"

His eyes lifted over my head, and I watched the soft lines around his mouth tighten. Curious, I looked over my shoulder, but before I saw who had put the frown on Zander's face, he was twirling me in a circle.

Zander leaned in, his breath minty and cool on my cheeks. "I think Zoe wants her dance partner back. She's giving me the stink eye. See you tomorrow."

All I could do was nod.

Zoe weaved in and around the crowd, making her way toward me and looking beautiful while doing it. "What did Zander want?" she asked. "I saw the two of you dancing."

"A date."

She didn't try to hide her surprise … or disappointment.

"It's not a big deal," I added, suddenly feeling like I had made a mistake. "Unless you don't want me to go out with him."

"No, that's not it. I just got the impression you were interested in a different one of my brothers."

"Well, then maybe *he* should have asked me instead of Zander."

She let out a long heavy sigh. "If Zander is interested in you, then Zane would never get in the way—bro code and all. Believe it or not, Zane isn't always a jerk."

Her words and disappointment hit me, and I knew I couldn't go through with the date. Maybe I hadn't given Zane enough credit or time. And I didn't want to lead Zander on. I wasn't that type of girl, because if I was being truthful with myself, it wasn't Zander I was interested in. Searching the crowd, I had to set this straight before I got myself into a love triangle between brothers. That was the very last thing I needed.

I excused myself and sidestepped Zoe, only to run into a roadblock. I smacked into something firm and warm and that smelled like the first frost of winter. Zane had found me before I'd had a chance to track down Zander.

Damn.

I'd clashed into an unmistakable shade of blue, his hands gripping either side of my hips, steadying me. Zane should come with a warning label. He threw off enough testosterone to draw the attention of every girl with a pulse in a twenty-mile radius. If you got all three Hunters together, the female population would be powerless.

I was drawn to him, whether I liked it or not.

His eyes were fixed on me, and he flashed me a wolfish grin.

In that second, I was powerless.

Gulp.

Zane twined our fingers, pulling me to him. "I think you owe me a dance."

I kept my face *almost* neutral, but ignoring the charge jolting from him to me was difficult for both of us.

"Be a gentleman." I heard Zoe warn, but it sounded so far away because my heart was throwing itself against my chest.

Zane's lips quirked up. "A little out of your element, Princess?"

The little network of cells in my brain started to function, my sanity returning. I was not about to let him kill the nice little buzz I had going. "Don't you think it is a sign that your family needs to tell you to behave?" I asked sarcastically.

He just stared at me.

I shook my hair. "Do you want to dance or just gawk at me?"

No matter how much I tried to be good, you can't keep a bad girl down. He needed a lesson. There was a brazen side of me I didn't know I had. I weaved my arms around his neck and started to move my hips. If he wasn't going to make a move, then I would, because standing in the middle of the dance floor was getting awkward. Zane already stood out in a crowd.

My body brushed his, and a tingle tiptoed along my spine.

He sucked in a low breath, proving I wasn't the only one who felt this strong connection between us. It was an affirmation that gave me courage I wouldn't normally have, but there was also the risk of this backfiring on me. What was reward without risk?

Safe, boring Piper—that was not me tonight.

I was no longer in control of myself, my body doing things I wouldn't normally have the lady-balls to do. I blamed it on that misty drink. Never drink anything murky.

Determined to get a response from stiffy, I turned it up a notch, pulling out moves that would not have made my mom proud. I wanted him to suffer. Rolling my hips against his, I placed my hands on the hardness of his chest. Those steely eyes began to burn like the center of a flame, the hottest point.

Holy smokes.

A dangerous smile curved his lips as he reached out his fingertips, tracing my plunging neckline. His touch seared a path of pure heat. It was a reaction I wanted, and boy, what a sizzling reaction it was. My entire body was humming, and I was damn sure it wasn't the drink. Uncertain what to do next, my hands drifted up his shoulders, little bolts of electrical current following my fingers.

Definitely not the booze.

I felt like I was radiating from the inside out. Zane was intoxicating. He was like nothing I'd ever had before. Dark. Sweet. Dangerous. Mysterious. I craved more.

He growled near my ear before looking down at me, eyes darkening. Black veins spidered around his long lashes. It was hard to believe what I was seeing through the sputtering of lights, but I knew I wasn't imagining anything. They were real. I lifted a hand—

"What do you think you're doing?" he spat.

"I think it's obvious."

His brows knitted together. "I need to get out of here." Dropping his hands from my waist, he spun around, grabbing my hand in the process. As we catapulted toward the exit, small crowds parted like the Red Sea, but Zane kept his head down.

Zane Hunter has humiliated me for the last damn time, I seethed with each step he yanked me about. I would never make a fool of myself over him again.

Bastard.

CHAPTER 11

We rushed toward the red exit sign, stopping only when we were outside. I more or less gave up trying to jerk out of his hold after a few failed attempts. He had a handcuff-tight grip on my wrist, and I took that as he really wanted me to go with him. Why? Beats me, but I got the feeling I was in trouble. As cool as it was tonight, my body managed to feel like it was on fire.

Zane took a deep breath, the muscles along his jaw thrumming. "Jesus, Piper. Are you trying to kill me?"

His dark voice wove itself into my belly, causing me to shiver. "You're the one who wanted to dance," I reminded him. "I was just being friendly."

He thrust his hand into his messy hair. "You got any *friendlier* and Zander would have ripped out my heart with his bare hands."

Confusion lined my brows. "What does Zander have to do with this?" He couldn't possibly know about the date. It was not a big deal. I didn't see how a date could cause him to act ballistic.

His jaw was clamped shut. "Everything."

We were standing toe-to-toe. Cold air blew along the back of my neck, but I barely felt it over the heat pumping between us. "As usual, nothing that comes out of your mouth makes sense."

"I should have stayed home tonight," he mumbled.

"Me too," I snapped back. "You know what? Forget this."

I had no idea where I was going, no idea where I was, and no clue how to get home, yet not even an act of God could have gotten me back into that club. And standing outside with Zane was no longer an option. I looked left and then glanced right. What I needed was an internal GPS.

I whipped around, taking off to the right. The direction didn't matter as long as it took me away from Zane.

"Piper!" he yelled. "Where do you think you're going?"

Far away from you. I picked up speed. What I wouldn't do for a Starbucks—something frothy, chocolaty with a kick of espresso. Damn dreadful island. There was no Starbucks here. No McDonald's. No Target. Like I said, it was a dreadful island.

Rounding the corner, I realized I no longer heard Zane calling my name. Good. He'd finally gotten a clue. I glanced over my shoulder just to make sure he wasn't following me. Coast was clear. I exhaled in relief and disappointment, but it was fleeting.

As I faced forward, a figure emerged in front of me. I jumped. "Goddammit, Zane." My hand slapped him on the chest. "You scared the shit out of me."

"About time."

My earlier confidence evaporated. "That's what you've been doing this whole time? Trying to scare me? Well, let me tell you ... you royally suck at it."

A hint of amusement filled his eyes. "Glad we cleared that up."

I let out a long frustrated groan. "You are single-handedly the most infuriating guy I have ever had the displeasure of meeting."

"Thank you."

One smartass comment and I was fighting a grin. "That wasn't a compliment, you baboon."

"Maybe not to you," he said. "I strive so hard to be infuriating. It's nice to know my efforts pay off."

"Your mother must be proud."

He caught my eye, giving me a gold star, bar-fight grin. The glint in his eyes was scary enough, but under the rough exterior, there was still a note of desire. "You haven't met my parents."

What did he mean by that? I shook my head, realizing I was never going to understand him—not just guys like him, but Zane in particular. He was a different species of male, which reminded me ... "We need to talk," I said, lips thinning.

He shoved his hands into the pockets of his jeans. "Well, what are you waiting for? Spill."

I couldn't sit still, so I started to walk aimlessly down the road, assured that he wasn't going to ditch me. Fumbling with the charm around my neck, there was no other way to say what was on my mind, so I just blurted out, "I know you're different." I waited a beat to see if his expression would change at my insane accusation. It didn't. "Yes, I know I sound crazy, and saying it out loud doesn't make it any less outlandish, but I've seen things I can't rationalize. So what are you? Vampire? Demon? Zombie? Frankenstein? I'm just spit-balling here."

He laughed, and the sound was husky, making the wide street seem too small.

"I'm glad you think this is funny," I muttered.

His long strides were no match for mine, but he slowed so he was beside me. "That's just it. It isn't funny, but you don't give up. You don't listen. I warned you, Princess."

That was all he'd done—warn until I was blue in the face. New tactic. "Why were you in my room?" I waited for him to deny it. He was going to deny it, right?

The longer the silence stretched, the less certain I became. Doubt weaseled its way into my head. Oh God. He had been in my room.

Zane didn't say anything, just pinched the bridge of his nose. I could practically hear each gear in his brain grind into action. "Why would you think I was in your room? Do you know what kind of security I would have to get past undetected to get to you? Raven Manor is practically Fort Knox."

I couldn't possibly tell him I had smelled his scent, or that I swore

I'd seen his blue eyes in the distance. Even in my head that sounded absolutely ridonkulous. "Come on, that wouldn't stop a guy like you."

He shook his head. "And you've got me all figured out."

I threw my arms into the air. "No. I don't. And that's the problem. You won't tell me."

"Some things are better left unsaid," he said, a chariness to his voice.

I was going to hit him. "You could have at least bought me dinner before you decided to screw me," I shrieked, fed up and not caring who heard me. My frustration level reached a new peak.

He moved. "Trust me, Piper. If I decide to screw you, it won't be in a public place."

My throat closed up as his face hovered near mine, my body hyper aware of him. "That's rich coming from you."

"What's that supposed to mean?" he asked, angling his head.

I licked my lips. "That you're a douchebag extraordinaire."

His eyes lingered on my mouth. "That the best you can do?"

"And you're a—"

In a blink, he suddenly had me pinned against the wall with that rock hard body of his. I told myself to keep my mind off his abs, which was like saying no to the last piece of bacon. Who could do that?

"What the hell do you—?"

A hand closed over my mouth, and he shushed me.

Oh no he didn't.

I gave him a monster glare, prepared to unleash verbal diarrhea, when I heard voices.

His hand was still covering my mouth, and I couldn't stop the dirty girl thought even if I tried. Not that I tried very hard. Once it was there in my head, it was stuck. I wanted to lick the inside of his palm. It would be so easy, just a quick swipe of my tongue. What would he do? Would that dark scowl only intensify?

The idea became a temptation too good to ignore. I must have made a noise, because his eyes flew to mine, and as if I didn't have a brain, he pressed a finger to my lips, making it very clear he wanted me to be quiet.

Wrong move.

Our current situation might not have been so titillating if his damn rock hard body wasn't plastered to every inch of mine. I challenge any girl in my situation to resist the urge to take a taste. Having his skin against my lips—no good. I wanted to take his finger into my mouth. What would Mr. Big Shot do then?

I hated that I found him so tempting.

His eyes were still attached to mine, and I watched dumbfounded as they darkened.

Oh shit.

I'd come to learn that with the appearance of Zane's unearthly black spider eyes came trouble.

Under a streetlight strolled two guys not much older than Zane and me. The difference: they made my skin crawl. I considered myself a good judge of character, and my bizarre intuition never let me down. Right now, it was telling me that these jokers were bad news.

Zane's body went rigid, and I started to feel my first inklings of fear.

There was a distinct leader, a blond with spiky hair who looked like he bench-pressed elephants for shits and giggles. His extra large arms were intimidating to say the least, but Zane didn't seem to notice. The other was scrawny with a dusting of freckles over the bridge of his slightly crooked nose. In what was becoming a habit, I looked to their wrists. Both of them had a tattoo of a blue sparrow. *I really need to figure out what these birds mean.*

Their shoes clopped on the blacktop, and they moved in jerky, excited movements. "Shit," Zane swore under his breath.

The beefy blond sneered. "Well, if isn't Death's favorite toy. Didn't expect to see you tonight."

Huh?

My confusion skyrocketed, but whatever nicknames these guys had for each other was the least of my worries. Slick and Sparky were eyeballing me in a way that had genuine fear spearing through my heart.

Zane shot forward, stepping in front of me like a shield. I tried not to be touched. "Blake, what are you doing here?"

Blake, the blond, turned down his lips. "Don't insult me. I know you have half a brain in that inflated head of yours. You know what I want."

"And you just thought I would let you take her?" His voice was laced with disgust.

Oh. My. God.

They were talking about *me*.

What did these lunatics want with me? The image running through my head wasn't pretty. For that matter, it was America's Most Wanted quality. All I could think was that this had something to do with my mom's *accident*. It was pretty darn evident they weren't looking to be friends.

I backed up, wondering how far I could get if I made a run for it. Otherwise, I was leaving my safety in Zane's hands. I stayed planted, taking my bet on Zane.

"What does it matter to you? Your brother's not around." Blake's smile lacked warmth, and I knew I was in a precarious situation. "We won't say anything. Scout's honor." He held up two fingers.

My stomach soured. "Oh yeah. That's convincing," I said dryly.

Squaring his shoulders, Zane mumbled, "Now is not the time for your particular brand of sass."

The thing was, I wasn't a hundred percent positive that Zane wouldn't just hand me over to these two seriously demented assholes. What they wanted with me, I couldn't even think about, because if I did, I would lose my shit.

Blake laughed, his buddy joining in. "Homegirl has attitude. Good. I like a little struggle and a lot of screaming."

I leapt forward. "Sick prick. No way am I letting you put a hand on me."

Zane captured me at the waist, pulling me against him. He kept his arms around me even as I struggled to break free. "Be quiet," he hissed in my ear and then raised his head. "If you know what's good for you, you'll take a hike, because my fist is begging to be in your face."

"Ooh," Blake mocked, putting his hands in the air. "The problem is you have something we want. Hand her over, and we'll all leave here without a scratch, except maybe the Raven."

Zane didn't like his answer. He growled low at the back of his throat. It was almost an animal-like noise. "You leave me no choice." Then he whispered in my ear. "Princess, do me a favor and stay out of the way."

He released me, and I felt so exposed without his arms around me. If—correction: when—we got out of this, Zane and I were going to have words about him manhandling me. I was not a doll to be tossed about. Just as I was shoving the blonde curtain of hair out of my face, Zane cocked back an iron arm and slammed his fist into Blake's jaw. The impact knocked Blake on his ass, sprawling him onto the blacktop.

My mouth dropped open.

I was seriously impressed with Zane's brawling skills, although I probably shouldn't have been. He looked like the type of guy who could do extensive damage with just his fists. "Wow, Rambo. I didn't know you had it in you."

"You have no idea what I'm capable of," he said ominously.

Derek, the scrawny one, interrupted what might have turned into another entertaining spat with Zane, bum-rushing toward us. Zane spun, clotheslining Derek in the neck. Sputtering, Derek went down to the ground with a *thwack*.

However, he didn't stay down long. Neither of them did. I blinked, and they were both upright and in Zane's face. This was bad, epically bad. How was Zane going to take them both on? He was strong, but two against one. The odds weren't in his favor, yet it didn't stop him. Scrambling to get out of the way, I pressed myself against a building, trying to make myself as small as possible. I should have been looking for a rock to slam over one of their heads, but in the heat of the moment, it didn't occur to me.

There was something not right about the way they fought.

Shadows gathered around Zane, and as I stared into Blake's eyes, there were flames dancing in his irises. That was of course on top of the web-like veins that circled their eyes. Blake's and Derek's were blue, Zane's black.

I was so intent on what was going on around their eyes, I didn't see the glint of a blade until it was too late. Derek flashed in the corner of my eye, a knife against my Adam's apple. My blood seemed to suddenly stop flowing. Zane had his fists full of Blake, beating the snot out of him, which left me with ninja Derek and his blade pressed to the base of my neck. I wanted to call out to Zane for help, seeing as the situation had taken a nasty turn.

Unfortunately, even the slightest move would draw blood. My blood.

I was pretty partial to every drop, and not breathing was the only way to ensure that blade didn't nick my pretty skin.

"I see this shut your trap," Derek said at my silence.

My bottom lip trembled. "Knives held at my throat tend to have that effect on me." I was surprised by how calm my voice sounded when I was quaking inside.

"Shut up," he hissed.

Did he know who he was talking to? My mouth was my only weapon, my greatest weapon. I wasn't trained in jujitsu. I didn't possess a black belt or any formal ass-whooping talents. I had skipped my defense class in gym to go get coffee with Parker.

Not such a bright idea now.

Christ, I could really use a maneuver to unman my assassin.

While I'd been scheming, Zane was still engaged in a one-on-one combat with Blake. No matter how many times Zane slammed his fist into Blake's chiseled face or stomped his boot into his gut, Blake got back up for more.

He was like a goddamn Terminator, which made me Sarah Connor.

I had also made the mistake of exhaling. "Ouch, you cut me." All that fear turned to rage. I couldn't believe the bastard had actually cut me. I might not have had any formal training, but I knew how to knee an asshole in the balls.

He went down like a sack of sprouting potatoes, groaning and calling me a bunch of vile names.

"Zane!" I yelled. No sooner had his name tumbled from my lips did I find myself face-planting into the ground. I hit the cement hard. Derek's hand snaked around my ankle, and I began to kick out with my other foot.

Son. Of. A. Bitch. Didn't see that coming.

At least I was finally able to gain Zane's undivided attention as he sent me a pointed glance, shaking his head. "I thought I told you to stay out of trouble."

Wincing, I blew the hair out of my face and looked up. "Yeah, well, plans change." I was going to be picking gravel out of my hands for weeks.

I didn't know what he had done with Blake, but he suddenly appeared over me. "Lucky for you, I'm adaptable." Zane hauled Derek off the pavement, dangling him in the air. The black veins surrounding his eyes began to grow. There was murder reflecting in his eyes.

For a brief moment in time, I thought Zane was going to kill him. His fists gripped the front of Derek's shirt as he held him against the brick wall, the tips of his feet centimeters off the ground. Zane was in his face, the knife no longer clutched in Derek's mitts. "I should rip the ribs from your chest, but if what you say is true, then take back this message. I will personally end anyone who tries to harm her. Is. That. Clear?"

Derek could only nod.

"Good. If I see you within a mile of Piper, you won't be walking away." He shoved Derek to the side.

Staggering, Derek limped down the deserted road, and I scanned the area behind me where I had last seen Blake, but his partner in crime was nowhere in sight. Not a comforting thought. I didn't know how he was able to sneak away without making a peep.

"Do I get a thank you?" Zane asked, not a bead of sweat breaking over his brow. Even his freaking hair still looked good.

I stood up feeling aches in places I didn't know I had. "For what exactly?" I replied, winded.

"I saved your life."

I rubbed my wrist, hoping I had done nothing more than sprained it during my fall. "And that brings on a whole new set of questions. Why did they want to hurt me?"

"You ungrateful brat," he grumbled. Obviously, fighting made him surly. "They weren't looking to just hurt you, Princess." He invaded my personal bubble, tilting my chin up with the pad of his thumb and index finger. The center of his eyes darkened at the sight of the tiny cut on my neck. "They wanted to kill you."

He wanted to shock me, but I'd pretty much come to that horrifying conclusion on my own. "Okay. And this is the part where you tell me why."

Utter silence.

"Say something. You owe me an explanation," I argued.

The mask came back on. "I don't owe you squat."

Frowning, I called it like I saw it. "Bullshit. Those guys weren't normal lunatics."

"Oh, so suddenly you're an expert in crazy?"

"After meeting you, I feel I could write a thesis on the subject," I snapped. I scooted to the left, putting distance between us, and my head swam.

"Hey, you okay?" He reached out, placing a hand under my arm. "Piper?"

I shook off his hand. "Yeah, I'm fine."

His shoulders stiffened. "You're angry at the world and hurt beyond belief, I get that, but I am warning you, Piper, it is a volatile combination you are playing with, and if you keep picking at it, it will only hurt you more."

"I don't need you to tell me how to live my life. You know nothing about me." Bitterness sharpened my tone.

His eyes softened. "I know you miss your mom and how much you loved her. I know how unfair you think it is that she was taken from you so suddenly, before her time."

He knew too much, making me feel vulnerable, which only pissed me off more. "Get out of my way."

"Piper."

The sound of my name from his lips broke me. Damn him. I wanted so much to hate him right now, as much as I'd hated the world these last few months. Between the threat on my life and the gazillion questions swimming in my head, I wanted to throw all my aggression, all my fury, and all my pain at Zane.

He was the only available target at the moment.

Instead, I let him pull me into his arms, and even more surprisingly, I buried my face into his neck, letting the tears fall.

I cried and cried—big, ugly, shoulder-shaking sobs, the kind that left you red-faced and emotionally drained. Tears made me angry. Tears were useless. Tears reminded me of a pain so intense I had almost lost my way, given up. I hiccupped, my chest heaving as I gathered my composure.

He held me through the whole ordeal, doing nothing but soothing me with the strength of his arms. His chin lay on top of my head, my face nuzzled between his shoulder blade and neck. The collar of his shirt was soaked, but he didn't seem to care. When the tears dried up, the scent of him teased my wrung-out senses. I tried not to dwell on the fact that I was in his arms or how great it felt. As my breathing evened, I dared not move, thinking I wasn't ready for him to let me go … or see the hot mess I'd made of my face.

Score one for Zane.

I traced the black crow on his wrist with the tip of my finger. It suited him. Ruthless. Powerful. Brave. Why did douchebag have to be one of his qualities? He had other less than redeeming traits, but remove the douche gene and he was my definition of the perfect guy.

I fought a yawn. Man, I was losing my night owl-ness.

Zane unfolded his arms and stretched. "Let's get you home. I think we're both wiped out."

That we could agree on.

CHAPTER 12

When the first cracks of nightfall came through the window, I stood in a towel, my hair dripping wet as I stared at the closet.

I groaned.

Tonight was my date with Zander.

This night couldn't end soon enough. Multiple times I had started to call Zander to cancel our plans. I had a bellyache; I needed to wash my hair; my grandma was sick—the usual cop-outs, but I couldn't do it. Every excuse I came up with sounded lame.

As I stared at my clothing options, horror filled me. I had no idea what to wear. Did he expect me to wear a dress? Even though I was dreading this date, I liked Zander, but definitely not enough to wear a dress.

I bit my nails, destroying my recently painted, shiny purple mani-cure. Half of my freaking closet was on the bed, the other half on the floor. It seemed stupid to be so indecisive about what to wear. Zander was going to have to be okay with me—skinny jeans, crop top, wedges, and all. I wasn't going to pretend to be someone I wasn't.

At seventeen, I was still trying to figure that out.

Hair and makeup went as spectacular as wardrobe. I wanted to lighten my usual dark makeup, but no matter what I did, I still ended up looking like I should be going to a rock concert. My eyes were large in the mirror. Wrinkling my nose, the tiny stud winked under the vanity lights.

I was nervous, but not with first date jitters.

Going out with Zander felt wrong, misleading.

I had just finished giving myself a Piper-you-got-this pep talk when a voice blared through the intercom. The mascara wand had come dangerously close to poking my eyeball out. Fabulous. Another sliver and my date would have been taking me to the hospital. That would have been a first date to remember.

It hit me as I stood up—one last glimpse in the mirror—this was my first legit date, and Zander was not the guy I'd pictured waiting at the bottom of the stairs for me. As my hand slid down the banister, all I saw were flashes of Zane. His eyes. His smirk. His electric touch.

I was literally two seconds away from running my ass back upstairs.

Okay. I was being stupid. There was no reason why Zander and I couldn't go out and have a good time, as friends. I just needed to make sure he understood that I wanted to keep our relationship in the friend zone. How hard could that be? He seemed like a reasonable guy, unlike Zane.

Zander cleared his throat. "Wow. You look great."

I flushed. "Thanks."

Seeing Zander in jeans and a polo shirt, I relaxed, glad I wasn't underdressed. He was punctual and charming. For no reason, I found both qualities annoying. As I left Raven Manor with him, I swore Rose was ready to plan our wedding. Her smile had never been so large, and there was a plan brewing behind those bewitching green eyes.

"Ready?" His warm smile put me at ease.

I nodded, looking forward to having a fun evening. And when the date was over, I would, as delicately as I could, let him know that we could be nothing more than friends.

He took me to the nicest restaurant on the island. His family happened to own it, which meant there was a good chance Zane would be working.

Ugh.

On the upside, at least the food was phenomenal.

The Black Crow was mesmerizing at night. Strands of firefly lights twinkled in the trees, and starlight sparkled off the deep, dark waters, making the ocean glow. There was soft music playing in the background, mingling with the harmony of nature.

We sat at a quiet table for two on the terrace. As I looked across the table, seeing Zander's slightly purple eyes flicker in the candlelight, I realized the ambiance was much more romantic than I'd bargained for.

What happened to not a big deal? This felt like a big deal. This felt like he was trying too hard.

By the time our drinks arrived with a basket of bread, the tension in my shoulders had shrunk. Carbs and fizzy carbonated drinks had that effect on me. I spent way too much time with my nose behind the menu, poring over my dinner choices, and I didn't hear the waitress return.

Zander laid a gentle hand over mine, and I looked up.

"Sorry," I apologized. "Um, can I get the ..." Eeny, meeny, miny, moe. I folded my menu and decided to be adventurous. "I'll have whatever he's having."

Zander lifted his brows in surprise and then ordered the prime rib, a salad with Italian dressing, and garlic mashed potatoes. The waitress scribbled on her little pad of paper before smiling. "You guys make such a cute couple."

I popped a hunk of bread into my mouth, hoping I didn't choke on it. I racked my mind for something to say after the waitress left, anything to break this dead silence. It didn't even have to be intelligent.

"Have you made any plans for college?" he asked, buttering a roll.

I latched onto the question. "Oh, yes. The future. I always thought I would go to art school, but I'm not sure anymore."

"You paint?"

I shook my head. "No, I draw. Anime mostly."

He blinked and looked at me like I'd just switched to speaking geek. "Anime?"

"Er, it's Japanese animation."

He chewed the bread slowly. "Cartoons ... that's cool."

Cartoons? That was offensive. It was so much more than drawing sweet Disney characters, but what did I really expect a guy like Zander to know about drawing? "What about you? Got big plans?" I took a sip of my cherry Pepsi, needing to wet my whistle.

"Family business." Zander was a few years older than me. I had assumed he was in college and home for the summer. I guess I assumed wrong.

Biting off another piece of bread, I replied, "Right. The club." My eyes did a quick glance around. "Is that what *you* want?"

Zander opened his mouth and then closed it. A moment passed before he shrugged. "Doesn't really matter what I want. This was what I was brought up to do."

What I heard was "life's not fair," and it made me want to dig deeper, find out more. "That hardly seems fair. Trust me, I get family obligations, but I think there comes a point where you have to do what makes you happy."

"You haven't met my father," he said. His tone told me all I needed to know. I'd hit a sore subject that was off limits.

Idiot. I leaned my elbows on the table. "Sorry. It's none of my business. I'm not passing judgment."

He flashed me a grin. "Why are you apologizing? I like that you feel comfortable enough to say what's on your mind. You don't have to tiptoe around my emotions."

The food arrived just then, saving me from sticking my other foot in my mouth—thank God.

Zander kept the conversation going, asking questions about Chicago, my life in the city, and school—the usual getting to know a person rundown. He asked if I had a boyfriend, and even though I thought of Parker, I still answered no. And when I returned the inquiry, he surprised me.

"Not anymore." He did a good job of quickly covering the flare of sadness, but not before I got a glimpse.

"Oh. I'm sorry. A recent breakup?" I winced, again sticking my nose where it didn't belong.

His chair scooted against concrete as he stood up. "Excuse me a minute."

I smiled. "Sure. Take your time."

Toying with the silver ring on my finger, I pressed back in my seat, admiring the view. There was a grand tree towering just off the patio. The branches swayed with the breeze. For a moment, I swayed too, like a woman coming out of a trance. I shook my head, staring at Zane.

In that second, I utterly forgot about the guy who had been sitting across from me moments ago. With those magnetic eyes and striking dark hair, I all but drooled.

He looked stellar in a pair of old, distressed jeans, his thumbs hooked into the front pockets as he stopped in front of me. "Hey."

There was no stopping the smile that split my lips and remained. "Hey, yourself."

Zane's smirk faltered as he noticed the empty seat. "You enjoying your date?"

Oh crap. How the hell had I forgotten I was on a date with his brother? What was wrong with me? "Did you want something?"

"Maybe, but I learned long ago I don't always get what I want." His voice was deep and rich.

Must ignore. Must ignore.

The last thing I wanted was to let Zane win and ruin a fine evening.

Fine.

And that was where the problem lay. My date with Zander was only fine. It wasn't exceptional or boring, but just okay—unmemorable, really, which wasn't fair to either Zander or me. Neither of us could push feelings that just weren't there. I liked Zander. He was nice, sweet, considerate, and a hundred other things Zane was not, but Zander also didn't make my blood hum or send a string of excitement through my belly. He didn't render me speechless at first sight. Zane did all that and more.

Damn Zane Hunter.

He'd ruined me for all other guys, and we hadn't even kissed. For all I knew, Zane could be a horrible, slobbery, tongue-down-my-throat kisser. But something told me he would be an extraordinarily amazing kisser.

I folded my arms. "Why are you doing this to me?"

"What is it that I am doing to you, Princess?" he countered.

It was a game, this back and forth between us. "This." I waved in the air from him to me. "I can't figure out if you like me or hate me. It's driving me crazy."

Zane's expression relaxed into a grin. "I don't hate you."

My lip pouted. "You have a funny way of showing it."

The grin reached his eyes. "Yeah, well, I didn't say I liked you either."

I seethed.

His hip bumped against the table as he leaned toward me. "It looks like you and Zander are having a good time."

Clenching my fists under the table, I dug my nails into my palms before I gave in and smacked him. "We are. *He's* a decent guy."

The jab wasn't lost on Zane. Amusement colored in his eyes. "Glad we cleared that up."

Lines creased my forehead. "I'm not sure we just had the same conversation, because I'm as confused as ever."

"Good. Then my work here is done." He shifted to leave.

"Why?" I blurted out.

His brows knitted, but he said nothing. Palms on the table, he inched toward me, lips quirking. "Because you're safer with Zander, Princess."

Neither of us moved. We were face-to-face, tingles spreading through my limbs. My heart did a somersault in my chest. Finally, he pushed off the table, running a hand through his hair. My mouth snapped open, but nothing came out. He took that as his cue to exit.

Against all common sense, I wanted to go after him. I had no idea what I was going to say, but I removed the white linen napkin from my lap.

Zander chose that second to take his seat, giving me a faint smile. "Dessert?" he asked.

My limbs sunk back down. "What?" Muddled, I was still reeling from my riveting chat with Zane.

"Do you want to indulge and get a slice of pie or cake?" he repeated.

I placed a hand over my belly. "Oh, gosh no. I don't think I could eat another bite. It was delicious though."

A soft smile curved his lips. "I'm starting to see why Zane digs you."

He caught me off guard. I didn't think he had seen Zane and me. "Uh. I don't know what you're talking about."

"It's pretty obvious. I don't think I've ever seen him look at someone the way he looks at you."

Awkward. I tried to make light of the situation. Sarcasm—it was my crutch. "What? With loathing?"

Laughing, Zander stood up. At his full height he was a good foot taller than me. "Not precisely. I think this summer just got interesting." He didn't seem to care that he was implying his brother had a thing for me, which only emphasized that all there was between Zander and me was friendship.

I didn't like the sound of that or the anticipation in his eyes. "What is that supposed to mean?"

He held out a hand. "I guess we'll just have to wait and find out. Ready?"

The problem was, I didn't want to play the waiting game. I nodded, placing my hand in his. There were no sparks that flew on contact, not like ...

I wasn't even going to think about him.

CHAPTER 13

The next two days it stormed a torrential downpour. Thunder roared over the turbulent waters, lightning cracked in the murky sky, winds howled like a sad wolf, and the constant patter of raindrops pelted the windowpanes.

I was going stir-crazy.

Being cooped up in this room and alone in this house, I was going to lose my mind. I pulled out my art stuff, hoping to occupy my mind. It was my usual escape. Not today. Every face, every pair of eyes, every set of lips all resembled one pompous ass. Zane.

Chewing at the end of my pencil, I stared down at the paper with its heavily drawn lines. In some spots, I had gone over the lines so intensely that it wore away the paper, causing a thin rip. And it was all *his* fault. My strange date with Zander hadn't helped. As soon as my mind began to drift, images of Zane plagued me. It was simple to blame my confused state on the trauma of losing my mom, but that wasn't the truth. The truth was ... I didn't know what the truth was.

That had to change.

If my life was in danger, I had a right to know why, and it made me wonder what kind of trouble my mom had been mixed up in. Had it followed me here? Was I safe? Where was my father in all of this? Gallivanting around Europe, while I dodged bullets.

Frustrated with this place, with my dad, with Zane, and with myself, I tossed the pencil in my hand across the room in a moment of rage. It hit the glass doors with a *whack*. The tiny tantrum did absolutely nothing to alleviate my exasperation and confusion.

But that was all about to change, because there was a figure staring at me through the glass.

Soaking wet, Zane stood outside on the terrace, peering in at me through a blurry curtain of water droplets. There was an amused smirk on his lips at witnessing my pencil toss. His cockiness almost made me leave him on the balcony, getting pummeled by the storm. I might have if I hadn't been bored to tears. Setting aside my pad of paper, I pushed off the bed and padded to the double doors.

I flipped the lock. "What are you doing here?" I demanded, tugging him inside my room by the front of his waterlogged T-shirt.

He shook his hair, spraying me with beads of water. "You want the truth, don't you?"

Frowning, I swallowed. He was offering me the very thing I'd been complaining about moments ago. Then why was I suddenly scared? "I think you owe me that much."

He let out a half laugh. "I did just stand in the rain trying to get your attention. That has to count for something."

"Maybe," I agreed, doing my damnedest not to be swept away by his dimples. "But first, let me get you a towel. You are making a mess of my floors." And then maybe my mind would stop having impure thoughts about Zane wet and how his shirt was so plastered against his chest that I could make out the lines of his abs.

Yum.

I scurried off to the bathroom, before I started to lick the water off his neck, and grabbed one of the white towels. Reemerging into the room, I tossed it at Zane who was flipping through the pages of my discarded sketchpad. "Hey!"

"Are these of me?"

"Do you always go through people's personal stuff?" I snatched the pad from under his grasp, tossing it facedown on the bed.

His grin grew. "Usually."

I felt infinitely red. "Why does that not surprise me?"

"Because you think you've got me all figured out, but you're about to find out how wrong you are." Something flickered over his face. Anger? Regret? Sadness? "I just hope when I'm finished, you won't be drawing me in a different light."

It was hard for me to believe he was worried I would look at him differently. "I doubt it can be worse than what I already think."

He worked his hand over his jawline, day old stubble shadowing his face. "Remember, you asked for it." Taking a step forward, he invaded my personal bubble.

My head tilted back, keeping my gaze latched on the most astonishing shade of blue. Our faces were perfectly lined up, and the glint in his eyes made it difficult to remember what we had been talking about. His hand slid to my lower back. "I have something to admit."

I pulled back a little, fighting a grin. "That you're an ass-munch?"

He chuckled. "Do you remember when I said I didn't like you?"

"How could I forget?"

He regained the tiny space I'd put between us, his hand following up the line of my spine. "I lied."

The muscles low in my stomach tightened.

His lips brushed against the curve of my cheek. "I think you are beautiful," he whispered, the coolness of his breath teasing my skin.

I bit back a gasp. That was not what I'd expected.

I forced my tongue to work. "Thank you?"

He lowered his head, our mouths a mere centimeter apart, and I thought for sure he was going to kiss me. His nose rubbed against the tip of mine, and my heart thundered out of excitement. There was also a different kind of emotion I couldn't identify. Whatever it was, it came out of nowhere—raw and potent.

"Piper?"

I shook my glossy eyes. "Did you say something?"

There was an intense, searing look in his expression. "You should probably have a seat," he said, dropping his hand from the small of my back.

"Uh, what?"

"Trust me. What I'm about to tell you will knock you off your feet."

Oookay. Now I was starting to get nervous. I sat on the edge of my bed, tucking my feet underneath me as he sat on the other side, putting distance between us. Good thing my senses were on overdrive from the almost kiss. It occurred to me that we were alone in my room, and my hands automatically went to my hair, smoothing the flyaways. I was rocking some serious second day hair. "What made you change your mind?" I asked, getting back to business. He had been very obstinate in his resistance to tell me anything.

He didn't smile or frown, only watched me with intense eyes. "I decided to stop giving a damn. It's becoming difficult to hide what I am, and you are in more danger not knowing."

"Why do I get the feeling you're trying to scare me? It's not going to work, you know. I have seen too many horrors to be frightened easily."

Lightning slashed wildly, illuminating the room. "Good, because what I am about to tell you not only puts me in danger, but also I am breaking a sacred oath. But before there is another attempt on your life—"

"Another?" I interrupted.

His blue eyes hit mine. "I'll admit, at first I thought you were playing with me, pretending not to know."

My heart trembled. "Know what?"

"I'm getting to it. This is just the beginning, Princess. There is no going back."

"I don't see how I have much of a choice. I'm involved whether I want to be or not. Tell me I'm wrong."

Pained concern showed in his expression. "I can't. You are the heart of it all."

A burst of fluttering panic tumbled in my belly. "Great," I said drolly. "Why me?"

"I'm working up to it."

I rolled my eyes. "That was a rhetorical question."

His brows dropped as he stared over my shoulder, several silent moments passing. "I never claimed the truth was going to be easy. It is going to seem damn near impossible, and honestly, I'm not even sure you will believe me."

Folding my hands in my lap, I replied, "Try me."

He rubbed the back of his neck, damp strands of hair curling. "I don't think I have a choice. Telling you feels right, no matter how wrong it is."

"What are you?" I asked, confused. He looked uncomfortable, and I suppressed the urge to tuck the stray curl behind his ear.

Zane let out a heavy sigh. "I am a weapon, a death reaper. My father is *the* Grim Reaper," he stated matter-of-factly, his eyes on me, watching for my grand reaction.

I gave him one. "Excuse me?" I shrieked. My hands no longer idle.

He combed his fingers through his storm-blown hair. "I didn't stutter, Princess."

I caught my bottom lip between my teeth, feeling irked by the stupid nickname he refused to drop. "Yeah, but I was hoping you were pulling my leg," I said lamely. "*Really?* The freaking Grim Reaper? That is the best you could come up with?"

His expression hadn't changed. Somber. Stagnant. Grim (pun intended). "I warned you." His accent came through heavier the darker his voice got.

I lunged off the bed, unable to sit anymore. "Well, I actually thought you were going to tell me the truth and not feed me some bullshit story."

He grabbed my wrist.

Wrong move.

I was feeling jazzed up. Now was not the time to lay a hand on me. Static bolted at his touch. I yanked back, expecting more of a struggle. Stumbling, I managed to keep on my feet without falling on my ass and looking like a dipshit, except I was closer to Zane. Much too close.

"Piper." He turned me to face him, my leg bumping into his knee.

"Look at me. Really look at me. Do you honestly think I would lie to you, especially about something like this?"

I cupped my elbows, trying to sort through the mountain of doubts. "No. I don't know," I retracted, my mind spinning. "I am not naïve or stupid, regardless of what you think of me." He'd already jumped to all sorts of wrong assumptions about me.

The heat from his thigh seared through the material of my jeans. Neither of us moved away. "The world is filled with impossibilities. Life itself is an impossibility. Why is it such a stretch to believe there are other beings that live among the humans?"

Every logical part of me was screaming *no*. "Okay, I'll play. What other beings are there?"

"How much time do you have?"

I shot him a dirty look.

"That was uncalled for," he said in what I guessed was supposed to be a sorry excuse for an apology. "I just can't seem to help myself around you. You tend to bring out the best in me."

My lips lifted partially. "I think we have that effect on each other."

Unknowingly, he twined our fingers together. "You've seen the proof. In your heart, you know that what I say is true."

Understanding dawned. "The eyes."

He rubbed the back of my hand. "There's that."

"What else?" I couldn't hide the interest from my voice. Once I'd gotten over the shock, the denial, my mind opened, and answers to a few burning questions began to unravel. Yet, it was still dream-like, surreal.

He gave a one-shoulder shrug nonchalantly. "I have superior ass-kicking skills."

"Oh, so you're like Dean Winchester," I added, being a smartass.

His blue eyes were baffled. "Uh, who?"

I shook my head, thinking if any place could use the skills of the Winchesters, it was this island. "Never mind. Obviously no one here watches TV," I mumbled. "Are there others like you?"

"More than you can imagine. I have been trained to fight from the time I could walk, honing my skills."

My mouth dropped open. Part of me was awed by what he was telling me. I was fascinated by him and had been from the first moment, but I was also leery. "I don't understand. How can that be?" I plopped back down on the bed, dazed.

"How is the sky blue or the grass green? How is the Earth round? It just is. Not everything in the universe makes sense. There is a Heaven. There is a Hell. And there are reapers. Life. Death. Chaos. Sometimes those lines get gray or even cross."

"You referred to yourself as a weapon. Why?" My heart pounded inside my chest as violently as the rain.

His hands rubbed down his thighs as he took a seat. "We all have a purpose. The death reapers—or Black Crows as many call us—are the only reapers that can destroy a soul. And when we take a soul, we absorb the essence of the soul. I told you from the get go I was trouble."

"Black Crow? Like the mark on your wrist?" The dots started to connect.

He nodded. "Most humans can't see spirits. They don't allow their mind to be open to such possibilities, such evil. But you, you've seen the horrors of the world. It makes the veil thin, allowing you to see what we keep hidden. Our marks. Our eyes. The color of our blood. All the things that brand us as supernaturals. There are four sectors: death, soul, phantom, banshee. A banshee restores the balance between sectors. Without the last, Earth would be nothing but pandemonium. Mankind would be extinct."

"Holy shit. Let me get this straight. You're saying there are ghosts running around? And you kill souls?"

"That's the gist. If we didn't do what we were trained to do, then the hallows would cause destruction this world has never seen. We keep the malevolent souls at bay, hunting them. There are souls who don't leave this realm peacefully and need to be destroyed. They are called hallows."

It was impossible to keep the doubt from my face. "You're a r-reaper." I couldn't even say the word.

A wall went up, his eyes hardening—and just when I thought we were tearing them down. "I am. And not just any reaper."

I could barely breathe. A reaper? Holy buckets. I almost preferred the world through my rose-colored glasses. Knowing there were *things* out there causing horror was giving me a panic attack.

"Just breathe," he whispered, rubbing my back.

The touch of his hand was comforting. "I'm okay. Keep going. I want to know more." Screw the ignorance blinders. I wanted to be able to protect myself, protect my family. "You said you train."

He nodded. "All reapers have particular skills."

"What are yours?"

"I'm deadly and precise. I'm never sick, and I heal. But my specialty is I can manipulate shadows, blend with them, use them, control them."

"Can *you* die?"

"Yes, I'm not immortal, but I resist most injuries. I would have to be gravely hurt—so close to death that my body wouldn't be able to heal."

That sounded gruesome.

Restless, I shot up and started pacing the room. This can't be real. Reapers. Hallows. Spirits. Millions of notions swarmed my head with each step—ideas I had never thought of before. My mom. Her murder. Was this connected? Had one of these so-called reapers taken her from me?

"Piper, slow down." He placed a hand on my cheek. I hadn't even seen him move. "Look at me," he demanded. "I know what you are thinking, and I don't know the answer."

My eyes lifted of their own accord, powerless to stop it. "Zane, everything you're telling me, I know in my gut that it's connected to my mom." There was nothing he could say that would convince me otherwise. My emotions clogged any rational explanation at this point.

His eyes darkened. "There's more."

I shut my eyes. More? Could I handle more? The grip on my control was held by a thread, but I was too strong to fall apart now; I had been through too much. My lashes fluttered open. He was so close I felt his minty breath on my face—tasted his scent. And for a minute, I forgot that he had something more to tell me.

Nodding, I pressed a hand to his chest, letting him know I was ready. He looked into my eyes and—

The bedroom door swung open, and I gasped, jumping away from Zane like I had something to feel guilty about, which I didn't. My eyes whipped to the doorway.

Joy.

Just what I needed.

CHAPTER 14

The look on Rose's face was one of pure annoyance. A tremble of power seemed to vibrate through the room, but I couldn't see it. Still, the hairs on my arms stood up, and I automatically rubbed my fingers up and down my shoulders.

"Zane, I think you've overstepped your welcome," Rose barked, a glint of disapproval in her mossy eyes.

Hell to the no. She was not going to kick him out. Over my dead body. "You can't just barge in here and demand he leaves." If there was one thing I hated, it was adults telling me what I could and couldn't do. They all thought they knew what was best for me, yet I was the only one who knew what I was feeling and what I needed.

Right now, I wanted Zane to stay. We weren't finished. I had many, many more questions, and I couldn't shake the hunch that Rose's unseemly arrival wasn't unseemly at all. How convenient. She'd showed up just in time to prevent Zane from revealing information about my family. I just knew it.

"Piper, I should go," he said.

My hand shot out and suction-cupped to his forearm. "Oh, no you're not." I turned to Rose, shooting daggers. "Are you spying on me?"

She gasped. Hell of an actress. "How could you think that?"

"I don't know," I said mockingly. "Maybe because this house has a security system more high tech than the White House, or because you're a paranoid old lady, or because there is a friggin' intercom in my bedroom. Have you never heard of privacy?"

Her chin lifted. "I do not know what kind of rules your mother allowed in her house, but here, boys are not allowed behind closed doors."

My expression turned sour. "You can choke on your rules." I think Rose and I were about to have our first fight, over Zane nonetheless.

In my room, now, Rose took up the whole space. "I will not be disrespected in my home." It could have been my rage, but Rose was glowing, a whitish aura surrounded her outline like a halo.

WTF?

Unsure, I took a step closer to Zane. "It wasn't my choice to be here, remember? Maybe it's best I leave." With that bold statement, I whirled around, intending to grab both Zane and my car keys, except . . .

My eyes did a quick scan of the room, just catching a flash of dark hair slipping out onto the terrace. Zane had bailed on me and was bolting down the stairs.

Coward.

"Zane!" I yelled, running out the double doors after him. Standing on the balcony, I watched the rain pepper down on the grass. Then he faded away like a chalk portrait, washed away by the storm. "Dammit," I muttered. Oh, he was going to pay for leaving me.

Drenched, cold, and fuming, the rain literally sizzled off my skin. I retuned inside where it was dry and faced Rose with an accusatory glare. I huffed and puffed, ready to blow the house down. "How could you treat him like that? Like he was pond scum?"

Her posture straightened, the ivory material of her dress covering her feet. "I did no such thing. The Hunters are personal friends of mine."

"I just bet. You don't have friends. They are all peons beneath your station, puppets for you to string about," I said, going in for the kill.

She softened her eyes, reaching out to touch my cheek. I jerked away. Her hand fell slowly to her side. "Whether you believe it or not, I am looking out for your best interests, Piper. Zane is not the kind of guy your mother would want to see her daughter with."

Low blow.

Laser beams shot from my eyeballs. "You don't know anything about my mom."

Her sigh was quite audible. "But I do know Zane a whole lot better than you. He is reckless, dangerous, and unstable—not someone I want alone with my only granddaughter."

I snorted. "Sounds like you don't know him at all. He saved me."

She lifted one perfectly groomed brow.

There. That had shut her up. "Yeah, you heard me. Two guys came looking for me. I don't know why, but Zane wouldn't let them near me. They fought, and if it weren't for Zane, I would probably be in a ditch somewhere, my picture splashed on the local newspaper. Is that what you want?"

A sharp intake of breath sounded in the room. Rose was stunned. "Interesting."

My mouth hit the floor. "I tell you that two guys attacked me, and you think the fact that Zane came to my defense is just interesting? I think that says something about his character, and even more about yours."

"Regardless, I am not surprised that he was able to properly hold his own. He was always a scrapper." The last word rolled off her tongue in a censuring tone.

I bit my lip. What I wanted to say was … *he fought so well because he isn't human, Grams. He's a trained weapon, a death reaper, born from the blood and flesh of the Grim Reaper. Wrap your silver head around that.* But I was pretty sure this was a secret I needed to keep, for Zane's protection and my own. So instead I said, "You're a joke."

She matched my pitch. "You are not to leave this house. Is that understood?"

"Crystal." Not that I actually planned to abide by her rules, but I couldn't have her breathing down my neck.

Not only was I frustrated and angry at Rose, but at Zane as well. What a dick move to leave me to deal with Queen Snob on my own. He could have stayed, or I would have left with him. At least then I might have gotten to hear what else he had to say.

The door slammed shut, and I was left to stew.

"WHAT'S the story with you and python arms?" TJ asked, sinking into the mahogany leather couch beside me. His hair was slightly greasy like he hadn't showered in a day or two. Boys. At TJ's age they were just gross.

I looked at him from the corner of my eye. "It's a short story called mind your own business."

TJ's lips lifted in a smirk that he'd tried to resist. "You're my sister. It's my biz-wax."

I sat forward. "You don't really want to know the details of my love life."

He snatched the remote off the couch where I had tossed it an hour ago. "He sounds like a douche, just your type."

"I take it you heard Rose and me?"

Kicking back, he placed his bare feet on the coffee table, linking his hands behind his head. "The whole island heard you."

I groaned. "Fabulous." Reclining, I laid my head back, turning toward TJ. "He's not as bad as she makes him out to be." Twice in one day I found myself jumping to Zane's defense, and I didn't really know why.

What gives?

I didn't know how I felt anymore. I hated him. I wanted him. My feelings were day and night, ranging from one extreme to the next in a blink. Finding out he was a supernatural destroyer of souls should have skewed my emotions one way or the other. It hadn't. I still found Zane provoking, mysterious, but underneath his moody cockiness was a primal protectiveness I found sexy. He captivated me.

"Of course *you* would say that. You want to jump his bones," TJ said.

I smacked him on the back of the head. "Watch your language."

His shoulders tensed. "Please. Stop trying to be Mom."

Ouch. That stung. It was an offhanded comment, but my first reaction was to tie his arms behind his back and smash his face into the ground until he screamed "uncle." Brothers sucked. "Someone has to remind you to put the toilet seat down."

Something flickered across TJ's face—worry. "Are you going to see *him* again?"

I took a few seconds to respond. "You know that saying, there is more than meets the eye?"

He rolled his eyes. "Yeah."

I pressed my hands to my knees. "Well, it perfectly defines Zane. No matter what you heard, he is not dangerous."

"What do you mean?"

"Don't ask questions I can't answer. If I tell you, I'll have to kill you," I teased. Logical explanations had gone out the window the moment I had learned that Zane was something other than human—a death weapon.

"You are so lame." He twiddled with a frayed piece of string hanging from the end of his shorts. "I don't like it when you fight. You're going to get us sent home."

I huffed a little, my nerves shot. "And that would be so bad?"

"I like it here." There was just the teensiest whine in his voice.

"You like being waited on hand and foot," I said. "Don't you miss your friends? Your room?"

He shrugged.

And I got it. Here, there were no reminders of what we had lost. It was easier to forget the pain, forget the sorrow. I couldn't blame him for wanting to be happy. At home my father moped around. I had left every chance I'd gotten for those same reasons—to drown my agony at the clubs with Parker. But TJ ... he had been stuck.

For TJ, I'd try. And by try I meant I would try harder to not get caught doing things that ruffled Her Majesty's feathers. "Want to

watch a movie on Netflix and have the kitchen make us popcorn?"
I asked.

"*Zombieland?*" we both said simultaneously.

Snatching the remote control before TJ, I sprawled out on the
couch with a smile on my lips. I needed a serious distraction—what
better than a zombie movie with my kid brother? He needed it, too.

When the movie ended, TJ was snoring logs on the couch. I
grabbed one of the knitted blankets and laid it over him. A piece of
popcorn tumbled from my hair, hitting the carpet, and I smiled. TJ
and I had spent the first half of the movie inconspicuously pelting
each other with popcorn bombs.

My hair was a buttery, salty mess—not exactly a hair treatment my
hairdresser would approve of. I had waited until TJ had dozed off
before breaking out my cell phone. Zane was on my hit list.

Waste of time. He ignored my texts, including my pleas to meet up
tonight.

Asshole.

Screw Rose's rules. I needed to know what else he had to tell me.
The unknown was eating me up inside. My finger hovered over his
name, and just as I was about to call, my phone dinged.

It was Parker. **Hey. You fall off the planet?**

I wasn't sure Raven Hollow was even in the same universe. **Something like that**, I texted him back.

Everything okay?

Rolling over on my back, I thought about his question. I was far
from okay but doing my best to pretend otherwise. The thing with
Parker: I didn't have to pretend. **No. But what else is new?**

Miss you.

Ditto. I watched the screen drain to black. Texting Parker brought
back memories of us in high school. The two of us staying up late,
scrambling to finish assignments I had put off until the very last
second. Procrastination was my middle name. Parker was the
smartest guy I knew. He was like the Einstein of Phillips Academy
High School. Being miles away from him made me realize how much
I had depended on Parker.

129

The phone flashed again. **Wanna talk about it?**

Normally, he was the only person I could talk to, and Parker might idolize Marvel superheroes, but there was no way I would ever get him to believe that Raven Hollow was filled with supernaturals. Anyway, the person I needed to talk to didn't have the decency to respond. **Not tonight. Rain check?**

On standby.

Nite. I set the phone aside and just lay there, concocting a variety of harebrained schemes. I had a pretty vivid imagination, and without Zane to fill in the blanks, my mind did a colorful job, all of which led down a dark, troublesome path. Good thing I liked trouble.

CHAPTER 15

Two things happened on the Fourth of July. My father texted me to wish me a "Happy 4th." *A month.* I'd been here a freaking month and that was all he had to say. So personal. Father of the year.

And Zoe invited me over to her house for Sunday dinner.

It would be the first time since Zane had been given the boot that I would see him face-to-face. He had vanished the last five days. *Poof.* Just gone. He was making himself scarce on purpose. For whatever reason, he'd reneged on giving me the answers I desperately wanted.

A splash of sunlight streamed across my bedroom floor, and my iPod was blaring as I wiggled into a pair of white jean shorts. With one hand behind my head and another out in front of me, I attempted what was supposed to be the sprinkler—a dance move that I only performed behind closed doors. It was a pathetic attempt, but I didn't care. This was the first time in a week, more like a year, I had done something silly, just for fun. The sprinkler wasn't the only poorly executed dance I butchered. There also was the dougie, and my personal favorite, the wobble.

A shred of the giddiness I was feeling was partly because I would see Zane, a dangerous feeling when it came to him.

There was a laugh that sounded behind me over the music, just barely audible. I might not have heard it if it also hadn't been accompanied by tingles skipping over my skin. I glanced in the mirror and saw my worst nightmare and my dream come true.

Zane.

Thank God I had a shirt on. Whipping around, my eyes narrowed. "What the hell are you doing here?" I squeaked, cheeks flaming. My eyes gobbled him up from top to bottom, convinced his entire wardrobe was jeans and black shirts.

He had the stupidest grin on his face. "Don't let me stop you."

I awarded him the stink eye. "Don't make me slam the door in your face." Grabbing the iPod, I cut off Panic! At the Disco in the middle of "The Ballad of Mona Lisa." It was one of my favorites.

God. How long had he been there?

He leaned a shoulder on the doorframe, enjoying the show. "Her Majesty let me in."

My face shot up. "What?" The iPod slipped from my fingers, crashing to the floor. "Shit," I muttered, bending down and examining the cracked screen. There went my tunes and my sanity.

"Nice job, butterfingers."

"Why would she do that?" I asked, pushing to my feet and dumping the useless device back on the dresser. "She had made it very clear that I was not to have anything to do with you. That woman has no scruples." She was messing with my head.

Picking up one of my perfume bottles, he took a sniff. "Trust me, I wouldn't be allowed to step a pinky toe in this room if Zander wasn't involved."

I blinked. How the …? I hadn't even seen him move. "What does your brother have to do with anything?" Bringing up Zander only scrambled my thought process.

There were shadows lurking in his eyes as he set the glass bottle back. "Everything."

Geez. It had only been one date.

Questions … too many of them. And I knew there would be a time and a place to bombard him, but not here, not in this house. But I could call him out. "I can't believe you ran out on me, and I'm pretty sure you left your balls behind."

A wicked grin slipped over his full lips as he slid his hands into his pockets. "Someone ate their bitch-flakes for breakfast."

"Coward."

"Brat."

"Zaney."

"Cute and unoriginal." His eyes gave me an all too slow once over. "Now that we got that out of the way, you ready?"

A flush crept over my body. "Now?" I skimmed the room, positive I was forgetting something. Shoes? Bra? My head?

"Yeah. Unless of course you're scared to be alone with me," he challenged.

Please. I was more afraid I might assault him with my mouth; I'd already insulted his manhood. "Well, what are we waiting for?"

His lips twitched. "After you, Princess."

"Oh, you owe me a new iPod," I said, grabbing my bag.

He chuckled. "You would try to blame that on me."

Shaking my head, I grabbed my cross-body bag and strolled out the door. I didn't need to look over my shoulder to know Zane was following me. My entire body was ultra-aware of him. Passing through the gardens, I rounded the corner of the driveway, my eyes looking left and right. "Where's your car? Please tell me you didn't walk here."

"Hilarious." He sauntered to the other side of my jeep and straddled a motorcycle, one of those fast doodads. "Hop on," he instructed, holding out a helmet.

Good God. He looked like total crush material, the epitome of a bad boy. I could work with that.

No. No. No.

You are not crushing on Zane Hunter. Not now. Not ever.

The little "save me Jesus" pep talk did nothing to dissuade my body. Looking at him gave me the warm fuzzies.

Someone fan me now, because it's getting hot up in here.

Fitting the helmet to my head, I secured the strap around my chin.

It was then that I came to the realization that I had to touch him. I had to more than touch him. I had to plaster my body against him like we were one.

Too much time had passed as I stood there gnawing on my lip.

He raised a brow. "First time?" The way he said the words made it sound like he was talking about my virginity.

Tipping my chin, I stuck my foot on the pedal and hoisted myself over. A quick jolt of static passed between us as my hands brushed around his waist. My thighs hugged his, and it took all my willpower to not sigh. I hadn't expected a motorcycle ride to be so … erotic.

His head turned to the side, bringing our faces mere inches apart. "Don't let go."

I swallowed, tightening my arms. His silent laugh rumbled under my death hold as the bike rolled forward. There was something to be said about riding on the back of a bike, the wind blowing over my face. I could do without picking the gnats from my teeth, but overall, it was an experience I wasn't likely to forget.

But that had more to do with the guy than the ride itself.

He pulled up to a modest ranch-style house in a soft, sunny yellow. It was bright and cheery. I had a difficult time picturing the scowling Zane living here. Well-tended flowerbeds grew under the windowsills and in giant barrel pots. A brick pathway led to a screened-in porch. There was a driveway filled with cars, but they were no obstacles for Zane's bike.

Warm and inviting—they were the first things that came to mind when I followed Zane inside. A wave of apples and spice scented the air. I was more comfortable here after five minutes than I had been at Raven Manor in six weeks. Eyes wide, I took in the lower level. The house wasn't cluttered, nor was it bare like the manor, but lived in. Family photos lined the walls and the stone fireplace mantel. The carpet was clean but worn from the goings and comings of a large family. A cat lazily slept on the back of an oversized chaise lounge.

I don't know what I expected a house of reapers to look like, but this was not it. This was normal. No creepy stairs. No dusty corners or giant cobwebs. No death chill in the air.

Zoe strutted down the hall with a sinister grin on her cherry lips. The color popped against her midnight hair and pearl white skin. "You're still in one piece. Glad to see Zane kept his word." She draped an arm around my shoulder, leading me the way she had come.

"Me too." I still found it impossible to think of Zoe as a reaper. Sure, she had a bad girl streak, but so did I. It was the black crow that flashed on the inside of her wrist that made it real.

"Mum is dying to meet you." She acted like nothing awkward had happened, so I could only assume Zane had told no one what he had revealed.

I kind of wished he had. I didn't trust my big mouth not to slip up. And plus, then I would have someone else to interrogate and reinforce the truth—a truth my mind was still balking at. I had spent the last week poking holes in Zane's story, unable to accept that the world wasn't as black and white as I was raised to believe.

Now I was meeting the parents. Not just any ordinary parents: the Grim Reaper and his wife. Dun. Dun. Duuun!

My palms suddenly started to sweat. Holy fudge cake the size of my butt. What was I doing? But before I could overthink it, a woman with raven hair and dazzling blue eyes appeared around the corner. She was the same height as her mini-me daughter, with a face makeup free, but she didn't need it. I stood frozen like a deer in headlights.

She put her hands on my cheeks, placing a kiss on each one. "It's nice to meet you, darling."

My nerves were getting the best of me, my smile wavering. "Thank you for having me, Mrs. Hunter."

"Call me Ivy." She had more of a lilt to her tone than her children, and she smelled like jasmine. It was a calming scent. "You're a gorgeous one, aren't you? No wonder my boys are taken."

I turned an ungodly shade of hot pink. "Not all of them." My eyes drifted to a frowning Zane.

Her bracelets chimed as she waved a hand in the air, smiling fondly. "Don't let his rough exterior fool you. Zane has the most heart out of the four."

"Ma," Zane complained.

She ignored him, looping an arm through mine, a gesture that reminded me of Zoe. She was the spitting image of her mom in both looks and mannerisms. Tiny crow's-feet appeared at the corners of Mrs. Hunter's eyes. "I hope you're hungry."

"Starved. I haven't had a decent meal since—" I stopped myself, unable to believe I had been about to mention my mom. There was something about Mrs. Hunter that made me forget the wall I kept up.

"Are you telling me they aren't feeding you up at the big house?"

"It's too rich for my taste."

She laughed, hearty and light. "I bet Rose is in seventh heaven with you finally home. She might not show it, but that woman thrives on strife and scandal."

I kept my face blank. *Home?* I didn't want to read too much into what was probably an offhanded comment, but Raven Hollow was not my home and saying so out loud, when they had graciously invited me into theirs, just seemed rude. Strife and scandal, huh? Those were two things I could definitely deliver.

I lost track of Zane as his mom led me to the back of the house. Out of sight, out of mind. However, it wasn't working. If anything, being in his home, I felt closer to him. Zoe was on the other side of her mom. As inconspicuously as I was capable of, I checked out Mrs. Hunter's wrists, searching for any sign of a mark.

None.

She was human?

Color me shocked.

Outside in the backyard, it smelled of barbeque chicken and baked beans—all the things I loved about summer. There was sun tea brewing in the heat on a brick paved patio.

Zander and Zach were seated at a wooden patio table large enough to feed an army, but I guess their family was like a small army. Zach tossed me a shit-eating grin like he had just pulled the prank of the century. And Zander ...

This was the first time we'd seen each other since our date. Other than a few texts back and forth, we had made no plans to go out again. He smiled sweetly at me, and I returned his grin.

At the head of the table was a man with dark hair, who had a dusting of white at his temples that carried into his trimmed beard.

I stopped breathing. This was Death. I was in the presence of the freaking Grim Reaper.

Gulp.

A chill flitted down my back. No surprise. He was the kind of guy I'd expect to put the fear of God into a person. *Play it cool. Don't embarrass yourself, Piper.*

A near impossible task when he just stared at me. I squirmed under his silver-eyed gaze, wondering if I had a booger hanging from my nose. Ay, caramba. That would only happen to me.

"The resemblance is startling," he said in a deep timbre that rumbled his chest. He was a big, burly man, reminding me of a teddy bear. "You'll have to forgive me. I wasn't prepared for you to look just like her."

He'd known my mom—that was evident—but the shock and fondness in his expression said he'd known her well. It was the first, and probably not the last, time I'd been told how much I looked like her. Still, it was a spike to the heart—a fresh, painful reminder that she was gone.

"It's a compliment." He scratched the end of his chin, eyeing me thoughtfully. "Tell me you brought an appetite. I am about to show these boys the art of grilling."

A uniform snicker rolled around the table. "Dad, seriously, you're only embarrassing yourself," Zach said, grinning.

He winked at me. "Pay no attention to my ungrateful son. Actually, it is probably wise to stay away from them all. Zoe is the only angel in the lot."

That brought on a new set of snorts.

Zoe beamed.

Zach placed his elbows on the table, steepling his hands together. "Dad is delusional."

Silver eyes dancing, he said, "I doubt Piper wants to listen to our family drama."

I cleared my throat. "Actually ..." I did. Very much so.

Mr. Hunter grinned. "I like this girl."

And that was pretty much how the night went—playful bickering and banter. Death was funny, warm, and had a deep belly laugh—all the things you would pretty much expect Death not to be.

I loved him.

I loved them all.

Savoring my last bite of sweet and tangy chicken, the button on my shorts was threatening to come undone. It had been a long time since I'd had a home-cooked meal not prepared by me, and I stuffed myself to the point of near combustion. Should have worn elastic pants.

When Ivy offered me a slice of pie, I regretfully declined.

"We are going to the docks to watch the fireworks. The island puts on quite an impressive display. You should come with us, if you don't already have plans," Zander offered.

None of the Hunters were quiet, but Zander was more reserved than the others. He had barely spoken two words to me since I arrived. It made me wonder if I had done something, or if he was more upset about the friend zone than I thought.

"Say you'll stay?" Zoe pleaded in a sultry way that didn't sound like a plea.

I had two options: I could go to the manor and watch the show from my empty shell of a room, or I could stay. The answer was obvious. "I would love to."

Fourth of July had always been a holiday I treasured. Sparklers. Smoke bombs. Unity. The Hunter's family dynamic made me envious and a bit sad. I missed this, having a family, the togetherness. Mine was broken and distant. Being with Zoe and her family was liberating. I felt alive again, and I didn't want that feeling to end—kind of a poetic justice.

I'd just had dinner with Death. How many people could say that? And I'd lived to tell about it.

Freaky.

The docks were only a few blocks south from the Hunter's house.

As we got up to leave, Zander was summoned by his father. I didn't give it a second thought, because Zane was hovering over me.

His hand slipped under my elbow, slowing my pace. "We'll catch up with you. Piper and I have unfinished business."

Zoe turned around and winked. "I just bet you do. Don't let Zander catch you."

"This is my hilarious face," Zane said flatly.

"Whatever," Zach called as he walked backward in the direction of the water. "It's your funeral."

Zane's lips quirked.

Funny, considering if he died, it could be one of his siblings reaping *his* soul. The thought of Zane dying filled me with terror, rising out of nowhere.

It was the coolness of his touch that pulled me from the darkness. "Hey, you okay?"

The chill that had trickled through me thawed. "Yeah," I managed. As long as he kept touching me, I would be more than okay.

He cast his eyes downward, meeting mine. "I guess that was overwhelming, meeting my father."

I pinched my index finger and thumb together so they barely touched. "Just a little. You didn't tell them that I know the truth, did you?"

He dragged his fingers through his tousled hair. "No. Not yet."

My heart turned over heavily. "Do you regret telling me?"

Zane's shoulders relaxed as he let out a resigned sigh. "I should, but ... I don't."

"Is it really that bad that I know?" I asked, not even realizing I had been leaning toward him.

We were in his driveway, shaded by a thick oak tree. "Depends who you ask. But don't ask anyone," he added as an afterthought.

"I kind of figured that out on my own, genius."

He lowered his chin. The sparkle that had been there for a brief second fizzled. "For both of our safety, we need to be honest with each other."

"I'm in danger, aren't I?" I barely breathed.

He watched me intently as he spoke. "You've been in danger since you stepped foot on this island."

I rubbed my heart, but it did little to ease the ache that had started to take up residence. "I don't understand. Who would want to harm me? Harm my family? I have a younger brother to take care of."

"You forget I have a sister."

"And a pack of hot brothers to look out for her." I closed my eyes unable to believe that had come out of my mouth. I really needed to work on my filter around this guy. It was sad.

"You think my brothers are hot?"

Duh. "That's not the point."

He blinked, and I told myself to not get swept away by the intense color forming in his eyes. "So, I can assume you also think I'm hot."

I made a noncommittal sound. "Like you need me to tell you that you are incredibly good looking."

A devious grin swooped over his lips. "You're right. I don't. But I am the better looking one, right?"

I rolled my eyes, done stroking his ego. He had enough puffery to last him for the next decade. How had this conversation gotten so bizarre? For the sake of my heart, I needed to steer us back onto safe ground. "But you have power. Why would you need to protect Zoe?"

He leaned against a car in his driveway. "Have you met Zoe?"

"Good point."

His eyes were sheltered, making it hard to read his emotions. "With all power comes responsibility, Princess."

I hopped on the hood of the car, grinning. "You stole that from Spider-Man."

Lips curled, he shifted his body to the side, his chest brushing my arm. "Doesn't make it any less true."

I bit the inside of my cheek. "Do you ever have fun with your power, or is it all just angst and business?"

"What do you know of fun?" There was a playfulness lighting his irises.

My emotions were all over the place, zinging and sending warning signals to my brain. I ignored them. "I invented fun. If you look up "fun" in the dictionary, it says Piper Brennan."

He laughed. The sound was darkly lyrical. "You are so lame."

"Yeah, well, at least I'm not boring."

"I've never really liked dull girls anyway," he said, brushing the hair off my shoulder.

I laughed. "Dull, I am not."

His eyes flashed. "Your dimple deepens when you laugh. It's damn sexy and very distracting."

"I hate to be disruptive," I said, flirting with danger.

I could just make out the darkening around his eyes as he leaned forward. "I can't stop thinking about you. You shouldn't be on my mind at all."

Those unearthly veins the color of ink encircled his eyes. They should have scared me. Instead, I found them hot—damn hot. My blood was humming, and I couldn't have made myself pull away, even if the earth was crashing down around us.

We were cheek to cheek. I felt him inhale, and then slowly exhale, the warmth of his breath fanning my skin. "You smell of the ocean and lilies. Why am I drawn to you?"

In that moment, I would have given my left arm to know how it would feel to have his soft lips pressed to mine. Just once.

But every fiber in my being told me once would never be enough when it came to kissing Zane Hunter. He was the kind of guy that would never stop with just a kiss.

And that was fine by me.

CHAPTER 16

He snatched me off the hood of the car so fast that I was still blinking when his arms came around me, his fingers splaying along my lower back.

"What the hell do you think—?"

That was it. My brain clicked off the moment his mouth clamped over mine. Those lush lips ground my mind into mush, and I was helpless to do anything but simply stand there and kiss him.

He should have tasted prickly and sour.

Oh, but he was damn sweet.

When my lips opened on a sigh, he dived right in, wanting much more. Not that I blamed him. He pulled me closer so our bodies became one shadow on the pavement. Sensations swarmed my system in an emotional overdrive, tiny bolts of pleasure spearing through my body from my head to my toes.

Holy hot lava.

There was something different about this kiss, about how he made me feel outrageously unique—like Zane himself.

I swore I heard him curse before he changed angles, teeth scraping over the bottom of my lip, and I almost let a whimper of bliss escape.

My mind still couldn't process that he was kissing me, that I was letting him devour me.

The simplicity of a kiss filled a basic need, except there was nothing simple about this kiss. How could it be simple when I was glowing from the inside out, excitement and unease dancing together along my skin? I might have fantasized a time or two about my first kiss with Zane, but sweet baby Jesus, the real deal surpassed any fantasy I could have dreamed up.

I managed to wiggle my hands out from our smashed bodies and dove them into the silky strands of his hair. I had to be out of my mind getting mixed up with a guy like Zane. Really, other than a summer fling, what more could we have? I wasn't staying; this wasn't my home. Not to mention, he was a weapon of death. Any relationship we had was doomed, but not even the prospect of our downfall could diminish the power of his lips.

His hands slid down my back and over my hips. Soft lips, firm body, skilled technique, and just a hint of mint on his tongue tangling with mine—that was what he offered. I felt myself sinking. All those awful thoughts I'd ever had about Zane, his rude behavior, all of it, just disappeared. *Poof.* With his lips on mine and his hands roaming over my curves, I only had impure thoughts.

His fingers skirted along the edge of my shorts, skimming my flesh. I murmured his name. And if we didn't part soon, things were going to escalate to an indecent level. Technology saved the day.

My phone vibrated in my pocket, humming between us. The vibrations were like an earthquake, jarring me back to reality. He eased back a little, so that our eyes met. Clarity broke through the haze of sexual tension, and just as quickly as he'd had me in his arms, I was not.

Falling back onto the car, I lost my balance, and if I hadn't immediately missed the feel of his arms, I would have been seriously irked, but I was too stunned by what had transpired between us. Black lines spread out under his eyes, trailing down his cheeks. They made him hotter. I wanted to reach out, pull him back to me.

The phone buzzed again. Retrieving it from the back pocket of my shorts, I thought about tossing it across the yard until I saw Parker's name across the screen. My heart sunk, reality crashing down around me.

"Let me guess. It's your boyfriend." Zane sneered, seeing my face fall.

I stared at the screen. "He's just a friend."

"You sure about that?" He couldn't hide the jealousy burning in his unnatural eyes.

"Don't make me vomit. One kiss doesn't entitle you to pass judgment. What? Am I not allowed to have a boy for a friend?" I snapped.

His eyes darkened to sapphires. "It complicates things."

"Whatever." I shook my head. I could not believe we were going to fight after sharing the most mind-blowing kiss of my life. "This is a stupid conversation. I'm not dating anyone, so can we talk about something else?" *Or not talk at all*, I silently added, my eyes shifting to his lips.

"Do you want a boyfriend?" His hand shot out, tucking a piece of loose hair behind my ear.

I stepped back, needing distance. "My life is too messy and complicated for a relationship." I would just screw it up somehow.

Challenge glinted in his eyes. "I bet I could change your mind."

What was going on? I angled my head, folding my arms. "This isn't a game."

"If you say so, but if it were …" He sent me a panty-dropping grin. "I'd win."

I couldn't prevent the heat from sweeping across my face. *Damn him.* "We should probably go."

He rocked back on his heels. "You're probably right. We wouldn't want to miss the fireworks."

I coughed.

We'd already made our own fireworks, but I didn't think it was wise to point that out. His eyes still shone with a glint of disorder. With just the right push, I knew we could be right back where we had been moments ago, his tongue sweeping through my mouth. It would have been a hell of a grand finale.

Get a grip, Piper.

In silence, we walked, heading toward the echo of lapping waters. The breeze frolicked through my hair, and beyond in the distance, I could barely make out the sound of voices. We made sure to keep enough space between us so we didn't accidentally touch.

The sand squished under my feet as we crossed onto the beach. It was a good thing he didn't expect conversation, because my mind was a million miles away—conflicted, all because of him and his life-altering lips. One minute he was as cold as ice and the next as hot as the surface of the sun. It would make anyone's head spin.

"Hello, gorgeous," a gravelly voice interrupted behind me.

I turned around. Zane already had his eyes pinned on a guy coming out from under the docks. Light from the lamppost streamed down on his pale-colored hair, the wind kicking up, blowing the long strands across his forehead. I guessed his age to be in his late twenties.

And I knew just by looking at him that he was a ghost, a spirit, or whatever they wanted to be called. For a split second, I panicked, not knowing if what I was seeing was real. Confusion scrambled my brain. Zane had clearly seen him, which, if I took a moment to process, would make sense if *he* was indeed dead.

Shit.

Zane stiffened, and my eyes immediately went to the stranger's wrists. If there was one thing I'd learned, it was that those little birdy tattoos separated the reapers from the rest of us. Sure as shit, a little blue sparrow adorned his left wrist. My brain had just barely registered what that meant when I felt tendrils of fear burrowing through my stomach.

He was a dead reaper.

The guy beamed at me. "Aren't you a sight for sore eyes? I heard you keep lethal company."

Zane snarled, a ghastly, primitive warning.

He nodded at Zane. "Reaper."

It was like a come-kick-my-ass invitation. "Zane?" I whispered hesitantly.

"It's okay," he assured me under his breath. "He's dead. A hallow."

145

If that was supposed to make me feel better, it failed. My first face time with a hallow—I was uncertain how I should be feeling or what I was supposed to do. Was Zane going to destroy this guy's soul? Technically, he wasn't human, the mark on his wrist saying otherwise, so did that mean he had a soul to take?

A sudden rush of brisk air stirred at the back of my neck, and my eyes turned to Zane. I gasped. Cloaked in shadows, he disappeared, only to materialize seconds later behind the ghost of the restless reaper. Zane was going to collect a soul tonight, and I was going to witness the whole thing.

Crap on a stick.

I wasn't sure I was prepared to witness Death's weapon in action.

What if I looked at Zane differently?

What if he grew an extra set of pointy teeth and ate the soul like a ravenous beast?

Wow. I needed to lay off the *Supernatural* episodes. This whole night was turning into a page out of a Dean R. Koontz novel. Unreal. Terrifying. Intriguing.

The ghost-spirit thing spun, but not before I caught a glimpse of panic as he realized he was about to lose his soul—the last grip he had to keep him here on Earth. "You're not the only one with tricks," he sneered.

Zap. He was gone.

I rubbed my eyes, determined they were deceiving me and what I was seeing wasn't real. Inhuman or not, people did not just vanish into thin air. *But Zane could move within the shadows,* my subconscious reminded me. That I accepted, but a dead person bending space didn't make sense. I might need to rethink how the world worked.

When he didn't immediately reemerge, I began to think I'd dodged a bullet. Of course, I was never that lucky. Fate had it out for me. What a bitch.

A slight twitch of Zane's brow was the only warning he gave.

I never saw him, but the moment his fingers wrapped around my throat, I knew I was in deep poo—the torrential, life-threatening kind. I couldn't breathe. Literally the oxygen was cut from my lungs as I gasped, struggling to fight for glorious air. I couldn't scream. I couldn't call for help.

No. No. God no.

I wasn't ready to die, if it was possible to die at the hands of someone who'd already kicked the bucket, but by the feeling of the hands squeezing my esophagus, I assumed it was very feasible. This idiot didn't know who he was messing with. I wasn't going to make it easy. Twisting and bucking, I went wild, trying to loosen his hold on me. All I managed to do was send us both tumbling to the ground.

The impact of the coarse sand knocked the air out of my chest, scorching my back in searing pain. *Son. Of. A. Bitch.* But at least his grubby hands were no longer grasping my neck. Greedily, I gulped air like it was an all-you-can-eat chocolate buffet and it was that time of the month. The taste was fresh and sweet, but didn't diminish the stinging burn. I started to cough. If I lived to see tomorrow, I was going to be sporting some killer bruises.

Thinking fast, I shoved the palm of my hand up his face at full force. On impact, I heard a nasty crack. Good. I hoped I'd broken his nose. My reprieve was short-lived.

Recovering far quicker than I'd anticipated, he pulled back his hand, bluish blood gushing from his nose. "You skan—"

Suddenly, the weight of his repulsive body was gone, and the sound of flesh being pummeled overrode the rising and falling of the ocean's tide. While I had been tangling with dead dude, I had forgotten about Zane. Vibrant, rare blue eyes met mine—a face so striking and so cold I knew I was safe.

"Looks like we're doing this the hard way. Keeps things interesting, and I'm looking forward to kicking your ass." Zane held the ghost at an arm's length, those dark veins spreading down his neck and over his arms.

Zane was wicked fast and deadly, his form flickering in and out, turning from shadow to human and back again. Blood pumped through my body so fast as the ground began to shake, trees and cars trembling. Zane threw his arms into the air, and a quick crack sounded, followed by a succession of several more.

Good God. I was going to think twice about pissing off Zane.

"I'm going to enjoy ripping the essence from your body," he growled.

Fireworks exploded in the distance, lighting up the sky, but I couldn't take my eyes off Zane.

"Piss off," the hallow hissed. "I'm not ready to let you strip me of my soul, Death Scythe."

"Well, that's unfortunate, considering you're dead," Zane replied, cloaked in darkness. "You don't think I can actually let you stick around, do you? Especially after that little stunt you pulled?"

"Change is coming. Can you feel it?" He jerked against Zane's bindings like he was having a seizure and was more than a little cuckoo.

Zane's eyes took on an eerie glow, and his jaw was compressed. "The only thing I feel is your essence. It's mine."

"Stick it up your ass, Hunter," he spat.

"Now there's an idea." Zane smiled coldly, grinding his knee into the hallow's chest. "You hurt her. You spilled her blood. And now, you will know my wrath. I might have shown you mercy, but now, it won't be quick or without pain." He placed his open hand over his heart.

And that was it. The hallow bellowed, unifying with the wailing winds and death.

The air kicked up, sand swirling around us in a tornado, lashing and spinning. A bright light erupted at the center of the hallow's chest, spreading until I felt the need to turn away, the brilliance blinding. Just at the moment, when I didn't think I could bear another second, Zane's darkness enveloped the light.

A part of my mind clicked off, and I was moving without thinking. It was a split-second decision. I wasn't brave. I was intrigued. "Zane?" My hand went through the shadows.

Oops.

I had expected to meet resistance, an invisible barrier, but my fingers skimmed Zane's arm. Touching him might not have been the smartest choice, not while he was severing a soul from a body. Electric tingles darted down my arm, and I felt something deep inside me.

A tug. A temptation. The shadows were cool and soft against my skin. Everything slowed down.

My body felt like it was shimmering from the inside out, murmuring with energy. I snatched my hand away, but not before I felt the power of destroying a soul. Scrambling backward, I gasped, falling on my backside.

When the light of his humanity finally flickered out completely, the body was gone as if he had been made of nothing but smoke and air—not a trace left behind but the aftermath of bruises on my neck and cuts on my back.

I had wanted the truth, but actually seeing it ... totally different than hearing or imagining it. I knew Zane was dangerous. I knew what he did. Yet witnessing it, feeling it ... All I could do was stare at him. "You really are a weapon."

Zane let out a strangled laugh. "That's what I've been telling you." Offering me a hand, he asked, "Are you okay?"

He'd killed him. I mean, yes, he was technically already dead, but he had ripped out his soul without hesitation. And as I examined how that made me feel, I realized I was grateful. He'd saved my life. Again. I put my hand in his without hesitation. "Thank you."

With an angled brow, he pulled me to my feet. "I never thought I'd hear those two words from your mouth."

There was comfort in him razzing me like old times. "Have you killed before?" I winced. "Sorry, dumb question. Of course you have."

"I've lost count. And there will be more. Many more." There was regret. He accepted what he did, but he didn't enjoy it.

Listening, there was only silence. No fireworks. "Guess we missed the show."

He glanced at his phone. "And you didn't run."

Searching his face, I asked, "Was I supposed to?"

Looking just a tad disheveled, he murmured, "You should be shaking in your boots, Princess."

I dragged in a deep breath that still tasted of Zane's kiss. "We're all full of surprises. Like you. You are prone to moments of great dickdom, but then you go and do something unexpected."

He touched me, a whisper along my cheek, sending a charge through my body so strong it stole my breath. "I don't think I'll ever understand you."

Thousands of tiny molecules surged inside me, a mixture of pleasure and pain. I didn't know what was happening, but it wasn't normal. My belly started to roll, my vision turned fuzzy, and my lashes flickered in an effort to clear the haze. Pointless. Before I had the chance to question Zane, I tipped over the edge into the unknown abyss.

He damn well better catch me. It was my last thought.

CHAPTER 17

More and more I'd been dreaming about the night my mother was murdered. I relived that moment as if I'd been there, watching her life being yanked away—the sounds of gunshots echoing down the street, the numbness that took over my body when I realized the wretched truth, and her blood staining my hands as she left me alone.

I screamed, desperate for help. Her body lay motionless on the blacktop, twisted at an odd angle. Fear and panic had made me useless.

But in my dreams, Mom blinked open her eyes, moaning in pain as she looked at me, a tear rolling down her cheek. She reached out a trembling hand, covering the side of my cheek. A river of warmth and love flowed through me. Weakened from the loss of blood, she couldn't hold her arm up, so she let it rest on my shoulder.

"Piper," she said. "It will be okay. You are stronger than you realize, much stronger than I."

My head swung back and forth, not wanting to hear this. She was wrong. So wrong. I was not strong.

Her hand squeezed my arm. "There is so much I never got to tell you, but there isn't time. Piper, wake up—"

My eyes jolted open.

Panting, beads of perspiration dotted my body, a fuzziness clouding my brain. Every limb felt leaden. I saw walls of purple and ivory, an antique dresser snuggled into the corner, and a furry white rug covering the floor beside the bed.

Not my bedroom. Not home.

I was in my room at Raven Manor, which meant my nightmare was still very real. My mom was gone.

I forced the dream to the back of my mind. It was then I heard the heated voices just outside my door. I knew them well.

Rose and Zane.

Even dead, I would recognize that holier-than-thou voice of Zane and the commanding voice of Rose. Like slugging through murky water, fighting to break free, the memories of what had happened tonight swam to the surface. There was no denying what I had seen. If I had been harboring any hope that Zane wasn't what he claimed to be, tonight had shattered that itty-bitty sliver of hope.

Curiosity got the best of me. Listening, I zeroed in, attempting to hone my snooping skills. They weren't that great to begin with, but luckily, Zane and Rose were making it easy, their voices rising.

"You shouldn't be here," Rose reprimanded.

I cringed, feeling a tad bit sorry for Zane.

"If I hadn't been there, she might not be safely tucked into her bed," replied Zane. "Someone has to look out for the brat."

Brat? I flung back the covers.

He was going to pay for that later, after I finished eavesdropping.

"What do you think I've been doing?" Rose countered. "I brought her here for that exact reason—to keep her alive, not for a meaningless fling."

Ouch. The hostility was evident; however, it was difficult for me to understand. That was more than a bee sting, and not in the least bit true. Whatever was going on between Zane and me, it was not meaningless.

"How long are you going to keep doing this? Lying to her? Keeping her in the dark? She deserves to know the truth, for her own protection," Zane argued. I could feel the increase in his anger.

Calm and collected, Rose replied, "Don't question my methods. I know what she needs, and right now she can't handle the truth."

"Shows how little you actually know your granddaughter," he scoffed.

She clucked her tongue. "You let your feelings clog your judgment. Feelings you shouldn't have, I remind you."

"It's not necessary. I know where I stand, but I'm done lying. I won't stand around and watch her suffer."

"And that's why you are not the right choice for her."

I was on the edge of the bed, literally afraid I might miss something imperative.

Frigid air seeped under the door. The chill rang in his voice as he spoke. "That's not what our souls say."

Huh? What did that mean?

Rose was silent for a fraction of a minute, absorbing the comment about our souls. I didn't understand what he meant, but it made my heart quicken. "That might be, but it doesn't matter. It's too late. The choice has been made."

"Bullshit," Zane spat. "You have the power to alter or even dissolve the agreement."

Her voice dropped to a whisper, and I nearly fell out of the bed trying to hear what she said. Damn it. Just when things were starting to get good, she had to go and ruin it.

The hinges on my door squeaked, and I scampered back onto the bed, snapping my eyes closed. I pulled the covers swiftly back up to my chin just in time. *Clunk. Clap. Clunk.* The scuffle of shoes sauntered across the wood floor, followed by the mattress dipping, but it was the scent of a misty rainforest that aroused my senses. Why did he have to smell so stinking yummy?

Soft lips brushed across my forehead. I kept as still as a corpse, forgetting to breathe.

"Piper." He rolled my name off his tongue. "I know you're awake. Piper?" Concern marked his voice.

I opened just one eye, making sure the coast was clear. No Rose, but I didn't delude myself into thinking she had gone far. After what I'd heard, I was actually shocked she'd let Zane in my room at all.

A rush of air exuded from his slightly tilted lips. "I thought I was going to have to perform CPR."

I smirked. "I just bet you would have liked that."

"And you wouldn't?"

I scooted up, resting my back on a pile of fluffy pillows. "Guess you'll never know," I said with satisfaction.

His lopsided grin spread an inch. "I could knock you out again if that would help."

A flutter took up residence deep in my belly and chest. "Just try it. You're already on my shit list."

His brow did that irritating and charming arch. "How much did you hear?"

My hand clutched the end of the blanket, twiddling with the knit. "Enough to know you owe me an explanation."

Ice blue eyes narrowed. "It would do well for you to learn to not stick your nose where it doesn't belong."

I was going to fly off the bed and kill him. "I heard her tell you—"

He pressed a finger to my lips and leaned forward, murmuring in my ear, "Be careful what you say. The walls here are thin, and you are treading dangerous waters, fiery one."

The warmth from his breath made me shiver, sending a ripple of annoyance down my back. I wanted to argue—patience not being one of my virtues. "Fine," I said reluctantly. "But I won't be put off for long."

"Tomorrow. Meet me at the docks of the club after hours." He flicked the end of my nose.

Frowning, I hugged a pillow to my chest, glaring. "You better not blow me off, Zaney, because I promise I'll hunt you down."

Standing up, a small grin pulled at his lips. "I might actually look forward to that." He walked backward toward the double glass doors. "Either way, Princess, just remember ..." his hand touched the doorframe "… I warned you." Then he slipped out the door as quietly as he had slithered in.

"Don't let the door hit you in the ass on the way out," I yelled.

The sound of his damn laughter carried in the wind as he strutted down the terrace stairs.

I PEERED out the large double doors, finding a sense of calm I hadn't felt in a long time. Despite the picturesque view—a garden flourishing with bold flowers and lush greencry, thriving in the summer's heat—my heart twisted.

Now that I'd had a taste of Zane, it was all I could think about. I was a smart girl, most of the time. I should have known that even a simple kiss with Zane would be earth-shattering. I wanted more. I wanted *him*.

Crap.

I was in trouble. Big, big trouble.

My heart was in jeopardy because of a guy who I wasn't positive I liked. Okay, I found him irresistibly sexy. Yes, I was drawn to him. But as a person, Zane was dark, moody, reckless, and dangerous. He killed. They might already be dead, but it still counted. He took souls. Zane was on another plane than me. I was still in high school, for God's sake. I wasn't prepared for him or the feelings he enticed.

He was complicated. He would complicate my life.

Speaking of, I was struggling to believe I had actually fainted. There hadn't even been blood or guts. I had collapsed for the first time because Zane touched me. It was laughable.

Night was in full bloom.

Fog brewed on the horizon, spilling into the ocean, gliding closer and closer to the house. I pressed my nose to the glass, the round, big moon setting my face ablaze. Zane was somewhere out there, possibly extinguishing and absorbing another soul. It was what he did.

And I was alone.

Doing nothing.

Just twiddling my thumbs, cursing his name, and trying to forget his face. I had no purpose. No meaning in life. I hated that I was stuck here, caged on an island, while my mom's killer ran free. I should be out there, looking for answers instead of pacing my room, cursing the four walls that kept me captive. Raven Hollow had the answers I needed.

Zane and Zoe, they could help. They had secrets. They had answers.

Making a rash decision, I crossed the room in purposeful strides, snatching my phone off the bed, and dialed Zoe. If I couldn't get what I wanted from Zane, then maybe I could get something out of Zoe. Like I said, patience wasn't a quality I possessed. It was going to be my downfall.

As I hovered over the send button, I rationalized my impulsive behavior by convincing myself that I needed "girl time." Utter bullshit, yet it didn't stop the muscle in my finger. Other than Zoe, I didn't have a single *girl* friend. All the girls I knew were petty, snobby, back-stabbing bitches. None of those were qualities I looked for in a friend. Parker was so much simpler. He never tried to steal a guy from me. There was never competition for who was prettier. He loved to gossip, but never behind my back.

Zoe was the exception.

She didn't make me feel self-conscious about who I was or how I looked. I didn't feel judged when we were together. Although I had only known her a short time, I felt a connection, a kinship. Zoe and I, we could be besties. She was the kind of girl I understood. I wondered if that was because she was sort of not human.

While I pondered the inner workings of female friendships, Zoe's voice came through the other end. "You better have a helluva good excuse for ditching me. And your tongue down my brother's throat does not qualify."

I giggled nervously. "I saw a hallow," I replied tentatively, the word sticking oddly on my tongue. "A reaper hallow to be precise."

"No shit," she said genuinely surprised. "You're alive, so that's a plus. And I would definitely know if you had died."

Dead air.

"Don't worry. Zane mentioned he told you," she informed me.

How could she be so casual about this?

"He's got such a big mouth, but at least that explains his shiteous mood," she chattered on. It was one of the things I liked about her—the constant stream of babble. "What I really want to know is what you guys were doing before the dead showed up."

"Uh." This was not the direction I had wanted this conversation to steer. "What makes you think we were doing anything?" I buried my head in the pillow, letting out a silent scream. My lameness had no bounds.

"When I asked Zane, he got all weird, more weird than normal, so it must be something big. And I'm putting my money on you, girl." There was no question. She was not going to give up.

This was not happening. I could always lie, but that was not the kind of friendship I wanted with Zoe, so I just blurted out, "He kissed me."

"Two scoops of shit." I heard her wrestling with the phone, taking it off speaker. "Sexy, I-can't-live-without-you kiss or friendly, you're-like-my-sister kiss?"

I groaned. "Are those my only two choices?"

"Stop stalling and spill your guts," she ordered.

She'd asked for it. "It was definitely friendly. Very friendly."

"Tongue down your throat?"

I made a face into the phone. "I can't do this."

She whistled. "Score one for Zane. So how was it?"

"Why do you have to be his sister?" I grumbled.

"Bitch, don't make me hurt you."

I sighed, finally giving up on the idea of privacy. "He is an exceptional kisser. There, are you happy?"

"Not quite. Man, getting dirt from you is worse than a takedown with a scorned soul." Zoe's voice crackled over the phone.

"He's your brother. You don't find this awkward?" I asked, propping myself up on my elbow.

"If it was Zach, totally gross. I'd question your taste in men." Her voice sounded closer to the phone. "But Zane, not so much. He's a damn dark mystery that attracts everyone with tits."

Doing a little wiggle dance in the bed, I sat up, pulling my knees to my chest, all while keeping the phone clutched between my ear and shoulder. Skill. "Are you guys allowed to date humans?"

"I take it you want to know if you can do the nasty with my brother?"

I wrinkled my nose, resisting the urge to hit my head on the nearest wall over and over again. "When you put it like that, it sounds dirty."

"Whatever. You like it," she said with a dry laugh. "You want to know if it is physically possible to do it? You bet my fine ass. Is it wise? Probably not. Zane is known to leave scars on the heart. In short, don't fall in love with him."

My throat got clogged. What if it was too late? But I didn't have the courage to ask what I couldn't admit to myself.

"Are you still there?" she asked. There was such a gap of silence she'd probably thought I hung up on her.

"Yeah, sorry." I cleared my throat.

"He's leaving, you know," she added.

"What?" I shrieked, bolting upright, throw pillows tumbling to the floor.

"I take it he hasn't mentioned it."

The idea of Zane leaving made my stomach fall sharply. "No. He failed to leave out that little bit of information when we were playing tonsil hockey."

Zoe giggled.

"Why is he such an ass?" I mumbled more to myself than her, the ball in my chest unraveling a little.

"Do you expect me to answer that?"

I smiled. "I'm pretty sure I can figure it out on my own. He's a guy. They're all assholes."

"Amen, sista," she agreed, a smile in her tone.

"Where is he going?" I had to know. How else would I stalk him?

There was another pause, as if she was deciding whether to tell me or not. "Away. For as long as I can remember, Zane has talked about getting off this island. He was supposed to leave weeks ago."

Oh. Well. Shit. "Why didn't he?"

"You showed up," she stated like it should have been obvious to me. It wasn't.

Why would I think I could influence such a huge decision on a guy who couldn't stand me half the time?

"The night I took you to the bonfire," she said, painting a clear picture in my head, "that was Zane's farewell bash."

I couldn't believe what she was implying—that I had something to do with Zane sticking around this island when he clearly didn't want to be here anymore than I did. "Come again?" That had been within the first week, and he'd despised me then.

"When you arrived, he decided to stay and make sure you didn't stir up trouble. In my opinion, the baboon doesn't want to admit he has *feelings* for you."

I wasn't sure what Zane felt for me, but I did agree he was a baboon.

After we hung up, I realized I'd completely forgotten why I had originally called. The answers to those nagging questions would just have to wait until tomorrow after all.

Tomorrow, I thought wistfully.

Tomorrow, I would drill Zane so hard … with questions obviously. Although my mind was thinking of something else entirely.

CHAPTER 18

Tomorrow felt like it would never come, and by the time I'd finally fallen asleep, the sun was just coming up. My eyes were so droopy I gave up the fight. Beauty rest was going to have to wait another day. Unfortunately, my body had other ideas. It refused to move, and if I was going to get those answers, I needed my legs and arms to function.

And my brain.

Maybe Rose had found her heart today, because I hadn't been disturbed, and after the ordeal yesterday, I figured she owed me. I was going to totally work it to my advantage, like in the form of sneaking out.

But first, I needed to get rid of my dragon breath. No one should be subjected to morning breath. I wanted to interrogate Zane, not kill him. Then coffee. Lots and lots of strong coffee. Not necessarily in that order.

It was a miracle what my body wouldn't do for a caffeine buzz. Though I moved more like a zombie, I was able to down my first cup of coffee, giving me the jolt I needed to feel halfway human. Making a quick pit stop at the bathroom, I brushed my teeth, washed my face, and applied a coat of mascara and lip gloss. Then padding back into the room, I dropped my clothes as I went and slipped into a pair of dark denim shorts and a forest green tank. The color did wonders for my eyes.

Zane might make my blood run from hot to boiling and he might confuse me in ways I didn't yet understand, but through all the ups and downs, I wanted to look smoking hot. It was a foreign feeling to me—wanting to look desirable for someone other than just myself.

Before I fussed another foolish minute, I grabbed the keys to Josie and left with a determination to unearth the secrets he was hiding from me—what the whole island was hiding from me. It was more than just reapers and restless souls.

My jeep rattled its way into the club parking lot, causing more ruckus than I would have liked. Poor thing needed a tune-up or a trip to the junkyard. The parking lot of the Black Crow was nearly empty, only a few other cars kept my jeep company. With keys jingling in hand, I strolled around the side of the building, my flip-flops smacking the soles of my feet. *Clap, clap, clap*—I loved the sound. It was the sound of summer.

A boat honked out in the bay as I walked onto the docks. Seagulls squawked overhead, but Zane was nowhere in sight. I sighed, kicking off my flip-flops, and sat at the edge of the wooden pier to wait. I would wait all damn day if I had to.

The vast waters imprisoned my gaze, slapping up against the wooden beams of the docks. Rising up, the water sloshed, spraying on my bare feet and legs. *He better not make me wait long—*

I didn't have to turn around to know he was behind me. Every nerve ending in my body was tingling, my skin flushing with anticipation, a feeling I didn't want. My mind and my body were at odds with each other. I forced myself to take my time, turning slowly, and used the extra moments to pull myself together. I looked him over intently, lingering at the angry cut on his cheek. Had that been there yesterday? Had he gotten it during the fight? I couldn't remember. "Let me guess. You had a hot date after you left last night and she got a little out of control?"

He grinned at me, sinful and lethal. "You could say that."

My belly went topsy-turvy as I stood up. Not thinking about what I was doing, my hand reached out, fingers skimming over the wound.

He winced, pushing my hand away. "It's nothing and will heal."

I wanted to tend to the cut, but I knew he wouldn't be receptive to my help, not in his current mood, so I shoved my hands into my pockets before I gave into the urge to touch him again. "All right, tough guy, have it your way."

"How are you feeling?" His dark hair caught a glint of the summer sun.

"Me? I'm golden." Or I might be if I could stop thinking about how nice touching him felt or wondering why he'd kissed me.

He saw right through me. "Liar."

"Why didn't you tell me you were leaving?" I demanded, more out of curiosity than him owing me an explanation, because he didn't.

He glared through lashes so black and long it looked like he wore guyliner. "Would it matter?"

I had come here to grill him about my family, yet the first thing out of my mouth was concern for him, and then I started acting like a slighted girlfriend. "I-I don't know. But that is not the point."

"What exactly *is* the point?"

You know those moments when your mouth and your mind didn't communicate? This was one of those God-awful moments. I was speaking before I knew what I was saying. "Is it because of me?" My voice cracked halfway through.

Wow. That didn't sound self-absorbed.

I knew what Zoe had told me, but I hadn't actually believed it. So obviously, I had to just blurt it out—force him to tell me I had absolutely not impacted his decision to hang around Raven Hollow for the summer.

He blinked and then grinned charmingly. "You?"

Now I was feeling like an idiot. My cheeks were burning. "Forget I asked. Zoe must have assumed."

"Zoe needs to have her lips sewn shut." He ran a hand over his jaw. "It's the only way she'll mind her own business."

I angled my head. I felt so ridiculous asking, but I wanted to know. Desperately. "Why didn't you go?"

"Don't worry. I had my reasons, and you didn't make the list."

Asshole. Why did he have to go back to being a douche? His bipolar attitude was giving me migraines. Only twenty-four hours ago he had kissed me, protected me, carried me home, fought Rose to stay with me, and today he was shutting me out, cutting me with his indifference. I wanted to call him a liar.

"Cat got your tongue?" he asked after the awkward moment of silence where I just glared at him.

I crossed my arms. "I'm sorry. Did you say something? I was too busy thinking of ways to stab you. Although, it might just be easier to push you over the dock."

He wielded his cockiness like a sword. "You might get your chance, just not today."

I stepped back, shaking my head. "This whole mysterious guy act is getting old, like yesterday's stale bread."

Suddenly, he spun, engulfing me in his arms, his hand covering my mouth. "Shh," he whispered into my ear.

My back was pressed against his chest. Ignoring his warning, I bit his hand. What could I say? It was a gut reaction.

"Dammit, Piper," he growled. "Why must you do everything the hard way?" He tossed me over his shoulder, and I squeaked as he hauled me under the docks. For a split second, I was fearful for my life.

Then I heard her voice.

Rose.

And she wasn't alone.

It took me a moment to place who was with her. Zane's dad.

What was Rose doing secretly meeting with Death?

Before I could think too hard on it, a cool, misty feeling came over me, chilling my blood. At first I didn't understand, not until I looked at Zane. Eyes narrowed, spidering with inky tendrils, he cloaked us both in the shadows, hiding us in darkness just as Rose appeared with Zane's father at her side. They were coming our way.

As soon as Zane noticed the docks were going to be the rendezvous point, his voice sounded in my head. *Whatever you do, don't scream.* Then he swept us over the side.

I didn't have time to question what he was going to do, or how he'd gotten inside my head, not when I was free-falling a ten-foot drop. Squeezing my eyes shut, I concentrated on the security of Zane's strong arms. I should have been wondering why he'd tossed us over the side of the pier, not how fan-freaking-tastic it felt being surrounded by him.

A cool vapor entered my blood, flowing through my veins as I held onto him. I knew he would never let go. There was an undeniable trust in him that came from … I didn't know where, but no matter what crap-ola came out of his mouth, he had only ever been there for me. When I got my wits back, we were wading in shallow water under the dock, and if anyone asked, I had no idea how we'd gotten from point A to point B.

Zane's back was pressed to one of the pier's wooden legs, and I was plastered to his chest. We were still covered by the shadows, darkness surrounding every particle of our bodies. It was a strange sensation, an indescribable feeling.

Or maybe that was his arms holding me.

Being this close to him scrambled my brain, but that was the least of my problems. The old wooden planks above our heads groaned as the last two people I expected to share a secret met.

Oh, please God, don't let them be having an affair. I mean Rose was old, but Death was like ancient.

No way could I handle that, especially since I had a love-hate thing going on with his son.

They were directly overhead, and I was afraid to breathe. Zane had gone to great lengths to keep our presence unknown, which led me to believe he was as surprised by this meeting as I was. What I might overhear scared me more.

Are you okay? His voice sounded again in my head.

I nodded.

Talk to me only through your thoughts. Got it?

I started to nod again, but then remembered what he'd said. *Okay.*

I was living in an episode of *Supernatural.* In what planet was it normal to be talking telepathically? Man, wait until I told Parker about this. We would both be questioning my sanity. Then I remembered ... I couldn't tell Parker about any of it.

It's so dark. I can't see a darn thing, I grumbled, forgetting that he could hear *everything.* Every. Darn. Thought. And that only made my mind drift to all the embarrassing things I didn't want Zane to know. Like how incredible his butt was.

That's the point, Piper. We're blended amongst the shadows, and with any luck, they won't spot us.

I couldn't help but wonder ... *Just how powerful are you?*

Those blue eyes sparkled in the dark. *It's better you don't know.*

Why?

For the same reason I'm protecting you. Power can be a coveted sin. There are those who would kill for what I can do or what I possess. If another reaper took my soul, he would inherit all my power.

I was just about to share a thought when I heard Rose. She didn't sound cheery. "Your son has been sniffing around my granddaughter, Roarke."

Roarke? Your dad's name is Roarke? I don't know why it sounded so strange. It was just weird that he had a name.

What did you think it was? Death?

Well, kind of.

There was a soft chuckle in my head.

"Isn't that what we want, Rose dear?" Roarke said in a humoring tone.

Her heels clicked on the timber. "Wrong spawn. I'm talking about the scythe."

"Zane?" Roarke thought it over for a few seconds. "Hmm. There did seem to be some friction between them."

Friction? I echoed. *Try more like warfare.*

Zane's eyes tapered to tiny slits. In the darkness, they were the only things I could see, glowing orbs of sapphire.

Oops.

Having him in my head was invasive. No thought was safe.

You'll get used to it, Zane responded.

Yeah right. My mom had said the same thing about ballet. I still hated leotards and slippers.

"It needs to end," Rose demanded.

"What makes you think Zane will pose a problem?" He wasn't the least bit intimidated and didn't strike me as someone who took lightly to being ordered about.

"He's your son," she said spitefully, no lost love between the two of them. "That's already a problem."

Death laughed—deep and from the belly. "She has your spunk." And like a switch, the amusement faded. "And she is going to need it for what is to come."

"I know," Rose snapped. I could picture her chin jutting out. "All the more reason she doesn't need the complication."

For all accounts, Death was a pretty reasonable guy. "Her life is already complicated. A little extra protection never hurt. I know my son. No harm will come to her in his presence."

"Except for her reputation. You and I both know how people of this town talk."

Mortified, I wanted to bury my head in the sand. I couldn't believe she had said that.

Zane snickered, hearing my silent groan.

In turn, I wanted to plant my fist in his gut. We'd see who was laughing then.

"I'm warning you, Roarke. He needs to keep his distance," Rose said with finality.

She was kind of scary, her tone taking on a choppy quality; however, Death was not in the least bit unnerved. "I can't promise. Zane makes his own choices, his own mistakes."

"Not when they put my granddaughter's life in jeopardy."

"Then you should have left her be, Rose."

She uttered a string of swear words that made me proud, followed by what I pictured was a grand exit. I listened closely, waiting for a sign that Death had gone on his merry way. Nothing. I didn't have supersonic hearing, but seriously, not a single peep. The boards didn't creak. There was no swishing of clothes. It wasn't until Zane released a shuddering sigh and dropped the veil of darkness that I knew we were alone. I blinked a few times, hoping the black spots on my vision would fade, but in the meantime, I placed a hand on Zane's chest, stabilizing myself.

"Is it safe?" I whispered.

Nodding, he peered down at me. "Yeah." He ran a hand through his hair. "They're gone."

Frustration whipped through me. "What the hell was that?"

He seemed to be wrestling with just how much to tell me, and I knew I wasn't going to like it. "I thought it was pretty obvious. Your grandma is going to do whatever she can to ensure we don't cross the friend boundary."

Too late. "That's not what I meant. How were you in my head? How was I in your head? Is it a reaper thing?"

A dabble of moonlight lit the side of his angled face. "Yes and no."

"Huh? Specifics."

"I wasn't finished."

I rolled my eyes. "Well, are you going to get on with it, or just torture me?"

"You are so—"

I pinched him.

He couldn't hide his amusement at my knee-jerk reaction. "You really are a pain in my ass."

"Zane," I growled, wading out of the water to the shore. I'd lost my flip-flops in the waves and couldn't care less. Sand sticking to my feet, I wasn't surprised to see Zane had beaten me.

"It's called soul symmetry," he told me.

"Is that like one of your super powers?" I was feeling prickly.

His lips twitched. "Funny. The fact that you can associate what I do with super powers shows how much you don't know about me, or how seriously dangerous you don't find me."

I shrugged, pretending I was freaked out. "You are just the lesser of two evils."

The bottom of his frayed jeans were soaked, but he didn't seem to mind. "I might not understand your logic, but you're probably right. And before you ask, soul symmetry is the converging of two compatible souls."

"Our souls mesh?" Sweet. Baby. Jesus.

"More or less. It synchronizes the wavelengths of our souls, allowing me to extend or share my abilities with you. But it only works when two souls are a match."

"Our souls are a match?" I asked in disbelief.

He tilted his face to the side. "Did you hit your head?"

My eyes shrunk, giving him a dirty glare. "Give me a second to process. This is a lot to take in. How did you know our souls were a match?"

"What does it matter?" he shot back. "I took a risk, and luckily, it paid off."

A risk? That had an appalling ring to it. "And if we weren't a match?"

If I hadn't spent hours studying his face in my head, drawing it on paper, I wouldn't have seen it, the smallest inflection of concern in his eyes. "I would have forced the symmetry. It would have been very uncomfortable. Painful even."

"Peachy. Sounds enjoyable."

He wasn't daunted by my response. "You and I might not always see eye to eye, but apparently our souls are in tune."

I brushed my hair back. "I'm not sure how I feel about you taking that gamble without my consent. Actually, it pisses me off."

The corners of his lips twitched. "No need to get your panties in a wad, Princess. It worked, didn't it? No permanent damage done. Not to be a killjoy, but we have bigger problems anyway."

Yeah, I couldn't get the sound of his voice out of my head. That was a problem. It had left a mark, and I was certain it would linger for days. Weeks. Months. He had the kind of voice that wasn't easily forgotten. Cursed accent.

Focus, Piper.

"I don't understand why I'm a target. Why would anyone what to hurt me? Hurt my mom?"

A fierce glow filled his eyes. "No one is going to lay a hand on you," he swore—half growl, half oath.

"You can't be with me twenty-four seven. Why do you care, anyway?"

"I don't know. I just do," he replied flatly.

My hands went to my hips. "That's not even an answer."

A muscle ticked under his eye.

"Okay, fine," I said, accepting he wasn't going to expand his thoughts. "But won't you be putting yourself in danger then?" Why would he do that?

"I'm a badass. There's no other way to say it. I'm the best at what I do. Too good, maybe." He wasn't bragging, just stating a fact. "You don't need to worry about me."

There was that arrogance again. "A badass, huh?" I stated, using my foot to brush the drying sand from my toes.

"Oh, you know it. I'm *the* badass. It's just—"

My lashes fluttered. "It's just what?"

His eyes flashed as he took a step toward me. "For the first time in my life, I wish I was something else."

Gulp.

Why did I get the feeling that his desire to be someone else had everything to do with me? "Why do you keep doing that?"

Stretching out his arms, he asked, "What exactly am I doing that is pissing you off so much?"

"Everything!" I exclaimed, my heel digging into the ground.

He wore a menacing grin. "You know you like me. Just admit it."

Humph. I would do no such thing. "I like you about as much as I like sardines."

Zane tipped forward, closing the space between us. "Don't make me make a liar out of you."

What could I say? If he kissed me right now, I wouldn't stop him, and I probably would have thoroughly enjoyed myself. "You suck."

He laughed. "Piper, we are suffering from the same affliction. I like you, but I don't *want* to like you. There's a difference."

CHAPTER 19

It was dark when I tiptoed into the kitchen. The huge house took some maneuvering, but I managed to get there without waking the dead or the sleeping staff.

My stomach rumbled, as if I needed a reminder that I was hungry.

Starved, actually.

Soul sharing evidently did that to me, not a pleasant side effect for my figure, especially when it was junk I was craving.

My taste buds sung when I spotted a box of Lucky Charms in the pantry. Score. The cereal pieces clunked in the bowl as I poured. Splashing on the milk, I grabbed a spoon and took a seat at one of the stools.

The first bite, filled with marshmallow goodness, was halfway to my mouth when Estelle walked in.

"Did you save me a bowl?"

I stuck the spoon in my mouth, grinning. "Maybe," I said, chomping.

She took a seat next to me, and I slid her the half-empty box. "So you're still sneaking out with reaper boy?"

My spoon clattered into my bowl. "What did you say?"

She bumped my shoulder with hers. "I thought he … As much time as the two of you seem to spend together, I just assumed he told you."

I shook my head, clearing the shock from my brain cells. "No, he did. I just can't believe that you know. Gawd, does everyone on this island know?"

Sneaking a marshmallow from my bowl, she said, "Pretty much."

"Even Rose?"

Swallowing, she confirmed, "Definitely Rose."

I couldn't believe it. But really, after what I'd overheard today, I shouldn't have been surprised. The bigger question was, why hadn't she told me? Why did she insist we stay with her? Why? Why? Why? "I think she is trying to drive me insane," I mumbled, pushing my spoon around in the cereal.

"Believe it or not, Raven Hollow is probably the safest place for you."

"Why? Because if I die, there will be a reaper close by?" I replied testily.

She grinned. "Morbid, but true."

Learning that Estelle and most of the island knew about the wonders of the world, I immediately thought about TJ. "What about my brother? Does he know?"

She stuck her hand into the box, forgoing a bowl and milk. "Nope, I don't believe so. He is way too absorbed with his Xbox, playing Diablo."

Amen to that.

I exhaled. "Good. Let's hope it stays that way." I turned in my chair now that she had my undivided attention. "Have you always known there were reapers?"

She popped a handful of cereal into her mouth. "I was born and raised here. There are many who never talk about it and think it's better to sweep it all under the rug. Then there are the elders like my Nana." Swallowing, she continued. "She explained the inner workings of life and death, educating me on the rules of the island."

"God, this is so surreal."

Tucking a foot underneath her leg, she shook a small pile of cereal onto the counter and nibbled on a pink heart-shaped marshmallow. "Raven Hollow is like the hub for reapers. They are free to travel where they please, go where the souls call them, but it is this island that they all come back to. Especially if they are summoned."

"Summoned?" I was on the edge of my seat.

She lined up the little pieces of cereal, grouping them by color. "Yeah. Now that is a trip. If you ever get the chance, you have got to see it. Imagine this tiny island crowded with the most lethal soul eaters."

"Nah. I'd rather pass. Does a summoning happen often?" Because surely, this was one convention I wanted to skip.

Her shoulders shrugged. "I don't know. It's only happened once in my Nana's lifetime."

My appetite vanished, and I pushed away my half-eaten bowl. "So you haven't actually seen one?"

"Nope, but the stories are pretty frightening."

This conversation was like watching a slasher flick before bed. Disturbing and fretful. I wasn't going to be able to sleep a wink tonight.

SITTING on my bed surrounded by discarded wads of failed sketches and a rainbow of colored pencils, the creative juices weren't flowing tonight. My mind was too busy, bouncing from one thought to the next, never settling.

I had not felt utter peace since I arrived in Raven Hollow. Coinky-dink? Please. I didn't think coincidences lived here.

Raven Hollow was filled with ghosts.

Raven Hollow was filled with secrets.

Raven Hollow was filled with death.

A text came through as I was gnawing on the end of my pencil. It was Parker. We'd been conversing back and forth for the last hour. It hadn't helped. Parker was like my security blanket—my crutch. I leaned on him—depended on him, except I couldn't share what was really on my mind. For the first time in our friendship, I wasn't able to open up and be honest with Parker. No way was I willing to get him mixed up in my messy, sticky, gooey life here.

He would never have believed me anyway.

So I kept our texts to safe, boring topics, like the weather, my non-existent tan, and whether or not I'd survive the summer. But what he didn't know was I meant that literally. It was always there, lurking in the back of my mind, that someone wanted me dead. My mom had been murdered, and I felt like nowhere was safe, but maybe being surrounded by reapers had its perks.

It was becoming more and more clear that my mom's death hadn't been a random shooting. Call it intuition, or the will of a determined daughter, but I knew there was something brewing and the reapers were involved.

A chill scurried over my skin, sending a wave of goose bumps down my spine. I shivered, and my pencil froze on paper. *What now?* Glancing up, eight beady eyes leveled with my nose. I let out a high-pitched shriek. From a thin web of string dangled the worst kind of intruder. A spider. Charlotte and her web had to go.

Darting off the bed, I did an epic heebie-jeebies wiggle dance, which sadly did nothing to stop the skin crawling. If anything, eerie joined the tingles, and I knew Charlotte and I weren't the only ones here. Fear became a tangible force inside me, and I couldn't move a muscle. Once I turned around, that would be it. There would be no going back, and whatever was waiting for me, I would have to deal with. On the other hand, it could be Zane. Or it could be …

Crossing my fingers and my toes, I took a deep breath and turned. *Oh God. Oh God. Oh God.*

A month ago, I would have thought I was seeing a ghost or a spirit, but I would have also assumed that someone had drugged me and what I was seeing was a figment of a bad trip. Now, I knew the world was full of shit I'd never fully comprehend and that thing outside my bedroom window was a pissed-off dead girl, looking to steal my soul.

I was pretty partial to my soul. I wanted it to stay intact.

So why did I find myself walking toward the glass doors? Why wasn't I running to find Rose? What was it about this girl that made me want to risk my life's essence?

As I got closer, a silent scream stuck in my throat.

It couldn't be.

Could it?

Staring through the glass, a full panic rushed through me. She wasn't a girl at all. Long blonde hair billowed in the wind, surrounding a face I knew as well as my own. There was a ghostly glow to her skin, a paleness that was unearthly. It was her clothes that cinched it for me. The jeans and the purple turtleneck were stamped into my memory.

I pressed my hand to the glass. "Mom?"

Even as the word left my mouth, I knew she wasn't really here, yet it still didn't stop me from doing something reckless. She was dead. In my head, I knew she was dead, that she wasn't really here, but seeing someone I had wished every freaking night to see again was a temptation I couldn't resist.

Restless soul or ghost, it didn't matter. I needed to talk to her.

My hand flipped the lock, ignoring that instinctual warning that was screaming at me not to open the door. She said something, but I couldn't hear, so I threw open the door.

I should have exercised more caution.

I should have known that karma was going to kick me in the gut.

I should have trusted my instincts.

Maybe they hadn't left me completely, because instead of throwing myself into her arms like I wanted to, I stepped out onto the terrace. "Mom, what are you doing here? How are you here?"

She said nothing, and the sad, concerned look in her eyes turned menacing. A dense fog blanketed her feet, rising up our legs. It was cool against my bare skin.

"Mom?" I said with hesitation, taking a step back. Prickles of unease and uncertainty tiptoed down my neck.

Then, like out of a bad science fiction movie, the figure that I desperately wanted to be my mom—dead or ghost, it didn't matter— started to blur before me. The lines of her heart-shaped face widened at the jaw, turning more round. Blonde hair turned a sassy red. She grew an inch or two taller and thinned out in the waist.

Bolting inside would have been a sane person's immediate reaction. Not mine. I stood there gaping like an idiot, eyes bulging and mouth hanging open. As soon as I saw the blue sparrow, dreaded reality set in.

Reaper.

I screamed for real this time, the tangy taste of fear coating my insides.

For all the good it did me.

There was no one around, nothing but twilight.

"You gave in so easily." She tilted her head. "I have to say I'm kind of disappointed."

"What do you want?" I asked in a much braver voice than I was feeling. Inside, I was quaking. The last Blue Sparrow I had encountered tried to kill me. She must be a shifter. That was pretty f'd up.

How could I be so dumb? So gullible? Why not give her my soul on a freaking silver platter for her to devour? I didn't have time to berate myself; she was advancing on me.

"Not much. Just your soul, little Raven." Her violet eyes flamed.

My window of escape was closing down on me, and then it slammed shut as my back hit the doorframe. *Shit.* All I could think was stall. "Why would you want *my* soul?"

An evil grin spread over her lips. "You have no idea, do you? That only makes this that much sweeter." Faster than I anticipated, she reached out, jerking me by my ponytail and snapping my head back. It felt like every tiny hair follicle had been ripped from my scalp.

I refused to cry out. Tears stung my eyes, and I bit my lip until the worst of it subsided. "You bitch," I cursed. Not exactly the smartest move when she still had my hair in a death grip.

She yanked again, leading me into the bedroom like a pooch. I swung out blindly, hoping I would get lucky and sock this loco reaper.

Ugh. I needed to work on my aim.

My fist sailed through nothing but air, causing me to lose my balance, which in turn tugged a handful of hair. Fire burned at my scalp.

I was going to be bald and dead.

Joy.

"You're pathetic," she hissed, a massive bug up her butt. As if she had to drive home just how superior she was, she shoved me.

I stumbled, nearly toppling onto the bed. My eyes frantically looked for a weapon as she lunged toward me, and in my panicky state, I did the only thing that came to mind. I threw my half full glass of Dr. Pepper at her face.

What a waste.

Glass shattered on the floor as she fumbled about, rubbing her eyes.

I bet that burned like a mofo.

She wiped at her sticky eyes, flinging dark liquid all over my lavender walls. Rose was going to pitch a fit. I scrambled around the bed, and she stalked me like a cracked-out panther, violet eyes glowing, accented by blue tendrils streaking past her fake lashes.

She pounced, catching me in the back with the sole of her canvas sneakers. I guess I should've been thankful the bitch wasn't wearing heels. I landed on my face with the grace of a drunk. Arms flailing, I went down hard, the floor scuffing my elbows and giving me a nasty burn on my cheek. Slivers of broken glass were embedded in my forearms and palms. Son. Of. A. Mother …

Lying flat on my stomach, I groaned, positive I couldn't move. My body was screaming in agony. The older you were, the harder you fell. This was nothing like falling off my bike at five.

Piper, take a deep breath.

Where had my lady balls gone? I wasn't going to let this vindictive hooker anywhere near my soul. My brother needed me. And I was far from ready to leave this world. Not yet. Not until I solved the truth about my family. About my mom.

And this skank, she might be my ticket.

She had known to use my mom to get to me, make me let my guard down. Now she was going to pay.

"And you underestimate me." I swung my foot out, catching her at the back of her kneecap, and watched her go down to the ground.

There was a satisfactory *thwack*, and she let out a howl of pain. "You stupid—"

Ha. Take that reaper bitch, a taste of your own medicine.

There was, however, a flaw in my retaliation. Her recovery time was a thousand times faster than mine. *Can't a girl catch a break?*

As I pushed to my feet, fully intending to find a sharp object, she bear tackled me, and the two of us went sliding across the shiny, glass-littered floor. I let out an *oomph* as her weight crushed me.

She choked out a dry, bitter laugh. "It's almost comical that you think you stand a chance against me. Your mother didn't teach you shit." Her hands shot out, pinning my wrists on either side of my head.

I'd just gotten my ass handed to me, but I didn't care about that. "What do you know about my mom?"

"I know she was a failure, running away from her destiny. She was a coward."

I bucked, my rage spiking. No one talked about my mom like that and lived. It fueled me, giving me the edge I needed. I didn't think at all, just reacted. Wrapping my legs around her hips, I rolled, gaining the upper hand for the first time.

The struggle was real.

Even though I was sitting on her chest, she wasn't making it easy, so I pimp slapped her. Hey, it was the only way I could think of to get her to stop from tossing me across the room. I was already going to be covered in bruises tomorrow morning.

A network of blue veins coursed down her face, and I knew what came next: my soul being sucked from my body. Man, I hated being right. She wasted not a second. A bolt of blue energy slammed straight under my boobs, her hand covering my heart. A starburst clouded my vision as the warmth in my veins began to freeze.

If I didn't do something fast, I was going to be entering the spirit realm sooner rather than later, but what? How did you stop a reaper from taking possession of your soul? If there had been a chapter on the subject in my mythology textbook, I'd obviously doodled through it.

They could be killed, echoed in my head. Zane had told me a grave injury was enough to take down a reaper, but did I have it in me to go through with such a vile deed?

She'd made it obvious only one of us was leaving here with her heart still pumping. I intended for it to be me. Full strength, I arched back, shoving both hands into her chest. "Screw you!" I yelled.

With a force I didn't know I possessed, she flew back, her red hair billowing around her as she slammed into my dresser. A loud *thud* followed by a *crack* shot through the room as she hit her head on the corner. Bottles of perfume and lotion fell over the edge, clunking off her head. Unblinking, she stared at the ceiling, motionless.

"Still disappointed?" I asked.

I waited for her to answer. Guess she was a little rattled.

Relief eked through me. I was alive, but it was short-lived.

There was a dead body in my room.

I very much doubted Rose would approve. Nor did I imagine her staff cleaned up such messes. I clamped my hand over my mouth. Suddenly, I didn't feel too spiffy.

My heart started hammering in my chest like crazy. I felt sick to my stomach and was pretty sure I was two seconds away from hurling all over Rose's Persian rug. The experience of killing was a different brand of hell, and it sent shivers to my core.

With trembling fingers, I made the call. There was only one person I trusted to help me in my current predicament. "Zane," I said shakily when I heard his voice. "I need you."

CHAPTER 20

I felt a warm tingle down the back of my stiff neck, and I forced my lashes up. Zane slipped soundlessly inside my room and threw the lock, ensuring we wouldn't be disturbed. My body wouldn't stop quaking. I was curled up into a tiny ball on the bed, knees pulled to my chest.

Oh boy.

This could go one of two ways: very bad or disastrous. What other choices were there when it involved a dead body?

At least he was here and I was no longer alone to face this somber problem. I hadn't known what else to do, but faced with calling Rose or Zane, I chose the greater of two evils. I mean, it made sense that a reaper would know more about disposing of a dead body. Rose might be blood, but with this, I trusted Zane more.

His eyes immediately sought mine, brows lifting and mouth hanging open. "I can't leave you alone for two seconds. I swear trouble seeks you out."

Zane's presence enticed two very different emotions inside me: relief and apprehension. It was weird that a reaper made me feel secure, but he did just that, and after the hellish night I'd had, I could use a safety blanket.

Before I had a chance to think about what I was doing, I was already in motion, springing from the bed and throwing myself into his arms. Later, I would be mortified. In my current distraught state, there was no room for self-consciousness.

His arms immediately encompassed me, and I buried my face into the alcove of his shoulder. "I don't understand what happened," I said against his neck, and then I was babbling incoherently, the whole messy affair coming out in incomplete sentences that made no sense, but somehow Zane got the general gist of what had gone down.

And while I was making a fool of myself, he managed to sit me down at the end of the bed. "You're hurt." His fingers moved over my achy cheek.

I grimaced. "At least I'm not dead."

His gaze flicked up. "That's more than we can say about her."

I dropped my forehead on his chest and let out a long *swoosh* of air. The fact that he could joke at a time like this made some of the tension ooze out of my body.

"Too soon?" he asked.

I lifted my head. "She is dead, right?" My hands wouldn't stop shaking, so I shoved them between my knees.

His jaw tightened. "Stay there."

After the night I'd had, I didn't even want to be a few feet from him. I was going to be stuck to him like white on rice. The moment he stood over the body, I wiggled to the edge of the bed, swung my feet over, and tiptoed beside him.

He frowned in concentration, eyes still on the oddly angled redhead. "I thought I told you to stay."

I shifted my feet, my fuzzy socks slipping on the floor. "I have a short attention span. She's dead, isn't she?"

Kneeling down, he placed a hand over her stagnant heart. "Very. Even her soul is gone."

"What? But I thought ..." My voice trailed off.

He shot to his feet. "That only a reaper could diminish a soul?" he finished, taking the words right from my closed-up throat. "That's true."

"But that would mean ..." The knot that formed in my stomach inched its way upward into my chest. "Why did she come after me?"

Zane frowned. "You're a target, Piper."

"What is it about *me* that puts a bull's-eye on my back?" I asked.

"Are you sure you want to know? You might not like the answers you seek."

Did I want to know? Isn't that what I'd wanted all along? The truth? Would I turn away from it because I was scared?

No.

I couldn't.

Not only for me but also for TJ. And for my mom.

"I want to know. All of it, Zane. I need to," I finally said, voice thick.

"Let's clean up this mess. Then we'll talk," he said.

I hoped that meant he had some kind of magical spell for that, because I really didn't want to touch her again. What I wanted to do was close my eyes, curl up in my bed, and forget this night had ever happened, but seeing the expression on Zane's face, I knew there was no genie in the world that could grant me that wish. "Okay. So how do we do this? Toss her in the ocean? Burn her on the beach? Or bury her body in the sand?"

He shook his head. "Princess, you watch too many *Unsolved Mysteries*."

I gave him a dry look. "Enlighten me."

Flexing his fingers, he said with a sardonic grin, "It would be my pleasure."

Without preamble, he laid a hand over her head. There wasn't a moment of hesitation in his movements. At first, nothing happened, but then, slowly at first, the floor began to vibrate. A willowy darkness spread down her face, and inch by inch, the darkness consumed her from head to foot. When she was covered entirely, a burst of light lit the room, blinding me unexpectedly. Such a strong contrast from the blackness, it hurt my eyes. As the light began to recede and my vision adjusted, so did the minor shock wave. But most importantly, the dead body in my room was gone.

"Holy shit," I whispered, staring at the spot where a body had once lain. There was nothing, absolutely nothing left of the girl who had attacked me.

He stood, his icy eyes glowing. "Magic has nothing to do with it."

"Show off," I muttered, hugging myself. I needed to sit down. My legs had started to wobble, and I could feel the color draining from my face.

"Piper," Zane scolded, "if you pass out on me now, it will piss me off."

I sunk against the wall, lowering my head, and closed my eyes. "I wouldn't dream of making you angry."

He laughed. "Yes, you would."

Deep breaths. Deep breaths. In and out, I told myself. The last thing I wanted was to have to stick my head between my legs. Glancing up, I locked onto the protectiveness shining in his glowing irises. I had just killed someone, and I knew I wasn't in trouble. The cops weren't going to show up on my doorstep with handcuffs. This was a different world—different rules. "Now are you going to tell me why reapers are trying to kill me?"

"I think you need some fresh air," he said, guiding me outside onto the terrace, his cool fingers at my elbow.

I took a huge gulp of the salty breeze washing over my face, a calmness seeping through my blood. He sat down with me on the top step, overlooking the ocean view. It felt good getting off my feet, breathing in crisp air.

Actually, I was feeling strangely tranquil, my shaky nerves gone.

Now that I thought about it, I wasn't feeling like a girl who had just killed someone. Analyzing what was going on inside me, I got a sneaking suspicion that Zane was responsible. My gaze zeroed in on his fingers casually laying on my arm. "Are you doing that?" I accused, pulling my arm out from underneath his.

His eyes tapered. "What is it you think I'm doing?"

I rubbed the tingling flesh on my forearm. "Why must you always answer a question with a question? It's infuriating."

"If you are talking about the wave of calmness, then yes. My soul is quieting yours." He glanced at me as if to gauge my reaction.

I didn't disappoint, my eyes bulging. "Your touch can do that?"

Zane glanced over his broad shoulder, pinning me with his intense, bright eyes. "For *you* it can."

The hairs on my arms stood up where he had touched me. I could still feel him. "Because our souls are in sync," I concluded.

He nodded.

It was obvious I had much to learn. "Can I do the same? For you?"

His mouth moved into a barely there smile. "In theory, if you knew what you were doing, you could."

Whoa. This weird vibe we had between us was becoming intimate, and I wasn't sure I liked it. Okay, I'll admit I had a thing for Zane, but this soul merger was on the verge of taking it to a whole new level. Still, my interest was piqued. "Show me."

"Piper, this isn't—"

I crinkled my nose. "Don't be such a stiff." Poor choice of words. "I want to learn."

He sighed. "There isn't much to it. Our souls seem to naturally align when we're near."

"Why do I get the feeling that isn't normal?" I butted in.

Propping his elbows on his knees, he intertwined his fingers. "Nothing with you is normal."

"Great," I muttered.

His breath stirred the hair around my face as he leaned close. "The trick is to think of something that relaxes you, keeps your blood pressure steady. That calmness will transfer through our linked souls."

"That's it?" Disbelief colored my tone.

"Not everything is complicated. Some things are just basic."

It sounded easy enough, and that got me thinking … "Does it work both ways? Could you feel my distress?"

His eyes clung to me like magnets. "You don't get the good without the bad."

I swallowed discreetly. Fabulous. The last thing I needed was to worry about my emotions every time he was near. It was bad enough that I couldn't control my hormones around him. Good grief. Did he know that? How my insides went ape-shit when I saw him? Just thinking about it made my cheeks flame.

Ugh. Of course I would have completely messed up relationships with guys. It must be part of my genetic makeup to date complicated, egotistical, and I couldn't forget, hot douchebags only. But that was a dilemma for another day.

Trying to maintain my cool, I focused on the dimple situated just to the right of his damn kissable mouth. It wasn't working. "Happy thoughts, huh?"

Voice low, he said, "That's the idea."

He waited in silence while I struggled to gain control over my emotions. It was easier said than done, but most things are. I could definitely make him feel pain, uncertainty, fear, because those emotions were taking turns ricocheting inside me.

This was a dumb idea. Lord knows, I was full of them, but this one might just take the cake. I weaved my fingers with his, and a flutter formed in my chest. Then I watched his brows rise. I wasn't a quitter. With a renewed determination, I cleared my mind. If I could just latch onto one happy memory ...

The color of his eyes went up a notch, and I thought, *Nailed it.* "Did it work?" I asked, hopeful.

"Don't I look happier?" He sounded sincere, but I wasn't buying it.

A short laugh bubbled out of me as I unfurled our hands. "Not really. But something tells me you're a master at hiding your emotions." Stretching my legs out, I crossed them at my ankles. There was a count of quietness, and the edge in Zane's eyes came back. I sighed. "Why do I get the feeling you are about to change my life? Kind of ironic after what I've done—after what I've seen. There's no going back, Zane."

The lines on his face hardened. "Do you want to take a walk?"

I didn't bother with shoes or care that I was in PJs and socks. It was well past midnight, and the beach was empty other than the creatures of the sea. Shadows misted over the water, and the whoosh and sigh of the winds harmonized with the lapping waves. The world appeared untainted. Unfortunately, I no longer was.

"Cute shorts," Zane said, eyeing my little black and teal polka dot shorts.

The moon shone at our backs as we walked down the beach. "Don't get any funny ideas."

The sinister gleam in his irises wasn't reassuring. He was, after all, the son of Death. Wickedness was probably hereditary. "I wouldn't dream of it," he replied. "Although I'm sure you wouldn't mind."

"Try me," I countered.

The deeper we went, the thicker the shadows became, and with it Zane's mood shifted. A thin fog slid over the sand, white as smoke. "I probably should have told you sooner."

"Told me what?"

Running a hand through his windblown hair, he said, "You have the mark."

A chill rippled through my heart. "I have the mark?" I echoed, confused. "What mark?" But I was afraid I already knew.

He flipped over my wrist. "The mark of a Raven." The pad of his thumb outlined a pale shape, and as his touch passed over my skin, the mark grew brighter.

There it was. A white raven etched into my skin. "What the …? How the hell? That wasn't there before," I murmured mostly to myself.

But Zane answered nonetheless. "Your mind wasn't open to the possibility."

My head snapped up. "What possibility? What does the mark mean?"

"You're a banshee, Piper."

Queasiness tap danced in my belly. That couldn't be. He had to be wrong. I stared at him, bewildered. "You're shitting me."

He made an air circle around his head. "Does this face look like I am shitting you?"

No, and that was what was scaring me. "This isn't funny, Zane. If I knew you were going to be an ass-wipe, I never would have called you." I threw up my hands. "I should have known better than to trust you."

I turned to leave, but his hand shot out, spinning me back around to face him. His hands framed my face, keeping me from running. "Piper—"

The moment he touched me, my sensibility went out the window. "There is no way I'm a-a banshee." My voice grew louder and louder as I punctuated each word with a shove to his chest. "Don't you think that's something I would know?"

Finally, fed up with the jabs to his pecs, Zane caught my wrist midair, eyes blazing. "I can't say why no one told you, but I assume since your mother never brought you to Raven Hollow, she didn't want you to know. Whether you believe me or not changes nothing. The mark is proof."

The immature teenager in me wanted to give him the middle finger salute and tell him to buzz off. But the near adult in me knew that if what he said was true, it wasn't something I could hide from. Confused, hurt, and betrayed, I wondered how they could keep such a secret from me.

"Haven't you ever wondered why your mom never came home?" he persisted.

Only a bajillion times.

"Why would she lie to me?" I retorted.

"Your mom was a reaper—a banshee, Piper," he pointed out as gently as possible. "And not just any reaper—a White Raven."

I tried to gauge his expression, but it was too dark, his expression hooded. "Is that supposed to mean something to me?"

"It should, but given that a month ago you didn't even know reapers existed ..."

We were close, and there was too much tension between us. "Yeah, okay, I get the point, but I'm still not convinced that a stupid mark means I'm a supernatural, soul-collecting freak." As soon as the words were out, I bit my lip, feeling like a complete jerk. Now who was the asshole? A hot flush swept down my cheeks. I wanted to take the nasty words back. I wanted to stuff a sock in my mouth. I wanted to apologize.

Zane's jaw tensed, and he took a step back. "Ask Her Highness. She's the queen of freaks."

Several non-polite responses lined up at the tip of my tongue, but I pushed them away. It was pointless arguing when my emotions were already out of whack-a-doodle.

"Maybe I will," I seethed, trying not to be hurt by the hardness radiating in his eyes.

He seared me with ice. "You're in danger, Princess, if you haven't figured it out yet. You need me."

I was in danger all right—in danger of making a complete and utter fool of myself. He might be right. Maybe I did need him, but before I could do any permanent damage to this thing we had going between us, I turned and ran. And this time he didn't stop me. I wasn't sure I wanted him to.

Then why did my heart feel so heavy? Why was I on the verge of tears?

There was only one thing I was certain of … I had been right. Zane had changed my world. My life would never be the same.

CHAPTER 21

I faked sick on Friday, staying in bed and vegging out on cartons of cookie dough ice cream. Okay, so I might not have been entirely faking. I did feel out of it, and who could blame me? I didn't want to do the "family" thing. Hell, I wasn't sure how to resume life after learning I was a reaper. A banshee. It was impossible to believe, and I still couldn't fathom it. I didn't feel like a banshee. I felt like me.

What did it mean? How did I move forward? What was I supposed to do? Start reaper basic training?

I couldn't think about it. I was still going to be whatever I was tomorrow. Life would be there with all its ups and downs. Today, I wanted nothing but bad reality TV and junk food. Today, I wanted to be normal. Well, as normal as I could be, because every time I closed my eyes, I saw that girl's face, reliving her horrible fate. In my dreams, there were two different versions of me: the normal me and the reaper me, except the girl always died. It didn't matter what I was; she always died at my hands.

Of course, I knew eventually I would have to deal with the possibility that Zane was telling me the truth. If he was, then I was going to have to take the bullet, swallow my pride, and apologize to the big jerk. He was my only link to this reaper life. I never thought I would have to utter the words "I'm sorry" to *him*. I could feel the words sticking in my throat.

Then again, it had never crossed my mind that I could be a banshee.

As difficult as it was to consider, it was harder to ignore the signs that I didn't want to be there, starting with the ghosts. I knew now that they hadn't been figments of my imagination. They had been very real souls, reaching out to me to help them pass on and leave this realm. If I had known that, I could've helped them ...

Would I have?

I'd like to think I would have, but that didn't explain why my mom would lie to me—let me believe that something was wrong with me. It was so hard to think ill of my mom. She had been my best friend, my rock, and the betrayal I was feeling stung like a bitch.

I nibbled on my nails, but it didn't stop my eyes from constantly glancing at my wrist. As much as I hoped the little white raven would be gone, I was disappointed each time. The usual distraction of reality TV and other people's drama did little to make me forget my own. TJ took one look at my face and kept on walking past the media room, knowing better than to haze me when I was in a mood. Rose must have known that something was up, because she showed up after I'd binge watched an entire season of *Keeping Up with the Kardashians*.

Seeing her, I quickly folded my arms, covering the little raven from sight. I expected a surge of anger, but I guess it had defused and turned into disappointment, regret, and confusion. To be pissed at her would also mean being pissed at my mom, and I couldn't muster up the feeling when it came to her. So I let it go. The anger would come again once I worked through the hurt of being lied to by the most important person in my life. I needed Rose to confirm Zane's story. Then I could figure out the rest. I deserved the truth from her.

Looking up as she took a seat beside me, Rose surprised me. I'd never seen her in something comfortable. She was wearing a set of black silk pajamas. A steaming cup of coffee was in each of her hands. "I figured if you were having a pajama day, so would I."

A small smile cracked my lips at the sight of coffee, of course. "I wasn't sure you even owned jammies."

Holding out a mug to me, she took a sip of hers. "What? These old things?"

I'd bet my measly savings that the price tags were in the garbage, but it was the thought that counted, and I had to hand it to her; she was trying. "It's a good look on you."

The skin around her eyes crinkled. "Having a rough day?"

I huffed. "More like a rough year."

"Everyone is entitled to a day for themselves. It is how you pick yourself up tomorrow that counts."

"Wow. You get that from a Hallmark card?"

She chuckled. "I never thought I would miss that sarcasm. It is funny the little things you miss."

I stared down inside my coffee. "I know what you mean."

Rose scooted to the edge of the couch, setting aside her cup. "She loved you very much, Piper, and whether you believe it or not, she was my world. Your mom did what she had to do to protect her family, and I lost a giant piece of myself the day she died."

My eyes began to well. It was so hard to talk about her, but I realized that Rose felt immense pain, too. We just both showed it differently. I might lash out in sarcasm and lose myself in the nightlife of Chicago, and Rose might be stiff and boring, but I was beginning to see it was as much a ruse as mine was. Underneath our pain and grief we were genuinely different people, but a lot alike. We might actually like each other.

I could hear my mom's voice encouraging me with her favorite phrase, "Don't let life pass you by, Pipes."

Just as the tears spilled over, streaming down my cheeks, Rose hugged me tight, and more shocking, I let her, until the tears ran dry, leaving me drained and utterly spent. I sniffed, blinking away the lingering salty drops, and pulled away. "I need to ask you something," I said, fidgeting on the couch.

Brushing the hair off my forehead, she peered at me under curious brows. "Anything, dear."

My stomach tightened. Rose and I were finally having a sincere moment, and I was going to ruin it. "I must warn you it's going to sound insane."

"Hmm." She pursed her lips. "This sounds serious." But the curve of her mouth said otherwise.

Her playfulness gave me a little confidence booster. "Here goes." My fingers fumbled with the charm dangling around my neck. "There is no easy way to say this, so I'm just going to say it. Are you a banshee?"

I expected her to laugh or give me her best jaw-dropping expression, or maybe a quick denial and then accusing me of doing drugs. She did neither. Any reaction would have been preferable to none.

The coffee was suddenly rolling around in my belly.

Oh God. Oh no.

One look at her calm, collected face and I knew. Dread pitted in my chest. There were these little palpitations skipping in my heart. She was a White Raven. And I ... I was a reaper. That was it. My life was over; the walls were crashing down around me. I slumped back into the couch, sinking darker into despair, and the tears were back, forcefully pushing to the surface.

"Zane Hunter, I assume?" she asked, not bothering to hide her disdain.

"So it's true?" I asked, even though she'd pretty much confirmed the worst. If I hadn't been so hung up on the discovery of being a banshee, I would have had something smart to say.

A heavy sigh expelled from her lungs. "I was planning to tell you. It just never seemed to be the right time. It was part selfishness on my part. I wanted more time to get to know you, but it was always my intention to tell you."

"Why didn't *she* ever tell me?" I insisted. It was my mom's silence on the matter that cut the most. I barely knew Rose, but my mom ...

"Your mom was running from her birthright in an attempt to save you. This life isn't easy and is often dangerous. She only wanted to protect you," she informed me, but it did little to lift the weight on my heart.

I wiped my palms on my yoga pants. "But you feel differently."

She nodded. "I do." Looking over my shoulder, she was lost in the past. "It was no secret that I disagreed with your mother. When she left here with your father, pregnant with you, I begged her to stay, but she refused to listen. Stubborn and so sure of herself."

I had heard this story before, but it took on a different meaning hearing it from Rose's perspective. "How did she really die?"

Her fingers pinched the bridge of her nose as she collected herself. I could see the emotions she kept in check float to the surface. "She left here thinking she was strong enough to protect you all. She wasn't. Your mom was killed by reapers for her power, but what many don't know is the power of a White Raven doesn't transfer to the reaper, but to the next descendant."

"To me?" I squeaked.

She nodded. "It isn't until the last White Raven is killed that our essence can be absorbed. There is an internal struggle among our kind. Many no longer want to follow the rules that have been in place for centuries."

"Oh God." I didn't know a ton about reaper politics, but I knew enough to know it was probably a bad thing. "This is all so over-whelming. I don't feel any different." But as I said the words, I glanced down at my wrist for the billionth time. It was still there.

Rose's eyes followed mine. "You can see the marks?"

I wanted to deny it, but what was the point? "Yeah."

She frowned. "For how long?"

Both of our coffees were growing cold, sitting untouched. "I don't know. Since I got here, I guess."

"Your powers are awakening."

My eyes bulged like a cartoon character's.

"Don't be afraid." She unclasped the filigree gold watch on her wrist, and it was no surprise that she had an identical white raven.

"I don't think I want this," I whispered, looking up.

Her eyes softened as she clasped a hand over mine. "Oh, Piper, I wish it were that easy."

That was her way of telling me I was screwed. "What about TJ?" It was second nature for me to be concerned about my brother.

"Our gifts are matriarchal. Only the females are born as banshees," she said, the picture of calm. At least one of us was, because I was freaking out inside.

"Banshee," I echoed, running a hand through my second-day hair. "How is a banshee different than Zane?" Not that anyone was like Zane.

Her lips thinned, and I got the feeling she didn't like that he was the first name that tumbled from my lips. "It's complicated. Ravens have some of the same abilities as reapers. We can decide what to do with a soul. Banish them, destroy them, or send them to the everlasting—their fate is in your hands. Ravens are the only reapers who have a choice. Crows only destroy. Sparrows govern the souls between Heaven and Hell. And Hawks choose who will die. But our greatest power is the ability to create. Not all reapers are born like you. Ravens choose souls worthy enough to become a reaper. Our sole purpose is to keep peace amongst our kind. Your call summons other reapers. Individual or all, it cannot be ignored."

My call, huh? That was a pretty sick ability—powerful. "You're their queen," I mumbled, thinking how everyone always referred to her as Her Highness.

She smiled. "In a sense, but I've never quite looked at it that way."

I didn't think now was the time to tell her that was exactly how they saw her. *Her Highness.*

Ooh, how I despised the nickname "Princess" even more. Zane wasn't just mocking my grandma's money, but who she was—who I was.

Now that I had those missing pieces, I didn't know what to do with them, how I fit into the puzzle. My brain felt disconnected. Rose must have noticed the wariness in my eyes, and she pulled the knitted afghan over my shoulders. I definitely needed the warmth, my body chilled to the bone. Stretching out, I snuggled deeper into the soft fabric and curled up into a ball. I must have fallen asleep, because that was the last thing I remembered.

I FOUND myself lingering on the front steps of the Hunter's house, pacing and biting my jagged nails. My nerves were wreaking havoc on my fingers, and I was in desperate need of a manicure. What was I doing here again?

Right. I was here to tell Zane that I'd acted like an idiot, and that I believed him. I knew what I was.

Raising my hand, I hovered over the doorbell, battling myself internally. *Just hit the bell, already. He might not even be home*, wrestled my subconscious. And so the argument went as I wore out the floorboards of Zane's porch.

I turned around, positive this time I was going to hit that round button, only my head was down, and I didn't see the wall of solid muscle until I rammed into it. Bumping into Zane's chest was like hitting a brick. I stumbled back a step or two, startled eyes glancing up. "Uh, hey."

His lips quirked. "Hey, stranger."

The Black Crow polo stretched over his shoulders, and I assumed he had just come from work. I attempted to regain my composure after that bumbling entrance. "Can we talk?"

He nodded. "Come on. No one's home."

"Oh." This was worse. Alone. With Zane. I just hoped my hormones could handle it.

I followed him inside and silently up the stairs, anxious to get the apology out of the way, and knowing Zane, he would soak it up. It didn't occur to me that we were in his bedroom until I was staring at his rumpled bed. My feet were planted on the carpet as my eyes roamed. Monochromatic tones of steel gray splashed over the walls, yet the room had warmth despite the cool colors. Bonus: it smelled like him.

Heaven.

And Hell, depending on how you looked at it.

Whirling around, I was just about to open my mouth when his shirt tumbled to the floor beside a few others. The blade-like cut of his body stole my breath. I drank in the sight of him. Shirtless—the wicked tattoo of a reaper's scythe, golden skin, and washboard abs. He was the epitome of a bad boy. And I wanted him.

Seeing him half naked made me feel like I was stranded on a desert, parched, and he was a tall glass of water. "What are you doing?" I barked.

Unfazed, he stood, brows wrinkling. "Showering. Is that okay?"

My cheeks turned hot. "Oh. I thought we were going to talk."

"We will. After I get the sweaty smell off my skin, unless you like it dirty." He flashed a quick menacing grin that was going to get me in trouble.

"I'll just wait here, I guess." I hated how squeaky my voice sounded.

When he got to the bathroom doorway, he halted and turned around. "Don't touch anything."

That was like an invitation. I rolled my eyes. "Like I would want to touch anything of yours. Boys have cooties."

I waited until I heard the water running, figuring it was safe. Not knowing what to do, I bit on my bottom lip while my eyes darted over his room. Two seconds went by before I could no longer contain my curiosity. I strolled casually to his dresser, running my hand over the smooth surface. The wood was stained in a metallic color, picking up grains of almost black. There was a pair of Ray-Ban shades and a handful of loose change. A framed black and white photo of his family on the beach sat under a table lamp. Typical guy stuff, mostly. I didn't know what I'd expected to find.

My curiosity satisfied, I sat on the edge of his bed, feet swinging over the side. The water was no longer running, but I could hear him fumbling around in the bathroom. It was relaxing, listening to him do mundane human things like brushing his teeth.

"I thought I told you not to touch anything."

I jumped. Zane was standing a few feet in front of me in sweat-pants and a shirt. At least he had a shirt on. I wasn't sure if I was feeling relief or disappointment. His hair was damp, eyes sparkling in the sunlight. "Christ. Don't do that," I snapped. His sudden appearance had startled me. Damn him and his stealthy movements. It was freaky how soundlessly he moved, especially for being so tall.

He wasn't smiling, but at least he didn't look like he was plotting my death. "What did I do now?"

Unfurling my fist, I replied, "Sneak up on me. I almost karate chopped your balls in half."

He winced. "You sure like to threaten my manhood."

Leave it to Zane to throw off my whole train of thought. "This is not going as planned," I mumbled, running my fingers through my messy locks.

"I find few things ever do when you're involved."

I sighed, fighting an eye roll. "I wanted to say sorry for overreacting the other night."

He tilted his neck to the side. "Which night?"

Taking a deep breath, I struggled to keep my temper in check. "You're going to be a jerk about this, aren't you?"

He grinned. "Maybe if I knew exactly what we were talking about. It's so hard to pinpoint. I seem to recall you overreacting nearly every time we see each other."

I stood up. So much for an apology. All I wanted to do was hurt him. "God, I can't believe I was actually going to apologize to you. Now all I want to do is ram my shoe—"

He was laughing.

All I could do was glare at him. "Do I even want to know?"

His eyes met mine, dimples playing peekaboo. "Not in a million years."

"Great," I grumbled. "Please excuse me while I find a wall to bang my head on."

The lazy smirk on his lips stayed in place. "So I take it you've come to terms with everything?"

There was something almost playful in his expression, and my internal caution alarm went off. He was up to something, and it both warmed and frightened me. "I talked with Rose. By the way, you're on her shit list."

Chuckling under his breath, he reached forward, tucking a loose wave of hair behind my ear. "When aren't I?"

The back of his knuckles brushed against my cheek, and I had to bite my lip to keep from sighing. A glow blossomed in my chest, having nothing to do with the simple touch and everything to do with the look in his gaze.

The air crackled with static, his blue eyes darkening. He was watching me so intently. I buzzed with anticipation as he closed the distance between us. His hand slipped behind my neck, drawing me forward, right up against him. "You missed me, didn't you?"

Then he was kissing me.

CHAPTER 22

I rose on my tiptoes to meet him, kissing him back with a hunger that surprised me. But sharing a kiss so wholeheartedly with Zane probably wasn't wise. Not for my heart. I gave into the urge to touch him, binding my arms around his neck, straining *toward* not *away* like a smart girl.

He crushed me close, his tongue sweeping over mine. Full body contact sent my senses into a chaotic hyper drive.

His breathing choppy, he pulled back slightly. "Open your eyes, Piper. I want to see you melt when I touch you."

My lashes fluttered open. The intensity I saw in him mirrored my own. There was something between Zane and me that I couldn't explain, so much more than a girl crush. His hands roamed down my sides and over my hips, but when his fingers flirted with the top of my shorts, grazing my skin, I could barely stand.

His mouth slanted over mine, and I caught his lower lip as I started to pull away. He took the kiss deeper, igniting those delicious sensations that made my body come alive. A heady blend of emotions warred inside me, and I kept telling myself this was crazy, even as I slid my hands to his chest. When his fingers inched under my shirt, every cell in my body warmed.

"I've never wanted anything as much as I want you," he growled against my lips, not all too happy.

My blood pressure went bananas. It couldn't possibly be healthy, but I doubted the way Zane kissed was healthy for any female.

Sweet mercy. Did they give out master's degrees for perfecting the kiss?

Things got a little heated. One minute I was on my feet, and the next we were on the bed. He pulled me into his lap. Or maybe I climbed there. It didn't matter how. What mattered was I was there, in his bed, and it was exactly where I wanted to be. Maybe if I was honest with myself, it was where I'd wanted to be from the moment I'd laid eyes on him.

The weight of his body pressed into the curves of mine. His chest rose as he drank me in. "This doesn't make sense." His hand came up, and he rubbed the pad of his thumb lightly over the bottom of my lip. "I shouldn't be attracted to you."

Mood killer. I pushed at his chest. Hard. "Thanks a lot, douchebag."

He let me go, staring at me with a frown. "That's not what I meant, Piper. Obviously, I'm attracted to you. I can't keep my hands off you. What I mean is, I *shouldn't* have feelings for you."

As if that was better. "But you do have feelings for me?" I asked, just to be clear before I gave him a black eye. I knew when a guy wanted me, and Zane wanted the heck out of me. My body was still tingling from his touch.

I was greeted with silence.

My response was a dirty look. "I'll take that as a yes. Why is it so hard to admit?"

Zane straightened up, dragging his fingers through his already tousled hair. "Because it will only hurt us both, and the last thing I want to ever do is hurt you, Piper."

Well, shit. When he said it like that, it alleviated some of the sting. I leaned into him, pressing my lips softly to his.

He framed his fingertips around my face. "This can't work between us," he said.

It felt like I'd just had a bucket of ice water dumped on my head.

199

"You sure know how to make a girl feel special." Disentangling our limbs, I crawled off him.

I got to the edge of the bed before his hand covered my wrist. "Just wait."

I spun around. "What? You want to dog on me some more?"

A muscle popped at his jaw. "I'm not trying to hurt you."

"Don't worry. You didn't."

He looked at me straight on, a tiny glint in his eyes. "You can't lie to me, remember? I can sense what you're feeling."

"This sucks." Actually, sucks didn't even cover it.

"It's not that I don't want you, Piper, because trust me, I do," he added.

"Then what's the problem?" I protested.

"It's complicated."

I was officially done. If he couldn't give me a straight answer, then he didn't deserve the time of day. I started to get up.

"Okay. Fine. But promise you'll listen. To all of it," he added, driving home the point that I wasn't to leave until he said everything he had to say.

I paused in the center of his room, contemplating. He'd better not make me regret this. Arms folded, I turned around. "You've got five minutes."

Zane leaned back, his head resting against the plush silver headboard. "There has been a lot of tension building between reapers—talks of a change in management ..."

This I had already suspected after talking with Rose. He was telling me nothing I hadn't already figured out on my own, and I didn't understand how disobedient reapers had anything to do with us locking lips, but I'd promised to be patient.

"So your grandma and my father devised a plan. Nothing good ever happens when the two most powerful reapers get together, but at that time, it was of little concern to me. That was before I knew you, before I knew what you were to me. If I had known ..." A fire leapt into his blue eyes, scalding. "I would have fought for you."

My heart backflipped. The possessiveness and fierceness in his voice made me shiver.

Several seconds passed as our eyes locked, and then he said, "I need you to know that there wouldn't have been a reaper or human alive that could have stood between us."

Sweet Mary mother of Joseph.

When he said stuff like that, I all but liquefied at his feet. Still, I was as confused as ever. Hearing him tell me he would have gone to the ends of the earth to be with me only made me want him that much more. I was in serious jeopardy of falling head over heels in love with Zane.

Fists clenched, he closed his eyes briefly. "They decided the best way to enforce the continued peace between sectors was to *join* our families."

My jaw hit the floor. "Let me take a shot in the dark. By join, you're referring to Zander and me?"

His eyes flashed. "Afraid so, Princess. You're betrothed to my brother, a deal signed and sealed by Death and bound by blood."

Ew. Why did everything supernatural have to be written in blood?

Me? Engaged to Zander? The hell I was. No one, I repeat, no one decided who I was going to marry but me. I didn't care if it had the stamp of approval from the freaking Pope.

I shook my head, dumbfounded. "You can't be serious."

Regret shone in his expression. "You have no idea how much I wish I weren't. It's an unbreakable treaty. On your eighteenth birthday, you are to wed Zander, thus giving you the power and protection you need to govern the rebel sectors. With our families combined, there isn't a sector or a reaper that would dare challenge our authority. My father stands behind your grandmother, but a marriage between Ravens and Crows will solidify our place without posing a threat to Earth." His little speech was monotone, emotionless.

I had a very different reaction. "I can't believe this. I'm not doing it. She can't make me marry him." I was barely out of high school, and Rose was ready to make me some guy's wife. A guy I barely knew. Zander was nice enough, but that didn't mean I wanted to spend the rest of my life with him. It would be like marrying my brother. There was no spark between us, not like the fireworks that went off when Zane and I were in close proximity.

He sat still on the bed, his knees bent. "Someone is trying to overturn the pecking order, which starts with taking out the Raven line. Your family is the weakest in numbers. There are only you and Rose left. The other sectors have countless. Rose is extraordinarily powerful, but even she can't fight off both the Hawks and the Sparrows singlehandedly. It would be a suicide mission. And don't take my head off for saying this, but you are no help to her. Not as you are. You weren't raised as a reaper and haven't even begun to explore the power that resides inside you, Piper. We have all been trained, either from birth or the day we were turned."

It sounded like Zane was trying to convince me that marrying Zander was the right thing to do. That *he* was onboard with me being with his brother. "So, you're basically telling me I'm useless and I should go along with this archaic plan."

"For now."

I leaned all my weight on one foot. "What does that mean?"

"Only you can change your lack of skills. Train. Learn to be a reaper, to protect yourself. Gain power from souls. You were born to be a leader. With someone as spunky as you, there has to be a fighter inside you. I feel it from your soul, the need to kick some ass. It's there. You only need to learn to tap into it. But, until then, the only way for you to survive is under the protection of a really stellar reaper. Rose chose Zander. She had hoped your souls would align."

"Souls? Zander's and mine?" I made a face. I didn't want to soul link with Zander. "But I thought *our* souls were a perfect match."

He gave a sour laugh. "That's the kicker, Princess. Our souls are mates. They are more than a *perfect match*. They resonate."

Frustration rippled through me. "Then why can't it be you?" Crap. Did that just come out of my mouth? Did I more or less just suggest that Zane marry me?

For freak's sake, what was wrong with me?

I wanted to find the nearest hole and bury myself.

"It can't be undone. The agreement goes beyond this realm, Piper. The best I can do is train you."

"Oh, that's rich." I didn't want a trainer. "What makes you think I would want you to help me?"

"Because I'm—"

"A prick," I supplied.

"I was going to say awesome," he mused.

"Your five minutes are up." I walked out the front door, floating on anger and humming with the knowledge that Zane wanted me but considered me off-limits.

Someone was going to pay. And I knew just who was going to be the lucky recipient of the storm churning inside me.

I WALKED AIMLESSLY AROUND TOWN. If I had gone straight to the manor and confronted Rose, I would have killed her. Or at least tried and probably gotten myself killed in the process. How could she do such a thing to me? Her own granddaughter? We had never even met until this summer, and here she was dictating my life—my future.

Rose had another thing coming if she thought I was going to do her bidding.

I was no one's puppet.

"Piper!"

I jumped at the sound of Aspyn's voice. "God, are you trying to give me a heart attack?"

I had almost forgotten how stunning Aspyn was. She beamed at me, not in the least apologetic for scaring the piss out of me. "I was just going to get my nails done. Keep me company. You look like you could use it."

I glanced down at my chipped polish that had been lingering on there for about two weeks. "Why the hell not?" It would give me time to cool off before I went commando on Rose's wrinkly butt.

The salon was inside a cute little house that had been remodeled for a business. We had no sooner wiggled into the leather chairs when Aspyn asked, "So, is he a good kisser?"

I held out my hand to the lady on the other side of the small table. She was rocking big 80s' hair and snapping her gum. Keeping my face as neutral as possible, I wracked my brain trying to figure out whom she was talking about. "Who? Zander? I wouldn't know."

A sly look crossed Aspyn's pretty face. "I was talking about Zane."

My stomach did a funny dipping thing.

She pressed back into her chair, one hand soaking in a glass dish with whatever amazing stuff they put in there. "Tell me the rumors aren't just rumors."

It was no surprise that gossip swirled around Zane's lips. "How did you know we kissed?"

"Small towns talk. And everyone is buzzing about you."

It had been such a long time since I had gotten a manicure I'd forgotten how boring it was. Aspyn's lively chatter kept my mind off the lady grinding at my nails. "Um." I squirmed in my chair, feeling the color heighten in my cheeks. "Is it hot in here? Do you think they have the air conditioning on?"

She laughed. "I bet he's an awesome kisser," she supplied, enjoying this.

It was sort of weird that she was asking. I had just assumed Aspyn and Zane had hooked up. "You mean the two of you haven't …"

She gave an un-lady like snort. "Nope. But not due to lack of effort on my part. I gave up on him. Apparently, I'm not his type, but you are."

There wasn't any bitterness in her tone, and I was glad, because I would have hurt her, which would have made me sad. I was starting to really like Aspyn. If I had to base his kissing skills on what I'd already experienced, I'd say that no one kissed like Zane. Great doesn't do his kisses justice.

"Oh. My. God. You did a lot more than kiss," she squealed.

My mouth dropped open. This was not the type of conversation I wanted to have with a crowd. I swear every ear in the place was leaning toward Aspyn and me, waiting to hear what juicy detail I would divulge.

Aspyn changed hands, and as the nail tech pecked away at her cuticles, I caught a glimpse of a familiar mark.

Aspyn was a Black Crow.

I scowled. "It doesn't really matter what Zane and I do, does it?" It was a chance, assuming Aspyn knew, but I figured in my current mood, I had nothing to lose.

"Hmm. I knew there was something eating away at you, and I don't blame you for being pissed. Not that Zander isn't a prize, but Zane's the jackpot."

"You're so not helping."

Aspyn chose a daring red polish. "I see your point. But ... I don't think you're the kind of girl who follows the rules."

She had a point. "I'm not."

"That's what I thought. So again I ask, is Zane a superior kisser or what?"

My lips twitched. I had to think that Aspyn had been put into my path today just when I needed that boost. She was absolutely right. Zane was a fantastic kisser.

CHAPTER 23

Home. Sweet home.

"Rose!" I screamed, her name bellowing through the glass palace as I stepped into the circular foyer.

Fat wad of good it did. I went over to the intercom system and stared at all the buttons. If I went searching for her, it could take all day. This was the fastest method. Spamming every button until they all lit up, I wanted her to hear me no matter where she was in the house. Even the bathroom.

"Rose." I flinched at the electronic sound of my voice. "I need to—"

"Piper? What is going on?" she demanded.

I spun around, a renewed anger whipping through me. "How could you?" My voice shook.

She stood in one of four doorways, dressed in a white flowing dress, arms crossed. "Why are you yelling?"

The condescending tone was like dousing fuel on the flame. My anger spiked, a haze of red clouding my vision. "You are a liar and a fraud. You never cared about me. All you wanted was for me to be an idle pawn in your pathetic attempt for power."

A normal person might have winced or displayed any emotion. Rose showed none. She wasn't capable of them. She folded her arms.

"It isn't power I am after. Believe it or not, I am trying to save your life."

"By making me marry someone I don't know! I don't love!"

Her silver hair was pulled into a bun as tight as her lips. "It's more complex; trust me."

"That's just it. I don't trust you. And can you blame me? All you've done since I arrived on this wretched island is lie to me, keep secrets from me. At least Zane has the decency to be honest with me."

"Why don't we have tea and talk? Soothe the negative energy."

Tea? Was she shitting me? Did I look like someone who wanted to drink tea? "Screw your negative energy. I don't want tea. I want answers. I want you to tell me it's bullshit." The woman was off her bloody rocker.

She let out an audible sigh. "Then let's step outside." Her arms gestured to the wide open door, a speckle of white feathered on the apples of her cheeks. "A walk through the gardens will do us both good and give us privacy."

"Whatever," I shot back. I was so worked up I could have run a marathon and not broken a sweat.

With loud, sullen strides, I followed her outside, sincerely doubting that smelling the roses was going to calm the turbulent storm inside me. As unattainable as it was, I still was holding onto a shred of hope that this whole thing was a cruel joke and Zane was just an a-hole.

Not worried about thorns or sharp rocks, she walked barefoot under the vine-cloaked archway. "It's true."

And there went my dash of hope, crushed by two simple words.

"Before the end of next summer, you will marry Zander," she stated without hesitation.

Just like that. No questions asked. *Fall in line, Piper, like a good girl.* She was bat-shit crazy. Before I could let a string of colorful swear words fly, she was rambling on, attempting to reason her actions. "If there had been any other way, we wouldn't be having this tiff."

Tiff was putting it mildly. I was a grain of salt away from losing my shit. "I know you're old, but for Christ's sake, this isn't the eighteenth century." A branch brushed against my leg, and I couldn't have cared less. "Explain to me why I should even consider marrying Zander, why I shouldn't take the next ferry back home." I wasn't convinced she didn't have an ulterior motive.

Then there was Zander. He couldn't have possibly agreed to this harebrained scheme, could he? He was just a pawn like I was, right?

I thought about our date.

Was this whole betrothal the reason he had asked me out, in a lame attempt to get to know his bride-to-be? I wanted to gag. The sweet, floral scent of the gardens was making my stomach churn.

"It is the only way to safeguard against chaos erupting," Rose said, plucking a petal from a nearby pink flowering bush. "If the rebels succeed in diminishing the last Raven, there will be nothing to stop them from destroying everything and everyone, including all the loved ones we leave behind."

I thought of TJ, Parker, and even Mrs. Youleg down the hall. "This is so surreal," I grumbled.

"I know this is a lot to put on your shoulders, but there isn't time to waste. I need you, Piper; although, I do wish that things had turned out differently and we'd been given the chance to bond as family should, to teach you. I was foolish to think that a summer here at Raven Manor could do that. The only choice we have left is for you to accept your fate. You are my successor. The last White Raven."

Dun. Dun. Dun.

There was such finality to her words.

The problem was, I was still hung up on being engaged. She had just taken a quantum leap in a different direction. One crisis at a time was all my brain could handle; dealing with my White Raven responsibilities would have to wait.

I sunk down onto a wooden bench. "Can we just back up a moment? When did I say I wanted any of this? I'm not sure I can even be a Raven."

Her eyes were sharp, and I thought I saw just a smidge of desperation. She wholeheartedly believed this farce of an engagement was her last thread of hope. "It's in your blood. Don't let your mother's death be in vain. We must stop the rebellion before it goes too far."

Low blow. How had I suddenly been thrown into the middle of a reaper war? "You can guarantee that if I agree, there will be no rebellion? No one will die?" I wondered if reapers believed in divorce. Something told me the answer was no. It was a till-death-do-us-part commitment.

"There is never a one hundred percent in life. The sectors wouldn't dare challenge you with the Crows at your side. The Black Crows are the strongest sector. And your children would reign without fear or struggle."

"Children?" I squawked.

Ah. Hell no.

When I thought about the father of my very, very distant children, Zander did not come to mind. I pictured a little boy with ice blue eyes and midnight hair, a miniature Zane.

This was bad.

She nodded, emerald eyes holding mine. "Of course. You must also produce an heir. It is your duty as a Raven and is written as part of the contract to ensure that the Raven line lives on."

I choked. Marrying Zander was one thing, but doing the nasty ... possibly more than once. Possibly more than one child. What if I had a boy? The heir had to be a girl. Uh-uh. Not good. The idea of sharing a bed with Zander felt like incest. We might not be related, but I couldn't picture us being intimate.

I shuddered. "That is a deal breaker."

She sat down beside me, trying to be patient and failing. "I know you have feelings for the troublesome Hunter."

It wasn't posed as a question. "And does it make a flying fig of difference?"

"No."

My whole body slumped. That was not the answer I wanted.

The sun sparkled off the whitish glow of her skin. "I can't alter the contract. A deal with Death is unbreakable. If I had known ..."

"I get it. You're not a fortuneteller. Your powers are limited." It was time to play dirty. "Did you ever think to wait and let me decide? That I might have been willing given a choice?"

Her green eyes flashed. Shocker. I had undermined her power, and she puffed her chest, kind of like a guy. "You have much to learn, Piper," she said, going all Yoda on me. "I did what I thought was best. I know Zane cares for you, but he was given an order. The first time I let it slide, but I only give one favor."

White hot fury yanked through me. "Don't threaten Zane," I growled through gritted teeth. "He has only been honest with me, which is more than I can say about my own blood. I wouldn't expect you to understand."

"You couldn't be more wrong, Piper. I've been exactly where you are now." She had her hands folded neatly in her lap, but the emotion in her eyes deceived her quiet disposition. "Roarke is my ... I guess you would say soul mate. Like you and Zane, our souls resonate."

I choked. "Zane's father?"

She nodded with a hint of a smile on her mulberry lips. "But I was already promised as you are. Whatever you are feeling right now, I can tell you I felt it too. And I don't regret the choice. Not in the least. I cared deeply for your grandfather. He made me very happy."

If that was her way of trying to pacify me, to show me it wasn't as bad as I imagined, she botched it. It was disturbing thinking about Rose with Roarke. Although I never knew my grandfather, he had passed before I was born, it seemed wrong to know he wasn't the love of her life.

"I'm not making any promises. I need time to think, but I need you to know it will be *my* decision. I won't be forced into doing anything I don't want to do."

I didn't wait for her to dispute. I just walked away, leaving her surrounded by her roses, petunias, and mums. Let her chew on that, stressing over what her reckless granddaughter would or wouldn't do. It was about time someone else besides me was in the dark.

ZANDER AND ME. Me and Zander. It went on a loop in my head, over and over again. I was lying on my back in bed, numb and petrified. Tears welled in my eyes. I didn't want this pressure, this burden, but here I was, actually considering throwing away my hopes, my dreams, to save those I loved.

It was a gigantic sacrifice. I knew Zander could probably make me happy; however, it was hard to settle when the dreams of a little girl wanted the head-over-heels-in-love deal. What about Zane? How could I marry his brother knowing what was between us? There was nothing calm or quiet about my feelings for Zane. If I married Zander, I would be connected to Zane, forced to see him at family gatherings. Could I do that? Keep my feelings for him hidden? The answer was no. What made it worse was I was sure his family already knew.

I didn't know who got the shittier end of the stick.

Zander? Zane? Or me?

We all got screwed. Three lives. Disturbed and toyed with.

No matter what choice I made, someone was going to get hurt. Someone would be disappointed. So yet again, I snuggled in for what would be another restless sleep at Raven Manor. I couldn't remember the last time I'd had a decent rest, and my body was starting to feel the weariness.

Then it hit me.

I might not ever go home, might never sleep in my room or see Parker. That had been Rose's intention—for me to stay in Raven Hollow. Sure, I might take trips back for holidays, but if I decided to embrace what I was, Raven Hollow would be my home.

What a drab thought.

I groaned and punched the pillow.

CHAPTER 24

"I heard through the grapevine that you were hanging out with Aspyn." Zoe made a distasteful face, like she was sucking on a lemon when she said Aspyn's name.

We were sitting at a local sandwich shop, Upper Crust, after Zoe called an emergency friend-er-vention. Normally, I would run for the hills instead of subjecting myself to any form of "girl talk," but any excuse to get out of Raven Manor, I was grabbing. "I take it you two aren't friends?"

She took a swig of her drink, the ice sloshing at the bottom. "Try arch enemies."

"Wonderful," I said dryly, picking at my turkey club.

As always, Zoe looked beautiful and put together. Her style was envious, maybe because she made it seem so effortless. Today she wore skinny dark denim jeans and a lightweight, floral tank top. The color made her glossy hair and smoky eyes look even more stunning. "Just promise me that you'll watch yourself around her. There is so much conflict among the reapers; I don't trust her."

"But isn't she a Crow?"

She plucked a kettle chip from her basket. "Not all Crows think it's a good idea to align our sector with the Ravens. Her family is among the more vocal rebels." This was why I wasn't friends with girls. Drama. I didn't want to have to choose between them, but Zoe was making an arguable case. Being the newbie, I knew next to nothing about the sectors or the people in them. And then she said, "She's been throwing herself at Zane since they could walk."

It was irrational jealousy, but I couldn't snuff the territorial feeling. So what if there was a stupid contract with my name on it? I couldn't change how I felt, and somehow the jerk had weaseled his way into my heart without trying.

"You know, if you keep scowling like that, those wrinkles will be everlasting." She popped the chip into her mouth, crunching away.

I rolled my eyes, picking up my pickle spear

"Cheer up, buttercup."

"I wish it were that easy."

"Is being a reaper that bad?" she asked between sips of her iced tea, eyeing me thoughtfully.

I shouldn't have been surprised Zoe didn't care who heard us. I, on the other hand, was still very uncomfortable with the r-word when it was in relation to me. It didn't matter much that everyone in the café was probably aware of my social status. Hearing her admit I was a reaper did very little to settle the pit that had taken up residence in my belly. Me? With supernatural abilities? It was laughable.

I stole a quick glance around before my eyes landed on my wrist. The little white raven was clearer now, which probably had everything to do with my gradual acceptance. "I don't know if it's good or bad. There is so much I don't know, don't understand."

"Ask away," she said. "I'm an open book."

Taking a bite of my sandwich, I chewed slowly, thinking. "What kind of, you know, abilities do you have, besides destroying and collecting souls?"

She grinned. "Because I have a twin, my skills are unique. Zach is my counterpart. I can erase memories, which is pretty freaking handy when humans see things they shouldn't."

"I'll say." I was a little bit in awe, but the idea of screwing with people's heads was sort of intimidating. It wasn't a power I would want to be responsible for.

Her eyes lit up with excitement. "Zach can restore them. He'll tell you he got gypped, but I'm not complaining. That's what he gets for being born four minutes earlier. Good things come to those who wait."

I toyed with my straw. "At least you guys know what you can do. I feel like I'm at such a disadvantage."

She shrugged, her silky hair falling over one shoulder. "You can learn. I could teach you," she said, like it was the brightest idea she'd ever had. "It would be so much fun."

Fun was subjective. I wasn't so sure spending the remainder of my summer training to be a reaper was what I would call fun. It sounded a lot like work. "Zane said he would help me, too."

Her dark brows rose slightly. "I just bet he did. You are the first girl Zane has ever offered to train. He's different with you."

"Yeah, he spends more time threatening me than the others."

Laughter erupted from Zoe, drawing the attention of every eye in the café. I couldn't blame them. She had a vibrant and sultry laugh. It deserved attention. "That's his way of showing he cares."

I sunk in my seat. "As much as I hate physical exercise, I might have to take you both up on the offer." I wasn't sure how much time Zane and I could spend together without ripping each other's clothes off or engaging in verbal combat. "I can't promise to be a model student, but I'm willing to give it a shot."

"You're a Raven. This shit will be second nature for you."

Glad one of us was optimistic. I squirmed in my seat, preparing myself for the question I was about to ask, but I wanted her opinion. "Do you think I should honor the contract that was made for Zander and me?"

Her aqua eyes shifted downward, her voice dropping to just above a whisper. "There's only a small group of trusted individuals that know about the contract. I wouldn't know if Zane hadn't confided in me. If you're asking what I would do in your situation—having to choose between my heart and my duty—I don't know."

That wasn't the answer I was looking for. "Is it selfish that I want more than just a peaceful arrangement? I want—"

"Love," she supplied. "Who doesn't? I'm not going to hold it against you." She reached across the table, placing her hand over mine. "We're friends, Piper. Things are different for us, but for you especially. I know how you feel about Zane. Any idiot can see it. Your souls literally go erratic when you're together."

Unease galloped across my heart. "Does Zander know?"

She nodded.

"Oh God." I dropped my face into my hands. "This is so weird," I mumbled, my voice muffled. How could I look him in the face without my cheeks turning the shade of strawberries?

She didn't miss a beat. "Zander is all about duty and not disappointing our father. He's had time to warm up to the idea, especially since he got a look at you. It helps that you're beautiful."

I snorted, not in the mood for flattery. "I just bet I'm the girl of his dreams."

"Do you own a mirror?"

"Obviously, I just prefer not to look in it."

"Well, I'm glad you finally know the truth," she said, her eyes taking on a catlike quality. "I wasn't sure how much longer I could keep my big mouth from blabbering. It's still hard to believe that my mind-your-own-business brother spilled the beans."

"He shouldn't have had to tell me. My mom should have." There I said it. As hard as it was, it was the truth. She should have been the one to sit me down and explain I wasn't entirely human. Finding out the way I had sucked.

"I'm sure it was a hard decision," Zoe said sympathetically.

"Maybe, but it doesn't change anything. I'm stuck in the middle of a supernatural war with a giant target on my back," I grumbled.

"You have a power coveted by many reapers. I can't say I envy you."

"Thanks, Zoe. That was extraordinarily helpful."

Elbows on the table, she leaned toward me. "My dad thinks that the Sparrows are behind the recent attacks on you. He has ears out in every state, listening to the chatter among the sectors."

That meant very little to me, other than that the Sparrows were the sector that had little blue birdy marks. "I'm telling you, Zoe, I don't think I can do this. I want to run. I want to go home, but *Rose* thinks that it is a bad idea."

"She's right, Piper. Out there, you'll have little to no protection."

"I still can't believe I need protection." Curious, I wondered what would happen if I tried to leave the island. Did Rose have guards posted at the docks, ordered to retrieve me if necessary? I didn't doubt it. I had lived in the worst parts of the city before, and I was in more danger here than I'd ever been there. How warped was that? I looked down at Zoe's plate and then at mine. She had managed to devour her entire lunch, while mine looked like a squirrel was nibbling on it.

"Are you going to eat that?" she asked, eyeballing my turkey club.

I pushed my plate toward the middle of the table. "Have at it." She had an appetite like a horse. "How the heck do you stay so skinny?"

She gave me a pearly grin. "High metabolism."

"Let me guess. Reaper perk?"

"Just one of many. You are going to love being supernatural. It's the shit."

Debatable. So far, being a Raven had caused me nothing but heartache and trauma.

She shoved the last piece of crust into her mouth. "Ready? Let's blow this joint."

I was right behind her. The smell of fresh bread wasn't sitting well with the pit of constant worry in my stomach and the ball of unfairness.

Tossing my drink in the trash bin, the door jingled overhead as I pushed it open and lifted my head. The door swung closed behind me as I came eye to eye with my fian … my fianc … I couldn't even think the word.

Awkward to the max.

Zander stood with the sun glinting at his back, picking up auburn tints in his hair. Surprise leaped into his silvery violet eyes, mimicking my own. He was wearing a pair of tattered jeans and a white T-shirt.

With the windblown hair and laid-back clothes, he reminded me of a surfer.

"Uh, hey." In the back of my mind, I was trying to figure out how I was supposed to act around him now that I knew. Did he know that I knew? Was he as angry and upset as I was? Did he think it was unfair too? Good grief, I was going to give myself a migraine.

His fingers combed through his hair. "Hey."

Zoe stifled a giggle. "Text me later?" Then she was out the door, walking down the street.

My eyes got huge. I couldn't believe she'd left me. Alone. With Zander. What the hell was I going to say to him?

Absolutely nothing.

"You don't have to avoid me, you know," he said as he leaned against the building.

"What? Why would you think I'm avoiding you?"

He angled his head, trying to see my face. "Because you can't even look me in the eye."

Right. I was still staring at the invisible spot on his shirt. "I'm sorry. I guess I don't know what to say to you," I openly admitted.

Several seconds passed before he spoke. "We should probably talk."

My gaze darted up, finally meeting his. "Now?" I screeched like it was the most horrible idea he could suggest.

He gave me an understanding smile, watching me. "If you want, but from the panic in your face, we can wait until you're ready."

The thing was I wasn't sure I would ever be ready to have the *marriage* talk with Zander, but I couldn't tell him that. "I'm sorry. I'm handling this whole thing horribly."

"It's okay. And stop apologizing. You have nothing to be sorry for. For the record, there is no right way to handle this."

"You're a good guy ... who deserves someone better than me."

He stared at me for a moment. Then his lashes lowered, sweeping his cheeks. "Because you have a thing for my brother?"

I opened my mouth and quickly clamped it shut, unable to believe what I had been about to blurt out. I hadn't even admitted to myself what my feelings were for Zane. This was not how I wanted it to go.

"Look, Piper, I would never force you to do something you don't want to do. I just needed to get that off my chest."

His understanding tugged at my heart. I nodded.

"Let me walk you home."

"Thanks, but it's not necessary. You haven't even eaten yet."

"It's not safe for you," he argued.

"I get that, but I need some time to myself, to think. There's a lot on my mind." Hint. Hint.

Indecision spanned in his gray eyes, and I knew he was debating with himself. It was sweet. Zander was nice. Too nice. With turmoil in his expression, he nodded and let me walk away.

I gave him credit. But the stroll along the beach helped settle my nerves. So it was only fitting that just when things seemed calm, the shit storm hit.

CHAPTER 25

Hunkered down in my hoodie, I shivered as a cold front whipped through the island, shaking the leaves above. It was unusual weather we were having. Dark, ominous clouds gathered above. Wind lashed at my face, whirling strands of my hair and pushing against me as I walked. A storm was in the works, approaching faster by the minute. When I'd left Upper Crust, it had been clear skies for miles. Now I was positive I was going to get caught in a downpour.

I began to regret not taking Zander's offer to walk me home. There was something eerie in the air, and it was giving me the creeps —solitude no longer something I sought. Picking up the pace, I had this urge rise up my throat. I didn't know what it was, but it was dying to break free.

As I whipped my head over my shoulder, prickles of paranoia skirted along my skin. Someone was following me, watching me from the gloom created by the storm. A shadow glided over the sandy beach to my right, moving far too quickly to be something of this Earth.

Reaper? Ghost? Hallow? All of the above?

Whatever it was, it was a sure sign of trouble.

Oh, goody gumdrops.

Just thinking about the danger that lurked at every turn of this cursed island made the back of my mouth fill with a metallic taste. It had been so stupid and reckless to venture out on my own. After everything I'd recently learned, I knew I wasn't safe, that there were reapers hunting me, and sure enough, they had come like a druggie searching for his favorite fix.

"Zane!" I screamed his name, not certain why. Or maybe I did know why. In the back of my mind, I heard Rose telling me my voice held power. I hoped she was right, because I was about to be in some hot water. The rational part of my brain thought there was no way he was going to hear me. How could he? As far as I knew, he was on the other side of the world, but I still couldn't stop his name from hurtling from my lips.

It was always his name that came to mind at any sign of trouble.

I stood frozen for a few blood-pounding heartbeats, the wind howling around me, dark clouds rolling overhead. Screw this. If I waited like a sitting duck for Zane to save the day, I was going to find myself surrounded and defenseless. There was only one thing left to do. I spun around and took off, knowing I needed to get out of there before whoever was out there found me. I ran fast—faster than I'd ever run before, the hoodie flopping behind me like a cape. It felt like my feet weren't even touching the ground, but I wasn't going to analyze my sudden speed and agility now.

But no matter how fast I ran, I knew whatever was out there was faster.

I could sense them gaining, swallowing up the ground.

Shit. Shit. Shit.

A dark, murky shadow appeared beside me, and then in a blink, it was in front of me. I braced myself, ready to ram my hand into any part I could land on. I wasn't going down without a fight.

When Zane's face materialized, I almost hit him just for frightening the living crap out of me. "You asshole." I shoved at his chest, hard.

"Now that's not any way to greet your knight in shining armor."

Relief and a smidgeon of hope flared inside me.

Zane.

OMG.

He was here. He came.

"What the hell is going on? How did you know? I think I am being stalked." My voice was rough and rushed.

"Slow down. One question at a time." He interlaced our fingers. "You called. I came."

When he said it, it sounded so simple, but regardless of what I'd been told, it was hard to fathom. I didn't have time to make sense of how he knew where to find me or how he knew I was in trouble. I stopped questioning the implausible. "Of course you did."

One dark brow curved, and then I watched as his eyes narrowed, gaze darting behind me, becoming all business. "Whoever wants you dead, they've sent a death party."

My eyes bulged. *My death?*

Woo-hoo. Let the fun and games begin.

I could feel myself beginning to pale, the blood inside me chilling.

Zane's cool hands pressed on either side of my cheeks. "Okay, Princess. Tone it down." His eyes cast downward, midnight hair thrashing in the wind. "You've got to get ahold of yourself."

I glanced downward, wondering what had him scowling this time, and sucked in a sharp breath. My skin was lit up like a damn disco ball. The veins throughout my body glowed in a pearly white. Panic surfaced in my eyes. "Don't you think I would if I could?"

He scratched at the scruff under his chin. "What the hell were you doing?"

"Uh." I struggled to remember. "I had lunch with your sister, and then I decided to take a walk, clear my head."

"I meant before I got here. You must have done something to trigger your powers."

My powers? "I-I was thinking about you," I admitted, meeting his mildly surprised expression. "Then out of nowhere the storm appeared, and I felt someone watching me." Little did I know that it was a small army of ... still to be determined. "So I, um, called you."

The color in my cheeks grew. Confessing that I had screamed his name at the first inkling of danger was highly embarrassing.

Comprehension dawned. "You picked a helluva a day to start being a banshee."

"I did not—"

"Shh." He put a finger to my lips.

I bit his finger.

Icy blue eyes flashed down at me. "Do you want to get us killed? We are about to have an audience who would be more than happy to stick a blade through your heart. Now be quiet."

"Can't you just …?" I made some slicing motions with my hands.

He sighed heavily. "Even I have my limitations. There are more of them than I am comfortable with. If it was just me, I could handle it, but with you … I'm not taking any chances."

I poked him in the chest with my index finger. "I'm not some useless twit, you know. I don't need you to defend me." A total lie. Wasn't that the whole reason he was here? Because I had summoned him to defend me? "More what?" I asked.

"Piper, you're making this very difficult." He stepped forward, putting his hand against my mouth, silencing me.

But it wasn't his hand that kept me quiet; it was the brush of his body against mine. I hissed, inhaling the dark, tempting taste of his skin. This was not the time to start thinking about how fabulous his body felt.

I watched as his face changed, spidering with darkness, and I knew he was trying to cloak us in the shadows. A familiar coolness raced over my skin.

Hallows. Zane's voice sounded inside my head.

What do they want? I asked, remembering to use my thoughts.

You, I would suspect. But hallows don't normally travel in packs. They were sent, most likely promised a deal to let them stay on Earth.

How dangerous can they be? It was an offhanded, sarcastic comment. One I wished I hadn't asked.

Plenty. Hallows don't follow the same laws of nature as humans. They're essentially dead. So pretty much anything goes.

Fabulous.

"Dammit," Zane swore, no longer in my head. "You're like a beacon of light, attracting every hallow in a mile radius."

Where my veins glowed white, his were black. Lightness and darkness—that's what we were, complete opposites. "I can't help it," I mumbled under his hand. "You irritate me." *Among other things,* I silently added.

He removed his hand from my lips, warning me with a one-brow glare to keep my mouth shut. Unfortunately, I'd never been a good listener. I opened my mouth, prepared to tell him to shove his warning where the sun don't shine, but I never got the chance.

He was kissing me.

Not a sweet, gentle kiss.

God no. It was a knee-trembling, knock-your-socks-off kind of kiss. Dear God.

Since meeting Zane, I'd learned a few things. One was that he always kissed me when I wasn't expecting it. I also realized he was just as good a kisser as I recalled. Electricity spread throughout my body as I kissed him back, not willing to let an exceptional kiss go to waste. What sane girl would?

I stood on my tiptoes, looping my arms around his neck. Zane's lips were both soft and hungry, and when he pulled away, I steadied my hands on his shoulders before I became a puddle at his feet. "Why did you do that?"

"Oh, for shit's sake. You're still a goddamn glowworm."

Mystified, it took me a moment to remember our predicament. He had kissed me to diminish my freakish glitter effect. And to think I'd thought it was because he found me irresistible. Silly me. "I'm sorry. What do you want *me* to do about it?"

"We're out of options and time." Inky veins encircled his other-worldly eyes. I knew that look. He was about to do something moronic.

"I'm scared. Is that what you want to hear?"

He gave me a cheeky grin. "Actually, it's not as gratifying as I thought it would be."

"What are we going to do?"

"*You* are going to stay out of my way."

I tilted my head, giving him a dry look. "What are *you* going to do?"

"Try to keep us alive."

"Zane!"

But he was already gone, camouflaged by the shadows that were so much a part of him. "We'll use the element of surprise, Princess," he whispered in my ear.

I forced myself not to turn around and look for him but stayed eyes forward on the impending group of doom. I could hear whispers in the winds, voices laughing and chattering. They were close. By the time the ghostly figures appeared, cresting over the hill, my heart was in my throat. I counted under my breath each wavering form I could see, and who knew how many I couldn't?

Seven.

A little excessive if you asked me. I was only one girl with not a single clue how to fight. Did they really think they needed seven dead ghosts to take me down? I didn't know if I should be flattered or insulted.

Zane whistled softly in my ear. "Tough crowd, babe."

I contemplated elbowing the air behind me in hopes that I would whack him. "So not helping," I said between clenched teeth. "You expect me to just stand here?"

"I need them closer."

Withholding the instinct to run, I waited, biting my lip. The sky ignited with a bolt of lightning. Fan-freaking-tabu-lastic. A mother of all storms was just what I needed about now. When it rained, it poured—dead people in my case.

The shadowy group paused on the peak of the beach, and a girl—I think she'd been a girl—lifted her arms, encased in a blue light. I thought she smiled, but I was distracted. The trees near me began to shake. A thundering groan echoed under my feet, and I started to sweat.

What the …?

"Um, Zane—"

Arms encompassed around me, taking me so swiftly to the ground, it took my breath away. Zane shielded me with his body, but he couldn't shelter me from seeing the destruction that raged. Large clumps of dirt rained down on us, branches whipped through the air, but it was snake-like roots growing at our feet and lashing at us that gave me cause for concern.

He wasn't kidding about defying the laws of nature.

I was certain the ground was going to open up and swallow us whole. When the trembles halted, Zane growled in fury as he rose, swathed in darkness. Stretching out his muscles, he cracked his neck, lips compressed into a hard line of anguish as he stood over me looking like the angel of death. "You okay?"

I spit out a rock, pushing to my feet. "Never better."

He glanced at me from the corner of his eyes just to make sure I wasn't lying. "At least you've stopped glowing." There was a cut on the side of his temple, seeping blood down his face.

I gave a half demented laugh. My moment of insanity was short-lived.

The girl from the hill was in my face, glaring at me. I hadn't even seen her move. "Gotcha," she snapped.

I jutted out my chin, not letting her intimidate me.

Zane flashed in front of me, shoving me behind him and blocking me once again with his body. It was becoming a habit. "Not yet."

"How ssssweet. You've come to die with her, Death Ssscythe," she taunted, obviously the leader of the ghostly bunch. She had a horrible lisp, a downfall of being dead and bitchy.

"If you know my name, then you know I'm not that easily killed."

I forced myself to not roll my eyes.

They had circled us from the east, west, south, and north. All the bases covered. Zane murmured words that were dark and musical, a hint of an ancient language. A low flame bubbled over the ground, and like a match thrown on a puddle of gasoline, fire swept down the beach, burning everything in its path, including two hallows. Their screams echoed over the beach.

"Run!" he yelled at me.

Zane had gotten his element of surprise after all. The only problem: I wasn't prepared. Running was out of the question. Not only were my legs not working, but there was no way in hell I was going to leave Zane. He could huff and puff his chest, but I still wasn't leaving him.

As I stood there staggering, Zane launched at the two charred spirits, laying one hand over each of their hearts, and within seconds, their bodies burst into a neon green light. Zane rolled to his left, narrowly avoiding a powerful blast of plasma. His eyes sought mine out. "Why are you still here?" he rumbled.

My knees were knocking. "I'm not going anywhere."

"Piper," he growled.

"Zane," I shot back.

"As cute as this lovers' ssspat is, my patience is running thin." The bitch was back and taunting us with her hostile prattle. "You think you can take usss all? Not even you, Death Ssscythe are that strong."

That name always made me shudder. There was an ominous note attached to it, but I couldn't deny that it suited him. Zane moved like a phantom of the night.

So. Dang. Hot.

I felt the ground quake beneath me, and I thought, *Not again*.

Bright bluish balls of fire formed on the palms of the guy standing behind the ground-trembling girl. They shot past her, fizzling directly at Zane and me. I ducked, but between the shaking ground and trying to avoid being singed, I biffed it, falling face-first into the grainy sand. Heat blew over me, the embers crackling in the air.

Each time I tried to regain my balance, the ground moved and I was sent back down, eating sand. Zane flung a bolt of darkness at the guy with blue fiery hands at the same time he engaged a hallow in one-on-one combat. Just as he landed a few solid hits, two more bastards launched at him. Arm outstretched, Zane clotheslined one and then struck the other with the bottom of his foot. The impact spun the greasy bastard around, and as he came back, something slick and oily shot toward Zane. He dodged, barely missing the sticky missile of ooze, and in the process gave me a heart attack.

"Jussst give up. You can't defeat usss all," the traitor hissed, and then Zane punched him squarely in the mouth. Suddenly he was too busy spitting blood and falling to his knees to shout anymore.

"Move, and I'll split you open from crotch to throat," Zane threatened.

My lips twitched.

I took a quick headcount. Two more hallows dispatched. It was impressive. Zane had singlehandedly destroyed four hallows in record-breaking time, because, let's face it, I was useless. That left three: fiery hands guy, ground-shaker girl, and the tank. The last guy bulldozed his way through everything, coming straight for Zane.

Stumbling to my knees, I pushed the hair out of my face. I didn't care that I had dirt in places it shouldn't be or that my hair looked like I had shampooed with sand. I saw what was going to happen next like it had been set to slow motion.

The tank charged straight for Zane, tackling him to the ground in a rage so potent it literally flickered around him in a haze of red and reached out, touching the world. Branches shook, sending leaves raining down in a path behind the Tasmanian devil.

I felt it in my bones—the jarring, teeth-rattling impact. Anyone else would have been knocked unconscious. Zane wasn't human, but that didn't mean he was impenetrable. His body went up, spiraling through the air.

"Zane!"

CHAPTER 26

My scream tore through me, amplifying my fear, and like a switch, my fear turned to anger and desperation. He landed in a bumpy heap a few feet away, his body twitching from electric currents. Blood oozed from his nose and the side of his mouth.

I tried to move, to run to his side, but I couldn't. Both my arms were being held, and no matter how much I fought, I was going nowhere. It was the girl with earthquake abilities. She yanked my hair, snapping my head back. *Skank*. I bit back a yelp.

She held my head so I was forced to look at Zane. The one who looked like a juicehead hovered over Zane. "It'sss over, little Raven," the bastard hissed. "He will die, and so will you."

Zane turned toward me, his eyes locking with mine. I would never forget the regret in that one look. Tears burned the back of my eyes, my sorrow cutting through me. He tried to sit up as I struggled to break free, fury flashing in his hardened gaze.

He should have taken the last of his strength to save himself instead of wasting it on me. The two guys advanced on Zane, tag-teaming him. A pulse of blue light zapped through the air, striking him in the gut and sending him back to the ground. Before he could catch a breath, the guy built like a semi rammed him in the shoulder. The two of them went sliding across the beach.

The sight of Zane lying unmoving and defenseless shattered every corridor of my heart. "No!" I bellowed, my hands flying to my mouth.

I couldn't lose another person.

I couldn't lose Zane.

This was so freaking unfair.

If I had been raised as he had, knowing what I was, what I was capable of, I would have been able to save us, give us a fighting chance, but as it stood, I would have to witness another person I cared about die.

The shadows around him and in his blood wavered, and I could feel his pain, his remorse. I didn't know if it was him or me opening up, but I knew our souls were grasping at one another.

At the last split second, Zane slammed his hand onto the center of deputy douchebag's chest. The look on the ghost's face was pure shock. He had underestimated Zane—something that was never wise.

I didn't think. Not about myself or the girl behind me. All I could think about was Zane. Taking advantage of the distraction, I gave one hard yank, breaking free from the hands that bound me. I knew I didn't have more than a few seconds before they caught me again.

Falling to my knees in front of him, tears fell freely down my cheeks. I pleaded with him with my eyes to not leave me.

"Give me your hand," he croaked.

I looked at him like he was nuts. Shaking my head, I put my finger to his lips. "Now is not the time to hold hands," I managed to say.

One arm extended out toward me. "Now, Piper! Trust me."

Heart breaking, I reached out, my fingers encircling his. His was cold, so very cold. With the slightest pressure, Zane wrapped his hand around mine and squeezed, as if to reassure me. A sob broke on my lips, the darkness in his veins flickering, but the coolness of his soul continued to climb up my arm, wrapping me entirely. I knew what he was doing.

Soul merging. Soul transfusion. Soul mishmash. Or something crazy like that.

He was sharing or giving me his powers through the connection of our souls and, in the process, using the last of his strength in some hero attempt to save me. Fool.

"No!" I shouted, shaking my head. "I won't let you."

He was not going to sacrifice himself for me. The harder I tried to pull away to break our connection, the tighter I could feel his grip. The jerk refused to let me go. I begged him, but it was useless. He was a stubborn mule.

It wasn't fair. Zane didn't deserve this, and I wasn't going to let him die because of me, to save me. What was the point? So what if he gave me his powers? I would still die. It would be all for nothing. Injustice and hatred pooled inside me, reaching to my core.

Power. The word filled me with anger. It was because of power that I was in danger—that I would probably die. I couldn't understand the purpose behind it—coveting power, trading a life for power. The reapers' greed for it was going to be their downfall, and I finally understood what Rose had meant—how important she was.

And then out of nowhere, something unexpected ... something unexplainable happened.

My head fell back. A pulse of light shot down the center of my chest, and intensity burned behind my eyes so brightly I thought I would go blind. Power like I'd never felt built inside me, my hair flying out around me. The impact left me energized, weightless.

Hope sparked.

I wasn't going to die today.

And neither was Zane. I refused to let him leave me here alone. Not going to happen, bucko.

It was only two hallows and me.

That was what I concentrated on—not Zane, not what had just happened, but on the two bitter spirits. I wanted them gone. I wanted them destroyed. I wanted them to pay. I wanted to wipe their very essence clean from this plane. Every fiber of my being was centered on them.

Power gathered inside me, coiling. White lightning filled my veins, shimmery and mystical. My power. Their destiny was in my hands. I saw the second they realized their death was imminent. I wanted them to know it.

Gliding to my feet, the sky erupted in a violent crack of thunder. The howling winds picked up in force, thrashing around me, but never touching me. Inside the light built and built, until I could no longer hold onto the cord. With a wild cry, I let it go.

I never touched them, but I felt the power leave my body and heard the gentle hiss through the air. Stunned, I watched as the pure white flash of light stayed true to its targets, slamming into the center of the unnatural beings' chests. Their figures spasmed, the edges of their forms rippling until there was nothing left but the flare of my power.

I stumbled backward.

Holy shit.

I couldn't believe it. I mean, yeah I'd wanted to hurt them, but wow, I'd actually done it. No one was more shocked by the discovery than me. I blinked.

"Piper?" Zane's voice was barely a whisper, but I heard him clearly.

My face spun toward him. He was sitting up, watching me with careful eyes. "You're alive." I released a tired breath. I thought I saw the corners of his lips twitch, but I couldn't be sure because I threw myself into his arms.

"Hey, take it easy," he groaned.

I let up slightly but kept my face burrowed in his shoulder. "Oh, sorry."

Strong arms trembled around me. "That's not what I meant. I can handle a hug. I was talking about that massive amount of power you unleashed. I've never seen anyone do that. You didn't even lay a finger on them."

I sat down beside him, our thighs touching. My lips turned down. "I'm more concerned where it came from. Did you—?"

He shook his head. "I wanted to, but you didn't cooperate as usual."

"Christ. Don't. Ever. Scare me like that again. I thought—" I dragged a shaky hand through my ratted hair. "I mean it, Zane. I don't know what I would do if anything happened to you."

He brushed his nose against mine, inhaling deeply. "I'm fine. You can't kill awesome."

I let out a part laugh, part sob. "Jerk." He knew just what to say to lighten the mood. Looking at him smirking, my heart quickened. He was going to be okay. We were going to be okay.

His eyes lit up, crinkling at the corners. "I knew you had potential, Princess."

"Awesome," I replied dully. Unless I couldn't count, that was four souls this summer. "I'd rather not ever do that again, if it is all the same."

"Admit it; you like it."

The thing was, I did like it, but I refused to bask in it. I didn't want this power or the responsibility, but the reality was still the same. "Why do I get the feeling that power like that doesn't come without a hefty price?"

His lips pulled into a lopsided grin.

***

I EMERGED from the bathroom freshly showered and hurting. The hot water had done very little to ease my bones and aching muscles. Zane had shown me into their guest bedroom, handing me a T-shirt that was probably Zoe's and a pair of fuzzy pajama bottoms to change into. They were warm, smelling clean and faintly of laundry detergent. I had tossed my ruined clothes in the trash, wishing I could burn them. They were a nasty reminder of a night I desperately wanted to forget for many reasons.

Zane was lounging on the bed, looking exhausted, young, and enticing. Dark, damp curls fell over his forehead and at the nape of his neck. He must have cleaned up while I was scrubbing away the grime, trying to erase any reminders. My skin was polished and as soft as a newborn's bum.

He had insisted I stay the night at his house, and I hadn't needed much convincing, but not because he was irresistible and scrumptious. In this case, it had nothing to do with how often I'd dreamed about being alone in a room with Zane with a bed. I stayed because I was being hunted and I was afraid. Who knew what was out there waiting for me? This was the safest place on the island.

"You okay?" I asked, sitting on the edge of the bed. The mattress dipped slightly under my weight as I inspected his face. The cuts were barely noticeable, and the yellowing of bruising was starting to fade.

"I'll be fine. Nothing sleep won't cure." He paused, eyes fixed on mine. "You could have just left me there and run, like I told you. You should have, Piper."

"I-I couldn't just leave you." The thought filled me with dread. I averted my eyes, not wanting to think about it. "I never would have been able to forgive myself." *Or forget about you*, I silently added.

He folded his muscles, lips thinning. "Still, you can't be so careless with your life—so reckless."

"I know," I whispered, but what I didn't say was that his life, in the heat of the moment, had been more important to me than my own.

"You saved my life. Thank you, Princess."

Hell must have frozen over, because he sounded sincere. Words stalled on my lips as I stared at him, goose bumps covering my arms. I didn't know what to say. "You're welcome" seemed so ridiculous since I really had no idea how I'd managed to zap the hallows into nothingness. I wrapped my arms around myself, peering at the closed door and then back to him. "Will you stay with me tonight?" Knowing it would put him in a compromising spot didn't stop me from asking. I didn't want to be alone, and he was the only person who could make me feel safe.

His brows wrinkled.

"I'm not trying to seduce you or anything," I quickly added, not wanting him to get the wrong idea. "I don't want to be left alone."

"I know. It's just—"

"Look, you don't have to," I interrupted. "Forget I said anything."

"Piper, it's because I want to that makes me think it's a bad idea." His voice was strained.

My belly did a twisting motion. "Oh."

He pulled back a corner of the blanket. "Come here."

I searched his face for a moment before climbing up the bed. He had scooted to one side, leaving me plenty of room, but I wanted to be close. We lay there side by side, staring at the ceiling, his arms crossed over his chest. A strange silence descended over the room as I picked at the gray blanket. I was hyper aware of him. His slow, steady breaths. The coolness radiating off his body. His earthy, rainfall scent.

Minutes ticked by. Unable to stand the quiet another nanosecond, I turned on my side, facing him.

He stared back at me, a crooked grin on his lips. "You should try to get some sleep."

I wanted to touch him. "Why is this so awkward?" I asked, grinning. It felt wrong feeling anything but apprehension after what had happened, but smiling relieved some of the tension in my limbs.

"Because the last thing either of us wants to do is sleep." He unfolded his arms and tugged me closer. I needed no persuasion. "That's better," he murmured, his lips brushing against my hair.

My chest squeezed as he tucked me into the nook of his arm. "I don't think I'll be able to sleep."

"You don't need to worry. They won't come back, not tonight."

"Encouraging, but that's not it." I pressed my cheek to his chest. "I can feel them. The souls."

"That's normal." His voice rumbled under my ear. "You'll get used to it the more you—"

"No." I shook my head. "I won't do that again. I can't."

"Piper, it's not something you can swipe under the rug and ignore. That's not how this works. Being a reaper isn't a choice. It's your birthright." He stretched out his legs, shuffling a bit to get comfortable. "Anyway, I doubt I'll get much sleep either."

I glanced up. "Why?"

His fingers brushed through my hair. A sweet thrill jolted over me. Such a basic touch, but every nerve ending in my body felt it. "You're glowing again."

Sure as shit, the veins in my arms were lit up a pearly white. I was like my own personal nightlight. Fabulous. I couldn't suppress the giggle. "I can't seem to control it."

He chuckled. "I don't mind. And you'll learn. You've already proven to be a quick learner."

"God, I still can't believe that was me back there." I absently placed my hand on his chest.

His fingers covered mine. "You were pretty badass."

"Was that a compliment? Hang on, I need to document this." I pretended to reach for my phone.

His arms wrapped around my waist, pulling me back to him. "Not a chance."

"Did you lock the door? The windows?"

A muscle flexed on his jaw. "There is not a reaper, a hallow, or a robber getting into this house tonight. Only an idiot with a death wish would come knocking on the Grim Reaper's door."

He was right. I was sleeping under a roof with four reapers and Death himself. There wasn't a higher level of security or a safer house in the country than the Hunter's.

"Now, close your eyes. I won't let anything happen to you. I promise."

My chest swelled, and my belly fluttered. It felt so good lying next to him. Calmness overwhelmed me, and I didn't know if it was Zane's doing or my soul just happy to be near him. It didn't matter.

I closed my eyes, my body tuckered out. Sleep claimed me as I was wrapped in the warmth of Zane, the beating of his heart in my ear. I never thought I would be drifting off to sleep beside the one guy I couldn't have and didn't like half the time.

The world was a messy place. And even after a night as terrible as this, morning would come.

MY EYES FLUTTERED open as the sun was cresting over the ocean. The rays streamed through the window, warming the room and washing over my skin, but it wasn't the sun that had my body on fire.

God no. It couldn't be that simple.

I was no longer on my side of the bed. Glancing under my lashes, half my body was sprawled onto Zane, our legs tangled together. One of his hands was under my shirt, splayed along my back. A sweet, hot tingle washed over me at the feel of skin against skin. It was pure wickedness how my body fit against his. Thigh to thigh. Stomach to stomach.

His heart beat under my cheek. I couldn't help but think that we looked like lovers who had just spent a glorious night together. And that made my breath quicken. I closed my eyes, and for a moment, I pretended. No obligations. No consequences. We were free to let things unravel between us.

What a time for my hormones to kick into overdrive.

Still groggy, I lay as still as possible, stealing a peek at his face and making sure only my eyes moved.

His thumb grazed along my spine. "Good morning."

I gasped, not expecting him to be awake.

He had not made a peep, which made me wonder how long he had been awake. Then he shifted, and I was suddenly on my back with Zane's body covering every inch of me. Thought was not possible after that. *Sweet babycakes.* Cool breath danced over my skin as he nuzzled the sensitive spot between my shoulder and neck. My pulse became erratic. I bit my bottom lip to keep from making a sound. If he stopped touching me, I was going to cause him bodily harm.

Gentle fingers inched across my belly, and I pressed myself against the length of him, shifting my knee between his legs. I traced the line of his jaw with my lips as he softly murmured something I didn't understand, but it didn't matter, because the lilt of his accent was lyrical. It made my heart patter.

He lifted his head, staring down at me with winter blue eyes in confusion. There was so much depth in the deep hue of his irises. Regrettably, they cleared, and I knew my fantasy was over. Without saying a word, he disappeared from above me, the door squeaking open. I stayed motionless, staring at the white painted ceiling, my heart thumping. My body was on fire, cheeks flushed, and I was well on my way to frustrated.

I tossed the covers aside, sitting up.

Zoe popped her head in and did a double take before a trouble-some grin split across her lips. "I came to see if you were hungry. Did you two …?"

"What? No." I cleared my throat, running a hand through my hair. "I mean, we slept together, but just slept. Not together."

She laughed. "You're cute flustered. Don't let Zander find you in here."

"Does everyone know he was in here?"

"It's no secret that the two of you can't stay out of trouble." The door shut, her giggle echoing on the other side.

I groaned, burying my face in the pillow. It smelled like him—cool, fresh, and complicated.

CHAPTER 27

"How did you sleep?" Mrs. Hunter asked me.

Zoe giggled.

Zach cleared his throat.

Zane scowled.

And I turned a horrible shade of pink. I hated pink. It felt like I was walking the morning-after shame, except nothing had really happened. A few nibbles on the neck and some wandering hands didn't constitute, in my book, as anything to feel guilty over, but it could have gone there.

"Better than I thought possible," I replied, pushing a piece of pancake around in my plate of syrup.

"I just bet," Zoe mumbled under her breath.

I elbowed her under the table, keeping a polite smile on my lips. "Thank you again for letting me stay."

Ivy collected Zach's and Zane's empty plates. "Anytime. You had quite the ordeal last night."

"I'm sorry about involving Zane." I risked a glance at him across the table. The frown lines around his mouth deepened.

"There is no need to apologize. I would have been hurt if you had not called for help."

She was too forgiving. Her son had almost died because of me. I didn't think I would have had the hospitality that she was showing me if the roles had been reversed. It made me realize that I was carrying around guilt. I was angry with myself for putting him in such a tumultuous situation.

Zander wasn't around this morning, and secretly I was relieved, but I did wonder if he had left early because of me. Had he done so to absolve me of the awkwardness?

If someone had told me I would be spending my summer with a group of reapers, I would have told them to go to rehab because they must be high. Yet, here I was, sitting at the dining room table, eating pancakes.

Zane leaned back in his chair. We hadn't spoken two words since he'd walked out on me this morning. And it was fine by me. I didn't have squat to say to him anyway.

Zoe, on the other hand, I had a mouthful to say to her—like making her take a vow of silence over what she'd seen. I didn't want to hurt Zander any more than I already had. Him knowing that I'd spent the night with Zane would only make things harder.

I had just grabbed my glass when my phone buzzed. Taking a swig of my OJ, I set the glass down and picked up my phone. The world dropped from under my feet. There were over a dozen missed calls and multiple texts from my brother. I could only think the worst.

With trembling fingers, I dialed TJ's number. He answered on the first ring, and I knew immediately that something was wrong. Very wrong.

"Where have you been all night?" he rasped. "I've been trying to call you." His voice was frantic, and his words were rushed and strung together. I knew TJ, and he had been crying.

An ache started in my chest. "What is it, TJ? Tell me what happened."

"Oh God, Piper. She's gone," he said.

"Who?" But I already knew.

"Rose," he croaked, a large lump in his throat.

I flinched. "What do you mean gone?" But I was afraid I already knew. Every eye in the room was on me.

"She's dead."

The world stopped. "I'm on my way," I said, paling.

"Hurry, Piper," TJ pleaded.

Zane was at my side. I hadn't even seen him move. "What's wrong?" His sudden rush to my side was duly noted by everyone in the room.

Zoe had a smug smirk seeing her brother hover over me like a guard dog, but it took one glance at my face to know that something had happened. "Hey, are you okay?" she asked.

Fear burned in my chest, like hot coals. "It's Rose. S-she's—" I couldn't say it. Not until I saw her for myself. "I've got to go." I quickly stood, the blood rushing to my head. The room began to spin, and black spots danced behind my eyes.

"I'm going with you," Zane announced.

There was a buzzing that started in my ears, and I wasn't sure how I was still standing. I glanced down. Oh. That was how. Zane was holding me up.

"Piper? Piper!" he said more forcefully.

My eyes snapped up to his, and I nodded. "Let's go."

I didn't remember getting into the car or the drive to Raven Manor. My car door flew open before the wheels stopped rolling, and Zane cursed behind me. I rushed through the front door, screaming TJ's name.

He was sitting on the stairs, his arms wrapped around his knees and rocking. I took a seat next to my brother, my heart splintering. "TJ, hey. It's me."

"Piper." His voice cracked. There were circles under his bloodshot eyes. "What are we going to do now?"

Placing an arm around his shoulders, I fought to find the right words. So many questions tumbled into my mind, but I didn't want to press him. "Don't worry about that. Are you okay?"

He stared at the ground, doing everything he could not to break down in front of Zane. "I don't think it will ever be okay again."

I couldn't argue with that. "Where is she?"

He nodded toward the winding staircase behind us. "Upstairs. In her room."

"And you didn't call the cops?"

"She made me promise to call only you. No one else," he said. "Piper, I don't understand. What the fuck is going on?"

I started to scold him for cussing but figured he deserved a break. "I wish I knew." I hated lying to him, but I couldn't tell him the truth. He had been through so much already, and telling him that Grams was a supernatural banshee would no doubt push him straight over the edge.

"She was fine. And then—"

"I know. I know," I crooned, rubbing my hand on his back. "Nothing about life makes sense."

"You don't understand. She was killed. Like Mom."

My eyes narrowed. "How do you know that? Did you see someone?"

"No. She told me. But she said there was no reason to be scared, that she had taken care of her attacker."

Zane and I shared a look. We both knew her assailant had been a reaper, and Rose had taken them down before passing on. But who had it been? How had they gotten into the house?

"Did she say who did it?" I asked gently, hating that I sounded like a cop. It brought back painful memories for both of us, being drilled by detectives. When a relative was murdered, the family was always the first ones under fire. Being interrogated sucked. Neither of us wanted to relive those moments.

"No." He sniffled. "What are we going to do?"

"You are going to stay here. I need to see her. Okay?"

"Don't. You don't want to go up there."

"I have to. Don't worry about me."

My hand paused on the banister as I struggled with wanting Zane to come with me or asking him to stay with TJ. It only took one glance at the tight lines around his face to know he wasn't going to leave my side. Sighing, I continued what felt like a ten-mile trek to Rose's room.

I pushed open one of the double doors, hinges squeaking like a siren in the quiet room. A horrible sense of dread shot through me, but I forced my eyes to look toward the bed. There she was. Her silver hair laying out around her, shiny and slick—

I turned my head and hissed, a gasp of horror shattering my core. Nothing had prepared me for the sight that greeted me. A shudder rolled through my entire body, followed by a chilling scream. Zane had me in his arms, and I pressed my face to his chest, muffling my cries. Lead settled in the pit of my stomach.

Blood soaked the strands of her hair, dripping down the sides of her face and neck. Her dress was more red than white. I couldn't think, not with all the blood. It was worse than the dreams.

She wasn't moving. I hadn't really expected her to, but I had harbored a small splinter of hope that TJ had been mistaken, that Rose wasn't dead, that she hadn't left me here alone. I had only just found out what I was and the vast scope of what it meant to be a White Raven. Now she was gone, and the world was going to go down the crapper.

"Zane." My voice was hoarse. "What am I going to do? She left me alone, and I can't take her place."

Tenderness filled his bright blue eyes. "You'll never be alone, Piper."

I rubbed my eyes, chin trembling. "I don't know the first thing about being *the* White Raven."

"You have me. When the Grand Matriarch dies, her powers go to her heir. To you," he informed me.

"That's how I was able to stop them." It all made sense. Rose, she had sacrificed herself to save Zane and me. I didn't know exactly what had happened here, but I knew if Rose hadn't given me her powers, Zane and I would probably be dead.

Zane's eyes glittered as he looked over my shoulder. "I was thinking the same thing. This had been planned. We had been the decoy and Rose the prime target."

Shock splashed across my face. "Oh my God." I felt my eyes grow to the size of saucers.

His gaze snapped to mine, churning with anger, panic, and sorrow. "Which means you are in more danger than ever."

"Oh goody."

"This is no joke, Princess. You must take her soul."

I gripped the front of his shirt. "What? Are you kidding?" Unbelievable. I couldn't believe he'd suggested I take another soul—Rose's soul.

"Only then can she find true peace," he rationalized.

My head moved back and forth. "I don't want to, Zane."

He framed my face with kind hands. "I know this is difficult, but you must. For Rose."

I panicked. He expected me to lead an entire race of reapers. Yeah right. Was he smoking crack? I stayed in his arms for what felt like hours, and I didn't want to leave his embrace. Wrapped in his strength I felt sheltered, cocooned from the world, because once I let go, nothing would be the same.

"Okay." I inhaled, stirring restlessly. After one long stare into Zane's starry blue eyes, I turned around, facing Rose's frilly snow white bed. There was not a bone in my body that wanted to do this. My feet felt like iron bars with each step I took closer. Pushing tangled waves out of my face, I glanced over my shoulder.

Encouraging lines pulled at the corners of Zane's mouth. "Just relax, Piper. Trust me. You can do this."

He was right. I sat on the edge of the bed, careful not to disturb her still form. Lifting my hand, it shook as I placed it over her heart. My chest heaved. She was cold, so cold, her lips a shade of purple-blue. "I don't think I can do this," I uttered, an emotional wreck inside, tears rolling down my cheeks.

"Close your eyes. Concentrate," Zane's smooth voice murmured near my temple.

I did as he suggested, letting my lids flutter shut. As soon as I did, I felt his shadows slide over my skin, relaxing my soul, and for once, I was grateful. If there was ever a time I needed a dose of Zane to calm my nerves, it was now.

When nothing happened at first, I felt a weird sense of disappointment, like I'd failed everyone who meant something to me. Mom. Rose. Zane. I was supposed to be this all-star banshee, yet I couldn't even reap a soul, not when I really wanted to. But hell, when I didn't know what I was doing, I could take out a whole pack of ghosts without lifting a pinky.

I was going to be the worst Raven in history.

Then, a bright light flared behind my eyes. It appeared I wasn't a failure after all. Letting my lashes flutter open, my skin was glowing like a megawatt lightbulb. I felt myself sinking, swarmed by this warm radiance filling me from the inside out. It was indescribable.

I took a breath, a little dizzily, and leaned back against Zane's chest. It was done. I was all that was left. I was the White Raven.

God help us.

Zane pressed a gentle kiss to my forehead. "You need to rest."

"I can't. Not now. I need to go see TJ."

"Piper, I will use force if necessary."

I gave him a bland look. "Zane, don't make me wish I hadn't saved you."

"TJ should leave. He is not safe here. It's too risky," he said, pacing the room.

"What? I can't just send him away. Where would he go?" I snapped back.

He shot me a "duh" glance. "To live with your father."

I snorted. "You don't know the man. He isn't capable of taking care of a cactus, let alone a fifteen-year-old boy."

"Look, we can argue about this until you're blue in the face, but right now, we need to figure out what to tell him."

"Oh right. The body." My lashes lifted. Rose, in true supernatural form, had disintegrated into nothing. Her body had erupted into light, giving one heck of a flashbang. "I'll think of something."

I knew he was right about TJ, but it would break my heart to send him away. He was a pain in my butt, yes, but he was still my brother. It was my job to look out for him, to keep him safe, regardless of how much it hurt me.

CHAPTER 28

I sneezed.

"How are you feeling?" Zane was kicked back on a chair in my room, his hands propped behind his head.

If I had a dollar for every time someone asked me that question, I would be a millionaire. "Same as I was the last time you asked."

His brow arched.

It wasn't like I didn't know I was damn lucky to be alive, or that I wasn't grateful for those who had sacrificed themselves for me. I was. And I should've been suffering from post-traumatic stress or depression, but I wasn't. Physically, I'd never felt better in my entire life, and my mental state ... well, it was working through some pretty deep shit.

"Have you thought any about what you're going to do with TJ?"

I was sitting on the middle of my bed, thinking that it was far too sunny outside. Only two days had passed since Rose's death, and it felt wrong for Mother Nature to be so cheery. "Yeah. And as much as I hate to admit it, you were right."

"Of course I was," he stated matter-of-factly.

I gave him a bland look. "Don't make me hate you."

"It would be better if you did."

"For who? You?" I replied flatly.

"Piper."

"Forget it." Why the hell had I thought it was a good idea for him to stay at Raven Manor for a few days until I figured everything out? I was beginning to regret that decision ... for many reasons, and not just because he was forcing me to deal with things I didn't want to. Only Zane's family was informed of Rose's passing; they were the only ones who knew of my new role in life. And that was how it was going to stay for as long as possible.

We all had agreed we needed to keep Rose's death on the down low. If it got out, the rebels would come at me hard and fast, and I was nowhere near ready to deal with the repercussions. This gave me time. And boy did I need time. It was a double-edged sword. I needed time to learn what others had had a lifetime to hone. I needed time to decide what I was going to do. I needed time to ensure that TJ was safe. And I was out of time.

I hated lying to TJ and sneaking around with Zane. No one knew Zane was spending his nights with me—not in the same room, but in the same house. Well, maybe not the entire night. His arms were the only things that chased the nightmares away. My morals felt like they had vanished. My mom would not be proud, but that was what she got for leaving me to deal with this gargantuan mess on my own.

I felt stuck.

If I left Raven Hollow with TJ, I would be dragging my problems along with me. I wasn't stupid enough to think that once I left this island I would be safe. They wouldn't stop hunting me, not until they got what they wanted.

My power.

A power I knew virtually nothing about. I didn't know how to control it. I didn't know how strong I was. I didn't know if I could do this. Lead a race of supernaturals?

And there was no telling who they'd hurt along the way. I had too many people I cared about back in Chicago to subject them to danger.

"You know you can't leave now."

I swear he could read my thoughts. "I know. It's just a lot harder to send him away than I thought."

He scooted the chair across the room so he was directly in front of me. Then his hands shot out, grabbing my ankles and tugging me toward him. I didn't even try to resist. It would have been pointless. If Zane wanted me closer, there was nothing that would stand in his way.

"Is this your way of telling me you want my undivided attention?"

His hands moved up on my thighs. "I can't imagine what you are feeling. Okay, that's a lie. I can feel what you're feeling, but that's not the point."

I tilted my head to the side, regarding him, curious what this was about.

"I want to make you a promise. There are many things I can't give you, but ..."

Didn't he know I didn't care about those things? I cared about him, for whatever crazy reason.

"... I will be your sword. I will be your shield. I will defend you until my last breath. This vow I swear freely, to be your weapon as long as you shall live."

I almost fell off the bed. Holy shit Batman.

I don't know what I had expected him to say, but that had most certainly had not been it. A monsoon of emotions slammed inside me, encompassing every space of my body, and I knew my skin was glowing. "Zane, what did you just do?"

There was a flare of intensity in his eyes that he tried to hide with a one-shoulder shrug. "Now you're stuck with me."

My eyes tapered, and the muscles in my legs tightened. "Explain."

"Does everything have to have a rational explanation?" he asked dryly.

"Does everything with you have to be so secretive?" I countered. My innards were still buzzing with ... I wasn't sure what it was, but I felt more connected to Zane than before. It was bad enough our souls were aligned—now what?

"Call it insurance. It's an ancient ritual rarely used anymore, a bond of duty. It will allow me to sense if you're in danger."

I shook my head, confused. "Why would you do that?" *A bond? Until I died?* It seemed so permanent, especially for someone who spent so much time pushing me away. That two-way soul connection we had was telling me there was more to it.

His eyes searched mine. "Do you really need me to spell it out for you?"

I swallowed, breaking the sweltering eye contact, and pressed my lips together. Was he finally admitting he had feelings for me? But that wasn't all I wanted from him, a never-ending duty to protect me. Still I would take whatever I could get ... for now.

He placed his hands on my hips. "A war is coming, Princess."

I lifted my head. "And which side will you stand on?" I asked.

Zane caught a piece of my hair and wrapped it around his finger. "I think that's obvious. Yours."

My heart accelerated slightly.

All I saw was Zane—the guy I was falling for. In that moment, everything changed. I knew what I had to do. What I was born to do.

PIPER AND ZANE's story continues in ...
   BLACK CROW

SIGN UP for J. L. Press and receive a bonus scene told from Zane's POV and a free copy of Saving Angel, book one in the Bestselling Divisa Series. You will also get notifications of what's new, give-aways, and releases.

http://www.jlweil.com/vip-readers

J. L. WEIL'S BOOK RECOMMENDATION THAT YOU DON'T WANT TO MISS!

IGNITED BY DESNI DANTONE

For seventeen years, Kris has bounced from one tragedy to another. When mysterious dark forces come for her, she is forced to go on the run with the man that has sheltered her from danger her entire life.

While keeping her alive, Nathan introduces Kris to a world in which not everyone is human and the battle lines between good and evil are clearly drawn. Kris's piece in the puzzle is something neither is aware of and, as they uncover the truth, neither is prepared for what they find. Overcoming twists and revelations that shatter both of their lives, they discover that nothing is as it seems and nothing, least of all their hearts, are safe.

From author, Desni Dantone, *Ignited* is the first novel in a tale of first love, adventure, and lasting friendship that will introduce you to an exciting new world as Kris discovers how she fits in it.

GET YOUR COPY FREE TODAY ON AMAZON!
Amazon Link: http://amzn.to/2cHaXBu

RUNES BY EDNAH WALTERS

GET YOUR COPY FREE TODAY ON AMAZON!
Runes
Here's a sneak peek inside ...

THE MAILBOX

"So unfair. My parents decided to limit my computer time again," Cora griped and rolled her eyes into the webcam. "But as usual, my best friend Raine has my back, so here I am with the next *Hottie of the Week*. Before I can give you his stats, I need a break, so I'll be back in a few." She pressed pause on the webcam, swiveled the chair around, and faced me. "Thank you. I'm starving."

I threw her a bag of potato chips, which she snatched in mid-air. Keeping the door between us, I dangled a can of soda her way.

"Come on. I'm not going to ambush you," Cora protested.

"Liar. Just remember, I'll unfriend you on every social network if you do it again, Cora Jemison," I threatened.

Cora pouted. "You're never going let me forget that, are you? One lapse in judgment, Raine. *One*, and I'm labeled a liar for the rest of my life."

"Just until we finish high school. Lucky for you, we've got less than two years to go." Melodramatic was Cora's middle name, which made her the perfect video blogger. I, on the other hand, hated seeing my face on video hosting websites, something she tended to forget when she got excited. "So, when will you be done? We have swimming, and I need to get online, too."

"Ten minutes, but I'm skipping today. Keith and I are going to watch our guys crush the Cougars. Go-oh, Trojans." She pumped her fist in the air. "Come with us, Raine. Please... please? You can help me choose my next victim for the vlog."

"I can't. I have an AP English report to write."

"Another one? That's, like, what? One every week? I knew sour-faced Quibble would be tough when he e-mailed you guys a summer reading list." She shuddered. "You should have dropped his class when you had chance."

"Why? I enjoy it." Cora made a face, and I knew what she was thinking. I needed a life outside of books. She said it often enough, as though swimming and playing an oboe in the band didn't count. I'd rather read than cheer cocky, idolized football players any day. Performing in the pep band during home games was enough contribution to the school spirit as far as I was concerned.

"Fine, stay at home with your boring books, but keep your phone with you," she ordered. "I'll update you during the game." She snatched the drink from my hand, opened it, and took a swig. "Thanks." She swiveled and rolled the chair back to my computer desk and turned on the webcam. "Okay, *Hottie of the Week* is in my Biology class. He's five-eleven, masculine without being buff. Don't ask how I know. A girl is allowed to keep some secrets, right?" She giggled and twirled a lock of blonde hair. "He's a member of the lacrosse team and has wavy Chex Mix hair, which is longer than I usually like on a guy, but he rocks it. Don't you just love that term? Chex Mix. Better than dirty blond, right? I stole that from Raine."

I closed the door and shook my head. Poor guy. By Wednesday, every girl in school would be speculating about his identity and his relationship with Cora, not to mention leaving snarky comments on her video blog. She thrived on being naughty, but one day she would cross the line and piss someone off.

Cora and I had been tight since junior high when I found her crying in the girls' locker room after P.E. She'd had such a hard time adjusting to public school after being homeschooled. Seeing her now, you'd never guess it. She was crazy popular, even though she didn't hang out with the in-crowd.

Downstairs, I got comfortable on the couch with my copy of *Grapes of Wrath* by John Steinbeck, tucked a pencil for scribbling notes behind my ear, and popped open my favorite spicy baked chips. Good thing Mr. Q had included the book on our summer reading list and I already read it once.

The ding of the doorbell resounded in the house before I finished my assignment. I grinned. Must be Eirik, my unofficial boyfriend. I jumped up, raced to the door, and yanked it open.

"About time you got he…"

I took a step back, my pulse leaping. In one sweeping glance, I took in the stranger's shaggy black hair, piercing Pacific-blue eyes under arched eyebrows, black leather jacket, and hip-hugging jeans. Either fate had conjured the poster boy of all my fantasies and deposited him on my doorstep or I was dreaming.

I closed my eyes tight and then opened them again.

He was still there, the only thing missing was a bow or a note with my name pinned to his forehead. Irrationally, I wondered how it would feel to run my fingers through his hair. It was luxurious and so long it brushed the collar of his jacket. His lips moved, and I realized he was speaking.

"What?" I asked. The single word came out in two syllables, and I cringed. *Lame, Raine.*

"I asked if you'd seen Eirik Seville," the stranger said impatiently in a deep, commanding voice as though he was used to giving orders, "and you shook your head. Does that mean you didn't understand what I said, don't know him, or don't know where he is?"

"I, uh, the third one." Could I be any lamer? Worse, warmth crept up my face. "I mean, I don't know where he is," I said in a squeaky voice.

"He said he would be at the house of…" he pulled out a piece of paper from the back of his biker glove, the fingerless kind, and read, "Raine Cooper."

"That's me. Lorraine Cooper, but everyone calls me Raine. You know, rain with a silent E," I said even though he didn't ask for an explanation. I tended to blabber when nervous. "Yeah, well, Eirik's not here."

"When do you expect him? Or should I ask when does he *usually* get here, Raine with an E?" the guy asked.

I bristled, not liking his mocking tone or the way he spoke slowly as though I was a dimwit. "He doesn't always come here after school, you know. You could try his house or text him."

Mr. Hot-but-arrogant shrugged. "If I wanted to use modern technology I would, but I'd rather not. Could you do me a favor?"

Use modern technology? Which cave did he crawl from? He spoke with a trace of an accent that had a familiar lilt. British or Aussie? I could never tell the difference.

He sighed. "You're shaking your head again. Did my question confuse you? Am I talking too fast, too slow, or is it me? I've been told my presence tends to, uh, throw people off."

I crossed my arms, lifted my chin, and stared down my nose at him. I was usually the calm one among my friends, the peacemaker, but this guy was seriously pushing my buttons with his arrogance. "No."

His eyebrows rose and met the lock of hair falling over his forehead. "No to what?"

"No, you didn't confuse me. And no, I won't do you a favor."

He rolled his eyes, plucked wraparound sunglasses from the breast pocket of his jacket, and slipped them on before turning to leave.

Yeah, good riddance. To copy Cora's favorite saying, 'he just lost hotness points'.

He paused as though he'd changed his mind and faced me, the corners of his mouth lifting in a slow smile. "Okay, Raine with an E, what do I have to do to make you play nice?"

Whoa, what a smile. I was still staring at his lips when what he'd said registered. I peered at him, hating that I had to look up at him. At five-seven, I was above average for a girl, but he was taller. Six-two or three I'd guess. Worse, my face stared back at me from the surface of his dark sunglasses, making me feel like I was talking to myself.

"Stop being rude and condescending for starters," I said.

He chuckled, the sound rich and throaty. Sexy. A delicious shiver ran up my spine. "I thought I was being extremely polite."

I snorted. "Right."

"Do I need to apologize?"

"Not if you don't mean it."

"Then I won't."

I debated whether to step back and slam the door on his face, but I couldn't bring myself to do it. One, it was rude. Two, I wanted to know why he was looking for Eirik. "Okay, shoot. What's the favor?"

"Tell your boyfriend that he and I need to talk. Today. In the next hour if possible."

That annoying, commanding tone got to me again. I mock saluted him. "Yes, sir."

He chuckled, then did something strange. He reached out and touched my nose. "Cute. Nice meeting you, Raine with an E."

Cute? Ew. I reached up to swat his hand, but he was already turning away. I followed him, not realizing what I was doing until I reached the driveway. Where was he going? He wore biker's gloves, but there was no motorcycle parked at the curb. He turned left, moving past our mailbox.

"What's your name?" I called out.

He turned, lowered his sunglasses, and studied me suspiciously. "Why do you want to know?"

"I don't," I said with as much distain as I could muster, "but Eirik will need a name to go with the message."

"My name won't mean anything to him. Just tell him the message is from your new neighbor."

My stomach hollowed out as though I'd jumped off a plane without a parachute. He couldn't possibly be my next-door neighbor. A week ago, the For Sale sign had disappeared, but I hadn't seen any moving truck to indicate someone was moving in.

Please, let his home be farther down the street. Several houses around my neighborhood had been up for sale the last year. Using a trip to our mailbox as an excuse, I continued to watch him. Nice walk. Too bad it was overshadowed by his arrogance. He passed the low-lying white fence separating our yard from our next-door neighbor's then cut across the lawn and headed for the front door.

Crap.

He stepped on the patio, turned, and looked at me, a mocking smile on his sculptured lips. I averted my eyes and pretended to sift the bills in my hand. As soon as he disappeared inside, I pulled my cell phone from my pocket and furiously texted Eirik.

"Who was that?" Cora asked from on top of the stairs when I entered the house.

I bumped the door closed with my foot and dropped the mail on the foyer table. "Our new neighbor."

She hurried down the stairs. "Eirik's old house or down the street neighbor?"

"Eirik's old house."

"Oh, I hate you. How come hot guys don't move next door to my house?"

"That's because you live on a farm in the middle of nowhere," I retorted.

"Yeah, whatever." She ran across the living room to the kitchen window and peered outside like an overstimulated terrier. "Where is he? Where did he go?"

I grinned. Trust Cora to provide me with comic relief. I collected my books, the empty bag of chips and soda can I had left on the coffee table, and followed her. "I told you, Eirik's place."

"Ooh, if he takes Eirik's old bedroom, he'd be able to see right inside yours and you his."

"And that's interesting because...?"

"We want to see him shirtless."

"Hey, don't include me in your craziness."

She made a face and mouthed the words I'd just said. "Oh, live a little, Raine. Seriously, sometimes I wonder how we can be so tight. You move slower than a slug when it comes to guys."

"And you go at warp speed."

Her jaw dropped. "Are you calling me a—"

"Male connoisseur... aficionado... nothing tacky." We laughed. Cora fell in love fast and often, and got bored just as easily. I was only interested in one guy: Eirik. He and I had been neighbors until last year when they moved up the hill to one of the mansions at the end of Orchard Road. I never worried about him seeing inside my bedroom. The thought of the new guy that close to me was, I don't know, unsettling. I dumped the soda can and bag in the garbage and started toward the stairs.

"It would be like old times," Cora continued, moving away from the window, "except with him instead of boring Eirik."

"Eirik's not boring."

"Is to. So what's Mr. Hotness' name? What did he want? Is he throwing a meet-the-new-neighbor party? First dibs on your plus-one." She looked at me expectantly.

I laughed, "No one throws that kind of a party around here. I don't know his name, and he was looking for Eirik."

"Pretty Boy knows him? He just lost hotness points," Cora mumbled.

"I heard that." I waited for her to catch up before I continued upstairs. "I don't get it. You and Eirik used to get along so well. Now all you do is snipe at each other every time you're in the same room. What happened?"

"He talks down to me, like I'm stupid or something."

"He does not."

"Does to. Today I asked him to help me with a math problem, and he looked at me like I was a slug masquerading as a human being. Then he smirked and told me to ask Keith. He can be so..." She growled, her eyes narrowing. "I wanted to smack him. I should have smacked him."

Cora was smart, but she tended to act helpless around guys, which drove Eirik nuts. Deciding not to comment, I pushed open my bedroom door, and my eyes went to the window facing our neighbor's. The wide window seat with its comfortable cushions was my favorite relaxing spot in the room. Outside, I preferred the wicker chairs on my side of the balcony. I was going to have to deal with my new neighbor whether I liked it or not.

Cora removed the cute little jacket she'd worn over her tank top, threw it on my bed, and walked to the window. She and I were about the same height, except she was skinnier and had bigger boobs. Throw in her blonde hair and gray eyes and you had every teenage boy's fantasy. I was rounder with brown hair and hazel eyes, nothing to brag about, but I wasn't at the shallow end of the beauty pool either.

"How does he know Eirik? Do you think he's going to go to our school?" Cora asked.

"I don't know *anything* about him, Cora."

She threw me an annoyed look. "Only you can talk to a hot guy and forget to ask important questions. I would have gotten everything from him, including whether he has a girlfriend or not."

She wasn't bragging. Cora was amazingly good at gathering information, and she could be relentless when it came to guys, which is great for a vlogger. Sometimes it was funny, but other times annoying. Like now. I couldn't tell her I'd been too busy making a fool of myself to say much to my blue-eyed neighbor.

"Are you done with my laptop?" I asked, settling on the bed. "I have to check a few things after I finish my report."

Cora glanced at her watch. "Keith will be here in ten minutes, so I just need a few minutes to respond to comments; then it's all yours." She glanced outside then at me then back outside again. "It's such a beautiful day. Let's sit outside on the balcony."

Oh, she thought she was clever. The weather was perfect, but I refused to be a groupie to that rude guy. "No, I'm fine in here."

Cora pouted. "Pwease... pwetty pwease?"

I shook my head. "I want to focus on my work. You want to talk to my new neighbor, walk to his house and knock on the door."

A thoughtful expression settled on her pretty face. "I might just do that."

"Good. Just remember, you have a boyfriend," I reminded her.

She grinned. "Yeah, but I'm a mere mortal with a weakness for guys built like gods. I could feature him on my vlog."

I hope not. He looked like the type who could tear Cora apart if she dared. "You don't even know if he'll be going to our school."

"I would if you'd bothered to ask him." Cora sighed dramatically and settled on the window seat with my laptop. Occasionally, she stared outside. I was tempted to ask her if my new neighbor was outside, which bugged me. I shouldn't be interested in any guy period. I had Eirik—or I would if he could get his act together and ask me out. I hoped his feelings for me were just as strong as mine were for him. As for Cora, her restlessness made it impossible for me to focus. I was happy when Keith picked her up.

Less than an hour later, I grabbed by swim bag and raced outside. I had ten minutes to get my butt to Total Fitness Club for swim practice. I'd swum varsity since my freshman year, but high school swim season didn't start until next week. Off season, I swam with the Dolphins. Luckily, Matt 'Doc' Fletcher, my high school coach, also coached the Dolphins. Kayville might be a small town in northwestern Oregon, but we had three high schools and three swim clubs, and the rivalry was fierce. Most Dolphins went to my high school, too.

I threw my bag in the front passenger seat of my Sentra, ran around the hood, and saw the right front tire. I had a leak? It looked low. Could I take a chance and drive it? Maybe if I drove carefully and slow? Coach Fletcher was anal about tardiness. Worse, my attendance this past summer had suffered because of Dad.

My throat closed and tears rushed to my eyes. Not knowing whether my father was alive or dead was the hardest part of my nightmare. I still remembered the last conversation we'd had before he boarded the plane in Honolulu, the horror at the news about the plane crashing into the Pacific Ocean, the frustration as bodies were recovered and none matched Dad's. I was losing hope, while Mom still believed he was alive. How could he be after three months?

Our neighbors no longer asked us if we'd heard any news, but I'd overheard Mrs. Rutledge and Mrs. Ross from across the street gossip about Mom, calling her delusional. Prune-faced hags. I hated that we lived on the same cul-de-sac.

I kicked at the tire as though the simple act would ease my frustration, then pulled out my cell phone and checked for text messages. There was none from Eirik, which meant I couldn't ask him for a ride. *I hope he's at practice in case I need help with my car.* I texted him before calling Mom.

"Hey, sweetie." She sounded preoccupied.

"I have swimming, but I think my front tire has a leak and—"

"I can't leave work right now to drop you off. I'm dealing with a mini-crisis, too. Skip swimming, and we'll take care of your car when I get home. Call Coach Fletcher and explain."

"That's okay. I can still drive it. It's a slow leak and should hold until—"

"No, Raine. If you must go, hitch a ride with Eirik or Cora. I don't want you driving with a leaking tire."

"Cora's gone to the football game, and Eirik is not returning my calls. I can't miss practice, Mom. Coach has a big announcement to make, and today's the last class before tryouts for varsity." I'd be mortified if he knew why I'd been flaky the last several months. I still hoped no one at school knew about my father, except Cora and Eirik. "You know how he secretly uses summer club swim attendance to choose co-captains. I don't want to be the first co-captain to be dropped after one year."

Mom humphed, which warned me she was about to switch to Mother Bear mode. "I don't care how he chooses captains. You've earned it. I'll call him and—" There was a cracking sound in the background.

"What was that?"

"Jared dropped a mirror." There was mumbling in the background, then silence.

"Mom?"

More mumbled words reached me before, "I'm here. About the coach—"

"Don't call him. I'll take care of it."

"Are you sure?" She sounded frazzled.

"Yes."

"Okay. I'll try to be home early. Six-ish."

That meant seven or eight. My parents owned Mirage, a framing and mirror store on Main Street. With Dad gone, Mom was pulling double duty and often stayed behind to clean up and get the shop ready for the next business day. I rarely saw her anymore.

I texted Coach Fletcher, in case I didn't make it on time, then slipped behind the wheel. The tire pressure should hold. *Please, let it hold.*

I backed out of the driveway and reached out to shift gears when my new neighbor left his garage, pushing a Harley. Shirtless. I swallowed, drooled. His shoulders were broad and well-defined. His stomach ripped.

He glanced my way, and I quickly averted my eyes and stepped on the gas pedal. My car shot backwards instead of forward and slammed into something, jerking me forward. Panicking, I hit the brakes and looked behind me.

"Oh, crap." Of all the mailboxes on our cul-de-sac, I just had to hit the Petersons'.

Cursing, I shifted gears, moved forward until I got off the curb, switched off the engine, and jumped out of the car. Everyone had their mailboxes imbedded in concrete, but not the Petersons. They had to go overboard and use a fancy, custom-made miniature version of their house. Now the post leaned sideways like the Tower of Pisa, with red paint from my car all over the white pole. Their mailbox was totaled, the mail scattered on the ground.

Someone called out something, but I was busy imagining Mr. Peterson's reaction when he saw his mailbox. He was a big conspiracy theorist. The government and people were always out to get him. He'd believe I deliberately knocked down his stupid mailbox.

"That looks bad," Blue Eyes said from behind me, startling me.

"You think?"

He chuckled. "From that snarky comment, you must be okay."

"Peachy."

I picked up the mail. He moved closer as he helped, bringing with him a masculine scent hard to describe. It bugged the crap out of me that I liked it. Worse, the heat from his body seemed to leap through the air and wrap around me in ways I couldn't describe.

My mouth went dry. The instinct to put space between us came from nowhere, but I ignored it. Only cowards ran when faced with something they didn't understand, and my parents didn't raise one. Still, a delicious shiver shot up my spine, and a weird feeling settled in my stomach.

I waited until I was in control of my emotions before turning to face him. I tried not to stare at his masculine arms and chest. I really did, but all that tanned skin was so inviting and begging to be ogled. I'd seen countless shirtless guys before. Half the swim team spent time in tight shorts that left very little to the imagination, but their bodies were nothing like his. He must be seriously into working out. No one could be this ripped without hitting the gym daily.

"My face is up here, Freckles."

My eyes flew to his, and heat flooded my cheeks. I rushed into speech to cover my embarrassment. "I, uh, I was just leaving to go to swim practice and... and..."

"I distracted you. Sorry about that."

He didn't sound sorry. "You didn't."

He cocked his eyebrows. "Didn't what?"

"Distract me," I snapped and snatched the mail in his hands. "Thanks. I was checking my text messages when I should have been paying attention to where I was going," I fibbed.

Amusement flared in his eye, his expression saying he recognized my explanation for what it was: a lie. He had incredibly long lashes and beautiful eyes. Sapphire came to mind but...

Grinding my teeth at my weird behavior, I started toward the driver's seat, going for that space between us before I did something stupid like reach out and touch him or continue gazing into his eyes like a lovesick dimwit.

"Aren't you going to tell them you hit their mailbox? I mean, it's against the law to flee a crime scene and all that."

I glared at him. "I will talk to them when they come home from work. For now, I plan on leaving them a note. Not that it's any of your business." I searched inside the glove compartment for a notepad or anything to write on, but found nothing.

"I could explain to them what happened if you'd like," he offered in a gentle voice. "You know, share the responsibility. After all, I did distract you."

Seriously, how could someone so beautiful and tempting be so arrogant and annoying? I counted from ten to one then said slowly, "I don't need your help."

"Actually, you do."

"No, I don't." I marched to my house, conscious of Blue Eyes watching me. Sure enough, when I looked back, just before I entered the house, his eyes were locked on me, an amused smile on his lips. What was he so happy about? And why couldn't he just go away?

I pulled a piece of ruled paper from my folder and scribbled an apology with unsteady hands, then went to Dad's home office for a large manila envelope. Times like this, I missed him more. My eyes welled.

I blinked hard and put everything from the Petersons' mailbox into the large envelope before taping my note on the outside. I'd have to figure out how to pay for a new mailbox. Mom didn't like me working at the shop ever since I broke a few mirrors last summer, and jobs were hard to come by because of the bad economy. Something would come to me once I was calmer. Right now, I just wanted to get my butt to the pool and lose myself swimming.

I paused to calm myself before leaving the house.

Blue Eyes was studying the damaged mailbox like an insurance adjuster. Why couldn't he go bother someone else? Or at least put on a shirt?

"Excuse me." I skirted around him and propped the manila envelope against the crooked pole.

"I can fix this before they come home," he said.

I eyed him suspiciously. "Really? How?"

A weird expression crossed his face, but his eyes were watchful as though he couldn't wait to see my reaction. "Magic."

"Magic?" My hands fisted. I was in trouble, and he was messing around. "You know what? Stay away from me, Blue Eyes. Don't talk to me or even acknowledge we know each other when our paths cross again."

"Blue Eyes?" he asked, eyebrows cocked.

"That's me *playing nice.*"

He laughed. "Look, Freckles—"

"Don't call me that." I hated that nickname. It was a reminder of the hated spots on the bridge of my nose and the teasing I'd endured in elementary school. I slid behind the wheel, started the car, and took off. I was careful not to drive too fast even though I wanted to floor the gas pedal.

I could see Blue Eyes watching me as he grew smaller and smaller in the rearview mirror, until I left our cul-de-sac and turned right. My day had just gone down the toilet.

I was twenty minutes late for practice and still pissed off at myself for overreacting to my nosey new neighbor. So he had a hot body and an attitude? Big whoop. He was the least of my problems. I had my family to worry about, my position as co-captain to defend, and a guy I was crazy about to convince I'd make a great girlfriend.

"Did you fix your flat?" Coach Fletcher asked when I walked to the pool deck.

"I'll take it to DC Tires after practice." I slid in the pool and joined the thirty members of the Gold Team. Silver and Bronze swam at five.

We had eight lanes, but two were reserved for club members, which meant we shared lanes, taking turns pushing off the wall and looping each other. I didn't see Eirik. He rarely skipped practice, so that was weird.

Following Coach Fletcher's instructions, I finished my freestyle warm up laps while the others worked on their backstroke. I attacked the water like it was my enemy, although I wasn't sure who I was ticked off at, me or my new neighbor. When I started studying the male swimmers and comparing their bodies to Blue Eyes, I knew I was definitely my own enemy.

"Since all of you swim for the Trojans, don't forget we have Ultimate Frisbee tomorrow afternoon at Longmont Park. We'll meet in the north field at four o'clock," Coach Fletcher said at the end of practice. "I sent your parents e-mails last week, so no excuses. This is supposed to be for the team, but we'll meet some of the new swimmers and discuss a few things. Tryouts start on the seventeenth, which is sooner than we usually start. Why, you may ask?" He grinned and paused for effect. "We'll be hosting Jesuit High and Lake Oswego on the twenty-ninth at Walkersville's swimming pool."

Everyone started talking at once. Others high-fived each other. The two schools produced the best swimmers every year and often won at state championships. We'd never hosted them before.

"In the meantime," Coach Fletcher continued, "I'll need volunteers to work with some of the new swimmers. Any takers?"

No one raised a hand. Coach Fletcher crossed his beefy arms and studied us with piercing black eyes. He was a short, stubby man with a receding hairline, who preferred to shave all of his hair, but took extreme care with his beard and moustache. "Come on, guys. I need volunteers."

I looked around and saw Eel's hand shoot up. 'Eel' was Jessica Davenport, our senior co-captain and our swim team bad girl. Sighing, I raised mine. A few more shot up.

"Good. You'll each work with a student the last thirty minutes of practice every day. If they need extra coaching and you want more time, let me know and I'll okay the use of the pool after hours."

"I have pep band practice every other Friday and won't make it to practice," I reminded Coach Fletcher after everyone left.

"We'll have someone sub for you. Where's Cora?"

"She wasn't feeling well when I saw her after school," I fibbed. Coach Fletcher's expression said he didn't believe me. I wasn't surprised. I sucked at lying.

"Tell her to text me."

"Sure. Did Eirik text you?"

"Yes. He explained his situation."

I frowned. "His situation?"

Coach ignored my question and looked at his watch. "If you plan to take your car to the shop, you'd better get going."

It was six fifteen, and DC Tires closed at seven. I didn't bother to shower, just changed and raced to my car. The air pressure held up again, thank goodness. At the shop, while they fixed the leak, I checked my text messages and responded to Cora's, which were funny. The game was close and could go either way, but she sounded like we'd already won. Cora had a way with words.

There were no texts or missed calls from Eirik, which was beginning to worry me. He never missed practice, and he usually answered my messages and calls. Did his absence have anything to do with the 'situation' Coach Fletcher had mentioned?

It was seven when I left the shop for home. I looked at my rearview mirror, convinced I'd heard the sound of a motorcycle start, but there were only cars behind me.

I entered my cul-de-sac, and the first thing I noticed was the Petersons' mailbox. The wooden post no longer leaned sideways, and the tiny house looked normal as though I hadn't hit it. Weird.

As soon as I parked, I hurried to the mailbox and studied it. There were no dents. No new nails hammered in. Nothing out of place. I touched the surface to see if it had been repainted. It was dry as the day Mr. Peterson had unveiled it. I pushed at it to see if it would lean sideways, but the vertical pole anchoring it to the ground was firm.

Where had my new neighbor found a replacement? The Petersons bragged about ordering the miniature mailbox house from some fancy homeowner's website, so there was no way Blue Eyes had bought it locally. Had he used magic? Yeah. Right. There was no such thing as magic.

GET YOUR COPY FREE TODAY ON AMAZON!
My Book

ABOUT THE AUTHOR

USA TODAY Bestselling author J.L. Weil lives in Illinois where she writes Teen & New Adult Paranormal Romances about spunky, smart mouth girls who always wind up in dire situations. For every sassy girl, there is an equally mouthwatering, overprotective guy. Of course, there is lots of kissing. And stuff.

An admitted addict to Love Pink clothes, raspberry mochas from Starbucks, and Jensen Ackles. She loves gushing about books and Supernatural with her readers.

She is the author of the International Bestselling Raven & Divisa series.
www.jlweil.com

J.L. WEIL

Stalk Me Online

ww.jlweil.com

jenniferlweil@gmail.com

Made in the USA
San Bernardino, CA
13 January 2019